The World of Tond

Companion Volume
to the "Tond" Series

Steven E. Scribner

Cover art:

Drennic art depicting a far-off land,

the four-pointed star of the Fyorian ahíinor,

and "The World of Tond" in both Fyorian and Karjannic

.

Table of Contents

Introduction

This book is for those who have read the *Tond* series. If you have not read any of those books, this one will make little sense to you.

If you have read the *Tond* series, or are in the process of reading it, or even if you haven't but are not dissuaded by the first paragraph above, then by all means, read this one. Or, you may wish to use it as reference material while reading the series.

You will find that this book is divided into two sections. The first part is all of the details the world of *Tond* which didn't fit into the series proper: the histories, cultures, arts, and languages of that world, as well as its geography and biology. (I had originally intened this to be a series of short appendices at the end of Book IV, but it grew into a book of its own.) The second section, somewhat shorter, is "meta-*Tond*": here you will find what I, as author, intended the series to say (and what I didn't); a discussion on the names of things; a couple of random chapters that relate to the series; and the beginning of a work in progress.

If you have any questions about the series or about the world of *Tond* in general, hopefully this book will answer them. If not, you may wish to wait for the sequel – a second *Tond* series may be in the works.

STEVEN E. SCRIBNER

Part One

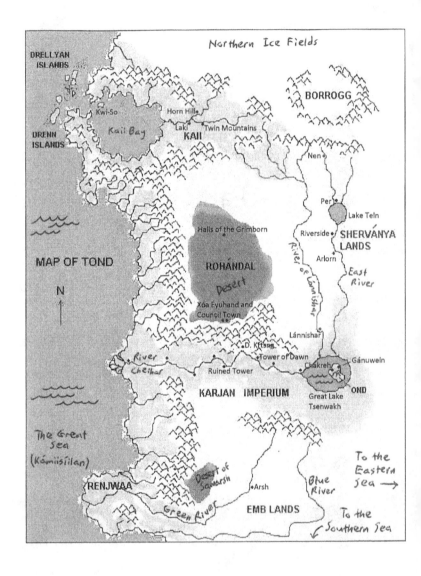

The Ecology and Geology of Tond

Due to the fact that natural "wormholes" open up from time to time between this world and Tond, any overview of the ecosystems of Tond must treat it as a subdivision of the ecosystems of this world. Most of the flora and fauna of Tond are also familiar here, though there appears to be a rather curious mix, i.e., here, camels and cactuses are not found sharing the same desert.

The geology of Tond follows that of known continental landmasses. A ridge of mountains is seen near the western coast, the result of collision between two large crustal plates. The mountain building is dormant at this time, though there was an enormous earthquake (Richter 9 or greater) recorded roughly six hundred years ago, centered in Rohándal but affecting nearly the entire continent. A third plate in the south of Tond is moving northeastward, creating a smaller mountain chain that intersects the larger one (this is the Mountains of South Rohándal, separating it from the Karjan lands.) The large peninsula of Renjwaa (actually a continent in its own right) trails behind it. In the wild north of Tond, geological forces were (and are) particularly complex and fragmented; there, several small plates moved in different directions, sometimes moving across volcanic "hot spots", and glaciers (Tond saw the same ice ages as here) carved out large valleys, fjords, and the archipelago of the Drennlands.

Flora and Fauna separate into roughly four zones, much like the zones that can be found here. In the north are the temperate forests and mountains; this zone continues along the coast as far south as the delta of the river Cheihar. In central Tond there is a large desert, the Desert of Rohándal, and a savanna, the Sherványa Lands. In the south are the tropical rainforests of the Karjan and Emb Lands, Tendh, and Renjwaa. South of this is the Southern Sea; legend tells of another continent far to the south, but it has never been explored.

THE NORTH

The thousand or so islands that constitute the Drennic Lands, the Drellyan States, and the Tashkrian Territories have been described as an evolutionary biologists' dream. Each island is separated from its neighbors by enough space to have developed one or more unique (endemic) species, but all are near enough to one another to share many species as well. The unique species are usually rather small and (to most people) rather insignificant, such as worms or sparrow-like birds; there are, however, two notable exceptions: the large flightless birds (known as *tsak-tsak*, from their sound) on Chkenjuksha Island, Tashkrian Territories, and the brightly-colored silver and blue trout-like fish called *nok-qor-ik* "bright ones" found only in Lake Nwok on the island of Ya-Hoik, Drennic Lands.

Like the mainland, each of these islands has a rocky or sandy shore and an interior ecosystem with grassy areas and forests. The ratio of the forested to the grassy area depends on the size and shape of the island; those that have less coastline have relatively less salty and windy air, and can support more tree and shrub species. This much is probably obvious. The forests generally consist of conifers and maples; the underbrush is ferns and a surprisingly large numbers of fruit-bearing shrubs and vines – these are the famed "berries" (Fyorian *sánatáalis*) of the north. (A favorite Fyorian recipe is *sánatar* "two berry" sauce, made from imported Drennic berries.) The trees and shrubs are in a symbiotic relationship with a soil-dwelling fungus, which increases the nitrogen content of the soil while growing on the roots or fallen logs of trees. The fruiting body of the fungus, resembling a mushroom, is poisonous to humans but fed on by several species of birds and rodents. Other birds eat the berries or leaves of several plants; there are also fifteen species of birds of prey, including hawks and a very large eagle. Rodent species include several types of mice and squirrels; there is also a unique carnivorous rabbit on the northern of the two peninsulas that surround Drennic Bay.

Further inland, there are much higher mountains; the tallest is the massif of Kalaelitaka (16,300 feet above sea level). The forests continue through much of this mountainous region, though they eventually give way to tundra as one proceeds east.

In the northeast, the mountains are lower but much more continuous. The exception is the enormous flat plateau of Borrogg, almost completely surrounded by mountains. In Borrogg, as elsewhere in the northeast, conditions are harsh. Cold dry winds blow from the ice fields in the far north; in Borrogg the temperature seldom exceeds 40 degrees F. Usually it is much colder. This is the realm of snow, tundra, and lichen-covered rocks; there are also several types of cold-adapted fungi that cling to stones, living off of the decaying bodies of insects and arachnids, both of which are common. Other animals are rare, except for several types of downy birds (including an owl), eagles, and unusually furry mice. There are no large mammals at all except for a unique genus, the so-called "lurkers" (Fyorian *wártala*). These are actually marsupials, like kangaroos, but made for the extreme cold; the "pouch" is concealed under thick fur, and long hair covers the entire body. Several types of lurkers have a turtle-like shell, impenetrable to the beaks of eagles (which hunt them). Lurkers are named for their habit of waiting unseen under or behind rocks or man-made structures, and grabbing their prey from hiding. The largest species of lurker stands erect and has been known to hunt humans.

CENTRAL TOND

Central Tond is unevenly divided into four ecosystems; the coastal forest, the mountains, the desert of Rohándal, and the Sherványa grasslands.

Extending southwards from the northern forests across a wide strip of land, the coastal forest, known by its natives as Dandwo (the word is related to Fyorian words for earth, such as "Tond"), is really a continuation of the forests of the north, though gradually the pines and maples give way to more tropical species such as palms and figs. The entire land is extremely well irrigated with run-off from the mountains. There are five major waterways and an untold number of tributaries. These rivers are inhabited by trout and salmon (particularly in the north); carp are found in the southern tributaries, and several unique species are found throughout. The abundant fish supports a large population of bears (in the north) and fishing cats (in the south); there are also many species of fruit-eating rodents and bats. Only one bird of prey is known from this area; this is the extremely intelligent "Eagle" of Tond – a remarkable bird, about the size of a large hawk, with a brown body and golden or white head. These birds are often domesticated, and when raised from chicks, develop an uncanny ability to understand human speech.

Some mention of the people in this forested region is in order. This is the wildest part of Tond, and some areas (far from the major rivers) are nearly uncharted. "Stone Age" tribes are known to live in several areas, almost completely isolated from the outside; those who are known about elsewhere in Tond are renowned for their ability to coexist with the land. It is said, for example, that a village of the Dorren people looks completely natural, and a visitor from elsewhere in Tond could walk right through it without seeing it. It is unknown how much this is true or just a legend (or stereotype).

Cutting off this wet green land from the interior is an unbroken chain of mountains; the highest in Tond (three peaks, known in Fyorian as Renyaldar, Tomolan, and Ar, are as high as the highest Himalayan mountains, though they are not near each other). These are the "Great Barrier Mountains"; no humans live even on their slopes, which are often very steep (a few isolated villages cling to precarious existence in the low-lying valleys). Mountain goats and wild yaks are found in the higher areas, though of course the tallest peaks are completely barren.

The mountains create a rain-shadow in the east; this is the vast desert of Rohándal. The desert has expanded in the last ten or twenty centuries at the expense of the grasslands; the Fyorians who live in Rohándal claim that the desert is partially man-made, though on accident – created in the general destruction of life during the Devastation.

Geographically the desert is an extension of the mountains that border it on three sides. It is a basin, thought not extremely low; at one time is appears to have been quite geologically active. There are several large lava flows. There are also sand seas and dune fields, and vast areas of fractured alkali badlands reminiscent of the most arid areas of the American west. The Halls of the Grimborn is near one of these, by a series of collapsed cliffs that may at one time have been an active volcano.

But what at first appears to be a barren land (a *Rohánd-dal* in Fyorian) has a number of fertile areas – there are thousand of springs and geysers, and (particularly in the south), the desert is dotted with oases. These are the famed *éyuhandis* of Rohándal, home of the Fyorians. Each *éyuhand* (singular) can be compared to an island; like the islands of the north of Tond, each has its own unique species, though nothing particularly spectacular. Around each oasis there are small fertile fields where wheat and corn can be grown, along with various types of gourds. These are the staples of the Fyorians, along with the edible cacti called *qenéila*, which grow wild just beyond most of the fields.

Inhabitants of the desert include various insects and spiders, reptiles, rabbits (considered a delicacy by the Fyorians), nest-dwelling desert-rats, and lizards. Most of these animals are quite drab in appearance, grayish or brownish; with the exception of the poisonous snakes and toads, both groups which often sport bright greens, blues, and reds. There are also diamondback rattlesnakes, the same species as in the American southwest. Plant species include shrubs and palms, all of which have durable seeds that can lie dormant for centuries if necessary, then revive when moisture is plenty. These plants are found in great numbers in and near each *éyuhand.*

Eastwards, the desert gradually gives way to grassland as the land rises and the weather becomes cooler. This prairie or savanna is the Sherványa Lands. The southern part of this region is heavily cultivated; this is the breadbasket of Tond. Sherványa farmers here grow wheat, corn, millet, amaranth, oats, and several other grains.

Northwards, the landscape grows wilder, with less cultivation, until it merges with the northern tundra. This large expanse of flat grassland is the home of herds of wild cattle and horses (some descended from domesticated animals that escaped into the wild). There are also rabbits (seemingly ubiquitous in Tond), rodents, and various lizards and snakes. Also found mostly in this area, but often drifting elsewhere north of the Karjan Imperium, is a wholly unique life-form not found outside of Tond: floaters.

Floaters (Fyorian *dányala*) are neither plants nor animals, and are usually thought to be most closely related to fungi (though recent evidence suggests that they may be a different form of life altogether; their cells actually closely resemble bacteria, rather than eukaryotic cells.) But, unlike bacteria, floaters are anything but microscopic. Their general outward appearance is a sphere, irregular potato-shape, or double- or triple-lobed blob, ranging from about ten to nearly one hundred meters around, and colored various shades of pastel pink, green, brown, or orange. Some types have stripes or geometrical patterns. Their most notable feature, however, is their ability to float in the air (hence their name). Each floater is in reality a living air bag, with a translucent organic "window" across much of the top surface. Sunlight filters in through the window and heats gas inside; this then expands, making the floater lighter than air, and it rises. At night, as the air cools, the floater settles on the ground, showing an ability (even with the apparent lack of sense organs) to avoid sharp objects or rough terrain. A network of filaments (roots? rhizomes?) then unfolds and penetrates the ground, taking nourishment from microbes. At dawn, the "roots" fold up or are retracted, and the process repeats.

SOUTHERN TOND

As stated above, the woodiness of much of northern Tond extends south along the coast through Dandwo to the River Cheihar, where it blends imperceptibly with the tropical rainforests of southern Tond. This vast area has not been well explored; much of the jungle is impenetrable. Rumors of the wildlife deep within include large apes.

As elsewhere in Tond, civilizations are found here along the relatively clear areas. The Karjan Imperium is located along the navigable banks of the river Cheihar, the Emb Lands occupy a drier area to the south, and the coast of the peninsula or Renjwaa appears to have been settled by people from a smaller continent to the west of Tond, between Tond and the original home of the Karjans.

Jungle plant species include palms, tree ferns, figs, mangroves, and many types not known outside of Tond. Orchids and other jungle flowers and vines, along with thousand of types of moss, grow in and on the trees. Insects are ubiquitous; larger wildlife includes five subspecies of tigers (the largest type is sometimes caught by Karjan hunting parties, returned to the Imperium and used for executing criminals; one smaller type is about the size of a lynx and is sometimes domesticated by the Emb).

In the middle of this wild land is a flat area, surrounded on two sides by low mountains. This area is a little drier (it even has a small desert, not nearly as large as that in Rohándal), and is appropriate for human habitation; Emb live there, as well as native Tondish (called the Tendh), cousins of the Fyorians. Both peoples have domesticated the camels that live in this small desert, though attempts to import the camels to the larger desert of Rohándal have failed.

Tond, then, like any large continental area, is a vast and varied land, and it has been settled by several peoples. Their history will be explored in the next chapter, "The Peoples of Tond".

The Peoples of Tond
(with a Brief History)

One ancient Fyorian name for Tond is *Áman Ványa nel Tánd*, "Land of many peoples". This is partially what makes the land of Tond interesting; even more so because only one of these groups show any connections with peoples in this world.

Describing groups of people, however, can be difficult. One has to be content with generalities ("This culture does so and so", "These people have skin and hair of such and such color") and yet avoid stereotypes – and often it is hard to tell the difference. And indeed, stereotypes abound in Tond just as they do here – the Karjans, for example, are often said to be fierce, and also fond of cooking, and also secretive. The Fyorians are said to be fat (despite their propensity for walking all over Tond), weathered-looking, and also to be bound by complicated written laws and oaths. These are just a couple of examples. Some of these stereotypes of course have their roots in actual aspects of the culture, but often they are distorted and/or exaggerated; and some are simply false, if not insulting (the Kayanti, for example, are widely known to consider the Drenn to be stupid).

What follows, then, is an anthropological attempt to avoid all such racisms and yet describe Tondish peoples and cultures for the person from this world who is probably unfamiliar with them. To the Tondish-born, this account would certainly seem simplistic and perhaps too general, but more details are of course filled in by the tale of Rolan Ras-Erkéltis, told elsewhere in this volume.

The peoples of Tond fall into roughly two groups, the Native Tondish and those from elsewhere. Both groups can be further divided into two groups. Of the Native Tondish, there are the Taennishmen, and everyone else. Of those from elsewhere, there are the Karjans and the Emb. These are only general labels for classification, however; it would be a mistake to consider the Taennishmen and other Native Tondish to be closely related.

THE TAENNISH

The Taennishmen are the most enigmatic group of Tond, indeed of anywhere. The myth of their strange origin is told in the Fyorian Song of Origins, and other places; all Tondish (and the Taennishmen themselves) agree that they are set apart from the rest of Tond. Anthropologists from this world have even theorized that they are either entirely mythical, or are not *Homo sapiens* at all but a different, probably superiorly intelligent, form of hominid. They have no obvious "racial" physical characteristics, and they almost always appear to be old but youthful in attitude and constitution.

Whatever they are, they have appeared in many Tondish legends and myths, often as the counterpart to the gods and heroes encountered here. This is part of their mystique; they definitely cultivate certain aspects of their culture to make themselves appear strange to outsiders. The 'magical' city that moves; the green robes; the seeming ability to appear and disappear anywhere; the supposedly unlearnable language; the mysterious *lumáaris* ("flock of lights") that they are sometimes seen to speak to; the eyes of no known color – all of these are of nearly mythological nature. (It must be mentioned that, though people from this world have had very limited dealings with one Taennishman named Nammar, none of these characteristics were noted except for the green robe.) The reasons for liking to appear so mysterious remain unknown; the Taennishmen themselves make no claims to be gods or even a special caste, and they steadfastly deny that there is any Taennish "magic" or "power". However, they do not deny being immortal, as is often said of them – this immortality is the result of their living in harmony with the *lumáaris*, they say, and they are subject to a kind of "temporary mortality" if they disobey it (they claim that this state is the same as that of other humans). Whether they are actually immortal or merely live extremely long life-spans (measured in thousands of years) is unknown – certainly Taennishland, the "magical" city that moves, was supposedly founded seventy-thousand years ago, and some of the Taennish are said to remember when it was built.

OTHER TONDISH

The vast majority of native Tondish are not Taennishmen, but belong to the race of Tondish peoples, the group that includes the Fyorians, Sherványa, Drenn, etc. This group of people is generally short and stocky, generally with blondish or brownish hair (tending towards reddish in the north) relatively long noses, brown eyes, and tan or light brown skin, tending towards a peculiar gray color in the north. More than one ethnic group in this world could be described by these characteristics; but they appear not to be related.

This Tondish race has lived in Tond for thousands of years and developed a bewildering variety of cultures, from the "stone age" tribes of the west to the vast interior empires of the Fyorians and Sherványa.

THE FYORIANS

The Fyorians themselves have no particular myth of their own origin. They have always been there, some say, descendants of those first thirty who crossed from Taennishland into Outer Tond (thus the mythical origins of the Taennishmen and other Tondish, at least, are connected). Archeological evidence suggests small settlements in Rohándal (then grassland) as early as ten thousand years ago, becoming much larger by about five thousand years ago, roughly beginning with the advent or agriculture in the area. This civilization grew until it covered the entire Rohándal basin. There are a few legends of conquerors from this early period, with resonant names like Káelrathaen and Sentálruthaen, but generally the Fyorian expansion was one of farming rather than conquest. The invention of writing spread the civilization even further; the Fyorians did not invent writing (a number of early scripts were in use all over Tond), but their standardized alphabet, the *talwehéinnaa*, put literacy into the hands of nearly everyone who could take some time to learn it. (It was somewhat more difficult in its earlier forms, with several hundred characters.) Writing was not to the Fyorians a secret to be guarded by a priestly caste (the presence of Taennishmen in the Fyorian courts was said to prevent this), and literacy approached, even in the early period, eighty percent – even in the absence of formal schools, because those who could read were encouraged to teach it to others.

Part of this was the result of the Fyorian religion, which was as bookish as any religion could be. The early oral legends, such as the Song of Origins, were codified into a book known as the *Tonílda*; all during the expansion of the Fyorian empire, various stories and commentaries were added to it. It was both a collection of literature and a holy writ; and it contained both sacred and secular material (the early authors refused to believe in a difference; much later, stories were broken into two books). The earliest sacred material dealt with a Creator God, *Teilyándal'*, and a series of minor dieties, *enkéilii*, made by this Creator. There are also tales of the "Sunderings" (*détaghun*), calamitous events brought about by humans, (or by evil spirits, or both), first by disobedience of the Creator, and later by outright malice. There are tantalizing hints of other mystical aspects of the Creator, such as a messenger called Shar. Other early tales, not in the *Tonílda*, mention the nature of the physical universe (divided into four elements, also made by the Creator).

A religion teaching that there was an act of creation has the possibility of coming into conflict with science when it arises. The interesting fact is that this did not happen in Tond. Apparently encouraged by Taennishmen, several groups of Fyorians formed monastic communities, intent upon learning more about the Creator God through meditations and prayers. One form of meditation was the careful observation of some small aspect of the material world;

this eventually led to a form of science. Observations and theories were at first recorded in the Tonílda, and later (as they became too voluminous) in other books; by the time Fyorian civilization reached its greatest extent (about a thousand years ago), science had developed to a high level. Industrialization had been introduced, though with a decidedly pacifist theme: manufactured and mechanical artifacts were made only to serve people, and few were produced as weapons. However, harm was inevitable because such manufacturing led to pollution and environmental degradation. To combat this, the Fyorian leaders at the time (supposedly influenced, again, by Taennishmen) proposed a fusion of technology and the Fyorian religion: destroying anything on the earth, whether on purpose or accidentally, was an insult to the Creator (this will be discussed in more detail below) and all possible steps should be taken to avoid producing harm.

All of the aspects of "modern" science were found in Fyorian industrialization and technology (if slightly different in minor details); theories included evolution and the big bang; techniques included genetic analysis and engineering, etc. None of these were considered to clash with the Fyorian religion. For an obvious example, the big bang was linked to the moment of Creation as told in the *Tonílda*; and in the Song of Origins, the first of the four elements created was *kullándu*, fire and energy. Scientific theory says that as energy cooled some of it organized into matter; the Song of Origins states that the second of the four elements created was *tandáalis*, earth and matter. Since time is one of the other elements (an aspect of *kewándii*, water and 'the flow'), the question of what happened before the Creation (or big bang) is moot – things can only happen before other things while time exists. Thus there is also no question about the origin of the Creator itself.

As stated above, the aspect of the Fyorian religion which most colored its relation to science, however, was its respect for nature. (Taennish philosophy always claimed that nature was not to be dealt with harshly.) At any rate, in the Fyorian view, one of the consequences of the Sunderings was to render nature hostile. Any type of hostility was included in this; the killing by carnivores, the death induced by microorganisms (which were theorized to exist centuries before they were discovered), and the aggression of humans. The four elements, the building blocks of nature, had become violent, and nature was full of sadness and pain. Nature was thus neither to be lived with in harmony (because it was violent and corrupted) nor subdued (because that was just another kind of violence); nature was to be healed. Fyorian science was thus often involved in finding cures for diseases not only of humans, but other living things as well; though most of the experiments were of a decidedly non-invasive nature (to cause pain to an animal was evil, as pain of any sort is evil).

The turning point in Fyorian religious history (and possibly Tondish history in general) happened in what became known as the Battle of Kondiláen. Kondiláen was a major city in the southern region of Rohándal, the seat of a challenge to the main Fyorian religion. In Kondiláen, one of the four elements, Kullándu (fire and energy, the first to be created) had been growing in popularity for several centuries. Its dual aspects of creativity and destruction were considered godly; by roughly one thousand years before the Devastation (see below) it had become a Shiva-like figure, a god of destruction and also creation (and procreation – sex). Although this religion also contained a respect for nature (the four elements were elements of nature), is was diametrically opposed to at least some of the main tenets of the main Fyorian religion – Kullándu had the destructive aspects that, in the Fyorian sense, had led to the Sunderings; and also because Kullándu was a part of nature whereas the Fyorian Creator God was always separate from it. (Kullándu was partially identified in Fyorian psychology as well. There existed a theory similar to that of the suppressed subconscious, with which Kullándu was identified. Since in the Fyorian religion, this "id" had been corrupted in the Sunderings, it was a source of cruelty and evil, and thus if deified, was an evil god.) The Fyorians from the older religion betrayed its peaceful tenets and became militarized, determined to root out this new religion from its core. Its main prophets were jailed and executed, riots broke out, Kondiláen became a war zone. The Taennishmen, apparently disgusted by the fact that the Fyorian religion had itself become violent, vanished for several years out of Kondiláen and out of Tondish history. Details are murky, but it is said that at this point, one or more persons appeared with the Sword of Law. What exactly the Sword is, or was, will probably never be known; it was certainly beyond any form of science or art of the Fyorians. Its origins were said to be with the Gleph (an unknown, almost legendary people); its main function was to read a person's intentions; any violent thoughts were repaid with that same kind of violence. A person plotting a murder, for example, would die if brought before the Sword. For nearly a year someone wandered the streets of Kondiláen holding the Sword above his or her head; its blinding light was said to destroy nearly anyone within sight. All of the prophets of the religion of Kullándu perished (though certain aspects of this religion later were absorbed into mainstream Fyorian thought), most of the Fyorian 'secret police' who were trying to round them up also died. The Fyorians of course countered that this was a reign of terror in itself; but in the end it was the wielder of the Sword who prevailed. After the slaughter, the Sword was placed in a glass case in the throne room of the Fyorian king (lest he too think violent thoughts) and criminals were brought before it.

Eventually the Fyorian empire recovered from the effects of this purge. Taennishmen returned; the Gleph, if they were ever in Kondiláen, seem to have scattered. Then came the golden age; whether it was related in some way to the use of the Sword is still debated. At any rate, violence in any form was simply not tolerated again, and the Fyorians were widely known as benevolent rulers, even in the farther reaches of their civilization where they were the minority. Fyorian culture began to take on its modern form; the *ahíinor* (originally scientists) devised machines which were to help the Fyorians rule peacefully; at the same time they began to wander all over Tond (much like the Taennishmen), teaching their ways of nonviolence, and spreading their religion and science. At its greatest extent, the Fyorian Empire covered all of Tond, yet it was never an empire in any sense of conquered territory. After the Battle of Kondiláen, they never involved themselves in the religions or politics of others – they merely presented theirs as an alternative. They also spread literacy; by about five hundred years ago nearly all of Tond could read and write.

Another, even more violent event was to take

place at the end of this golden age, however. In the century from six hundred to five-hundred years before the present (the century which became known as *sekúnn nel tókaa* "time of trials"), the Fyorian Empire fell apart under the threats from the rising Karjan Imperium, an accumulation of deadly weapons (sparking periodic warfare), raging epidemics of the skullpox, another religious war, and finally, the Devastation. This calamitous century will be covered shortly; in the mean time, the other native Tondish (influenced by the Fyorian empire) should be discussed.

THE SHERVÁNYA

Living in a vast eastern plain are the Sherványa, close relatives of the Fyorians. They are not mentioned in ancient texts such as the Song of Origins; therefore it is presumed that they split off from the Fyorians in prehistoric times.

Archeological evidence shows settlements in most of the Sherványa lands before the establishment of the Fyorian empire, so perhaps it was the Fyorians who split off from the Sherványa. At any rate, early Sherványa culture is documented in the journals of king Ayeyámushei, who had his scholars collect "all Sherványa lore, legends and history, as it is not told by the Fyorians and/or in the Tonílda". These half-legendary accounts contain much that is questionable for its historical accuracy (such as the tale of the twin brothers Shántilan-Tarion and Kétaman-Tarion, who fought over whether the city of Lánnishar should be ruled by themselves or Taennishmen), much that is obviously mythical in nature (Queen Mayeyamusei, who invented wings made of feathers and flew to the moon), but does present a fairly accurate portrayal of

27

Sherványa culture itself during this early period.

The Sherványa Lands were then, as they have continued to be until today, divided into innumerable small city-states (*beshándin*). These probably corresponded to the territories of stone-age tribes that inhabited the same regions much earlier.

Each of these city-states was surrounded by miles of farmland, and each was governed by a king or overlord of some type. This was much like a feudal system; however, it appears that in most of the city-states at least, the "peasants" (*kúmánya*) were free to move or settle where they pleased, as long as they continued their farming and were a benefit to their chosen city-state. In this way, it appears, several of the city-states grew larger at the expense of the others; two in particular reached populations of nearly one million (by far the largest cities in Tond) by about the time of the Battle of Kondilaen. These were the "Great Cities" (*rávishiilan*) of Lánnishar and Arlórn. At this stage the Sherványa economy became rather unstable, and the two "Great Cities" raised armies to attack and subjugate the other smaller communities, seizing their land and assets. These campaigns of conquest were successful; by the time the Fyorian wanderers began appearing in the Sherványa lands, there were three kingdoms: Lánnishar and Arlórn in the south, and in the north by lake Teln, a smaller confederation of scattered city-states, centralized with its government (and army headquarters, mostly to counter aggression from Arlórn) in Sen, on the south shores of the lake. The expanding Fyorian Empire naturally saw a threat in the huge Sherványa armies, and attempted to equalize the population of the Sherványa lands by settling in some of the smaller (conquered) city-states and offering to pay higher wages to farmers who would work for them. This sparked off scattered battles and brief wars, but the Fyorian values of non-violence had already taken root, and the Sherványa (never a particularly warlike people to begin with, according to most accounts) eventually stopped fighting. Lánnishar and Arlórn are still the largest Sherványa cities, and they still have their own armies – as do all of the other Sherványa cities – but these are mostly for defense (against much more aggressive groups, see below). The three kingdoms have been dismantled, and now each Sherványa state is self-sufficient and surrounded by farmland, much as they were in the oldest tales.

Racially the Sherványa resemble the Fyorians, though they tend to be somewhat taller and lighter (with blond hair, but brown or green eyes – like the Fyorians, almost never blue). Their language is closely related to Fyorian (see the chapter titled "The Languages of Tond"). Their culture is somewhat diverse, the result of centuries of fragmentation and then assimilation and later fragmentation again, but there are certain similarities seen throughout the Sherványa Lands.

In Sherványa culture, great importance is placed on music, poetry, and art. The music is usually described as a "contemporary" (i.e. new) sort, though obviously having ancient roots; the trance-inducing "Nocturnal Music" is one of the greatest forms of musical expression in Tond (see the chapter titled "The Arts of Tond".) Much of the art is based on complex interpretations of floral and botanical motives (the result of centuries of farming?). As hinted by the existence of trance-inducing music, there is also an interest in "expanded" forms of consciousness, both "natural" trances produced by, for example, hypnosis; and other also the use of various (locally-grown) hallucinogenic drugs. The most common of these is hemp, which is also used to make ropes and belts, also worn by the Fyorians, and (by a secret process) paper. In previous centuries the paper apparently still contained some of the hallucinogenic agent besides the fibers; it was sometimes smoked to "obtain divine influences". This may be a part of an older non-Fyorian religion (there are traces of a polytheistic religion, now archaic, in the Sherványa region). The practice has all but disappeared in recent times; the paper is now made only from the fibers. Sherványa clothes are generally of a simple type, rolls of cloth wrapped around the body and tied with ropes or cords; these garments are said to look somewhat comical to the Fyorians.

THE PEOPLES OF THE NORTH

"The complex history of northern Tond can be summarized as a tangle of events and peoples so confusing that even the locals get it all mixed up." So writes the Fyorian *ahíinor* Sheldran, and this, though a stereotype, is fairly close to the truth.

Far away from the large empires and kingdoms of the south, there are as many as three-hundred tribes, each occupying a town or territory. In such an area, border skirmishes are likely.

The western islands are the home of the Drenn, the Drellians, the Chashk, and the Tashkrians, to name only those peoples who number above ten thousand. Roughly half a million Drenn, the largest of these groups, occupy an archipelago to the west of Kaii Bay. These scattered people are actually a group of many cultures and as many as fifty different languages; the label "Drenn" refers to their hair color (almost the only constant in this diverse group) – *dren* is Fyorian for a ruddy, reddish-orange color; Drenn is a plural of this word (when used as a countable noun, "someone or something of that color"). The Drenn do not object to this stereotyping – most Drennic languages also contain a word *Drènn or Drèünn*, sounding very similar, which means "heroic". Living on islands, they are of course familiar with boats, and are often fishermen; they are also known for eating imported grains (such as rice) from much farther south (see below). Their various cultures all place an importance on epic narratives; often told to the accompaniment of music; their loremasters, the *Chelloi*, can recite tales that last for days on end. In traditional Drennic cultures there is also an interest in "veiled and unveiled reality" (*qód lô qód àk xúut*), the idea of personal secrets which may be shared with others or, conversely, may remain forever "veiled" (*qód àk*) in a single person's mind. Every Drenn carries a leather pouch attached to a belt around his or her waist; kept in the bag are "veiled" personal secrets and items (unusual seashells, stones, etc.) which were considered to be omens if found after making important and difficult suggestions. If one has made the right decision, something beautiful and unusual may be found; if the wrong decision, something grotesque or ugly, such as a deformed fish, might be found. Only the beautiful things are kept. This idea of finding portents in nature is quite at odds with Fyorian/Taennish thought, which sees nature as corrupted (though, as written by the Fyorian Táldusar, "Some truth gets through") – native Drennic religions (there are several) are rather shamanic and nature-based. The "veiled and unveiled realities" may be related to this, but they could also be a product of the Drennic Islands themselves – shrouded in ever-changing mists, the islands are hidden and revealed and often seem to change shape in the fog.

The Drellians, related to the Drenn, live on a less scattered archipelago farther north. Little is known about them, though Fyorians have wandered into their realms several times and report of hospitality and delicious cooking.

The Tashkrians and Chashk are two tribes of a people related to the Karjans of the south, though they apparently arrived in Tond much earlier, and they have accepted the Fyorian/Taennish religion. Like the Karjans, they are taller than "native" Tondish, and have black or dark brown hair and blue or green eyes. Eyes of *chud* (see below) are unknown. The Tashkrians and Chashk have often been at war with each other, and they have fortified their islands (scattered loosely between the Drennic and Drellyan lands) with tall stone towers. The largest of these in called *Kwiizats ag-Kweghan* in Tashkrian and *Kvaaz Kveranni* in Chashk – The Tower of the Star (Karjannic *Hwatsats Kwehlen*). Standing on a small island in the center of the two peninsulas that form Kaii Bay, it (along with the island) forms the "Guardian of the Bay". It is interesting to note that, as of late, the Tower has been the dwelling place of a high-ranking Fyorian *ahíinor*. Many of the other island towers are in ruins, since the Tashkrians and Chashk have moved many times in the past – there are scattered stone block and half-constructed "sea towers" (some actually built just offshore) almost everywhere in the Tondish north, giving these misty islands a mysterious, almost Arthurian, atmosphere.

Further inland live the Kayántii, in many small cities

and villages along the rivers in Kaii. This area is heavily forested, and for centuries the Kayántii have been building an elaborate system of roads connecting their cities. Besides this, the Kayántii are known for their gigantic stone buildings (discussed in the chapter titled "The Arts of Tond"), which rival the Karjan towers in size and surpass them in beauty. They are also known for a unique style of stained glass (also discussed in "The Arts of Tond").

Racially, the Kayántii look much like the Drenn, though their language has a much different melody. The first mention of them occurs in the *Tonílda*: "Kayánta was the son of Kyémen, and he had three sons and two daughters; they settled in the lands of the north and their descendents are called the Sons of Kayánta; they call themselves Kayántii." (Book three, the Song of Genealogies, section fourteen). They appear in a number of the Fyorian "Location Histories" as well. Their history is very long and complex, full of wars and golden ages and times of famine. There have been many hundreds of Kayántii kingdoms. At present they are essentially unified under King Katúleyakamankati, who lives in a small palace at Kementáreyawaa in eastern Kaii, although many small landholders actually hold most of the power in the countryside and the towns are more or less lawless. This lawlessness reflects the fierce independence of the Kayántii way; it does not necessarily indicate violence (though lynch mobs and vigilantism is not unknown, as Tayon Dar-Táeminos found out!) – more often, laws are decided upon by town councils when needed, and then discarded after their usefulness has decreased. An example was the War of Lakakeilátia, where a certain group of ruffians distinguished themselves by wearing white hoods. Another group, determined to rid the towns of them, donned red hoods to brand themselves as the enemies of the White Hoods. A town council was called at Lakakeilátia, where it was decided to outlaw all colored hoods. The result was that the potential violence was defused, and the ruffians, disgusted that they could not longer wear their badges of intimidation, broke up. About fifty years later, the ban was repealed, and hoods of all colors became a Kayántii fashion.

The Kayántii's most famous custom, mentioned in many sources, is that of the Morning Horn; on the hill of Kenáekikabérika ("Hill of the Hornblower") is a large horn, thrust into the ground so that the bell of the horn protrudes out of the side of a cliff over the city of the same name. It is blown every morning at sunrise by a woman who lives on the Hill; the first Hornblower was elected when the horn was given to the Kayántii by the Taennishman Nemral, and the position has been passed on from mother to daughter through the generations.

THE KARJANS

"Out of the setting sun they come, the untied wolves, to strike with speed and fang, to pierce the sweet earth of Tond, to bludgeon and to corrupt..." So wrote the Fyorian Séndral in a tale that nearly became part of the Tonílda, if the Taennishmen had not disallowed such slanderous writing. But when it was written, it did sum up popular Fyorian feeling about the newest arrivals in Tond. The Karjans were conquerors from their beginning, and they viewed nature (the "sweet earth") as also something to subdue or destroy if necessary. This naturally brought them into contact, and bloody conflict with, the Fyorians.

The roots of the conflict can be traced back

centuries, to that mysterious continent in the far west, original home of the Karjans (and most likely other peoples). That continent has never been explored or even seen by anyone from this world; all that is known is that it is probably close to Tond in size, and it lies across the Great Western Sea, farther west than a smaller continent known as the Western Crescent (for its shape). The people who lived there, including the Karjans, are of a different racial stock than those in Tond, being generally taller and slimmer, and having dark hair, blue or green eyes, flat noses, and pale skin.

Karjan literature goes back to that half-mythical land, and certain details of its early history can be discovered. In the north-east of that continent lay a river, larger than any in Tond; a watershed basin nearly the size of the Amazon. It was, however, covered with grasslands and small forested areas, much like the north of Tond but less mountainous. Here lived the earliest civilizations, and little is known of them, except that they must have been related to the Karjans and spoken other "Karjic" languages (two other such languages, Chashk and Tashkrian, are also found in Tond). At any rate, one of these civilizations began to conquer and enslaved its neighbors quite early; within a hundred years of its earliest records, this city-state of Tsokra-Chgren ("Dwelling in the South") had grown to nearly a million people. There are records of what might be Taennishmen in the courts (enigmatic references to *pfanj gratsang* "strange wanderers from the edges of known lands"); but apparently they were slain in some kind of uprising (some say it was because of a conflict over the enslavement of other peoples; the wanderers apparently did not tolerate it).

Tsokra-Chgren stabilized into a large community

broken into several castes. At the bottom were the *tadrek*, the slaves' slaves; next were the *tsadrek*, the slaves, then the *hakrit* farmers, *pfretang* traders and merchants, *kooshark* servants of the upper classes; and the three upper classes themselves: *hutark* priests, *tsajuk* warriors, and *hrakezh* royalty (all caste names given in their singular forms). A few minor castes were also mentioned from time to time. It was the *hutark* priests who were formative of the next stage of Karjannic civilization.

The Karjan pantheon consisted of about sixty gods and goddesses. The priests divided these into two groups, the *Kaetark* gods of creation (whose names always began with *Gaejtark-*) and the *Linaen* gods of destruction (whose names always began with *Hlijnaen-* or *Rijnaen-*). Each of the *Kaetark* had a *Linaen* counterpart, and these were often at battle. About seven hundred years ago, a priest named Kmchadk noticed what appeared to be a logical fallacy; if the creative and destructive deities were truly equal, then everything that was created would be immediately destroyed, and the universe would not exist.

From Kmchadk's observation, three new sects of the Karjan religion developed (as well as several minor variations). The first of these, taught within the lifetime of Kmchadk, was based on the teachings of Hrenchuk, and was rather Buddhist-like. Hrenchuk thought that the universe had not been created, it always had been, and the creative and destructive deities were manifestations of a tendency to move in cycles of birth and death. Another variation was taught by Ch'pfarshdook about a generation later; he thought that there must be a *third* set of deities to compliment the other two; these were the *bojtnk* gods of balance, who prevented destruction from coming to things that were newly made until they had fulfilled their destiny – a destiny which was a sort of cosmic law that was an intrinsic property of the universe itself. This form was, for roughly a century, the most popular form of the Karjan religion in Tsokra-Chgren, bringing something of a positive message in a universe that seemed all too dark and arbitrary: if a man lived long enough to fulfill his destiny, then that destiny itself must be good.

It was another variation that eventually brought the Karjans to Tond, however. About six-hundred years ago, a priest named Chgrenchwok taught that the original versions of the religion were closer to the truth; the universe had been created, and the Kaetark and Linaen forces were equal, or nearly equal. However, one of the Linaen had, at some time in the past, "defected" to the creative side, thus tipping the balance towards creation, allowing the universe to be made. Chgrenchwok did not say that he knew which god this was. Its name was given by the prophet Tarshkn, who had a vision "while staring into a flame at midnight" (*ach ts'hei'antwo kruk ach pfrel*), about ten years after Chgrenchwok had begun his teachings. In his vision, Tarshkn saw a fiery god with wings of an eagle, reaching out to conquer nearby lands, and thereby "creating" a true Karjan empire. That god was Gaejtark-Bad'hani, the god of war, originally Hlijnaen-Bad'hani, the one who had "defected" to the creative side.

There were of course military ramifications. Tarshkn's vision also included a mythical origin in which the Karjan people, or more specifically the three upper castes, had been made closer to the forging of the universe from metal in a great cosmic fire, and thus were closer to perfection – the gods had been made first, then the Karjans, then other peoples, then the rest of nature. The gods had a plan to move everything closer to perfection, Tarshkn said, by eliminating those things that had been made later. In the end, only the Karjans would remain, who would be accepted to the plane of the gods; and all of the other, more imperfect things, would pass away. It was up to the Karjans, however, to begin the process.

Thus began a savage holy war. (The Karjans had had a tendency to divide their mythology/history into great "ages", each said to be ruled by a *katark* power and then ended, often violently, by the corresponding *linaen*; this was the beginning of the present *bad'hahnwekh* or "age of war".) Tarshkn's followers, named the *Gaejtark-Bad'hanani Tsajuk*, "warriors" or "teeth" of Gaejtark-Bad'hani, first overran the royal courts of Tsokra-Chgren, and Tarshkn crowned himself *hmagj-hrakezh*, "eternal emperor of all greatnesses", and began his campaign to conquer the world. His battle cry was *Kayef grechdaemwkh arjala*, "We come to conquer all of you who are inferior to us", which meant the rest of the world. The arguments were circular; in one of Tarshkn's writings that survives to the present, he comments that the people who lived to the north (a tribe called the Thregg) resisted the Karjan invasion, thus proving that they were not clever because they did not realize that they were *supposed* to be obliterated.

It appears that Tarshkn's armies conquered most of their native continent, except for some scattered peoples who were too well armed or lived in inaccessible areas. Then Tarshkn, by now quite old, and his servant Vdraetk, set their sights elsewhere. (Incidentally, Vdraetk was the inventor of the Karjan custom of drinking blood from killed victims to gain their strength. Life force was carried in the blood, he said, and so it was the Karjan right to claim all of the life force from inferior beings which they conquered, so it could be put to "better" use. Two *tsajuk* objected, not that this was a barbaric idea, but that blood from "lower" humans was tainted because of its imperfection. Vdraetk had them killed, and he drained their blood and drank it.) At any rate, the conquering continued – there were rumors of a land to the east, and if it existed, then it too should be taken. Tarshkn and Vdraetk sent ships to search for it (the Karjans, even then, were great sea adventurers) and armies to take it if it was found.

That continent was, of course, Tond. Tarshkn's armies landed first at Fish Island, slaughtered every member of a tribe that lived there, set up a camp, and from there voyaged up the Great River (Larniisíilan, which they renamed Cheihar). At first they met with little resistance; despite the warnings of the Taennishmen that "Trálgor had been unleashed", the Fyorians were in their golden age and knew little of threats from outside.

Within twenty years, that had changed. Ship after ship or Karjans arrived, and they began to build towers along the banks of the Cheihar, on the site of cities that they had destroyed; the idea was apparently to build completely over them and wipe out their memory forever. They built their capital, Hwatsats Hragezhi, the Tower of Kings, in less than fifteen years over the Fyorian town (and *mechana* factory) of Rendrél, using the labor from several thousand slaves they had captured from the island of Ond. And then they began to look northward to Rohándal. The stage was set for the "time of trials".

FYORIANS, KARJANS AND THE DEVASTATION

As often happens when conquerors arrive, disease (to which the conquerors are immune) follows. In this case, it was the skullpox. Its etiology is unknown; probably a virus, perhaps related to either dengue or Ebola. It apparently came from the Karjan continent, and to them it was little worse than the flu – usually nothing more than an annoyance, though outbreaks of deadly strains had been known. To the native Tondish (except the Taennishmen), however, it was a scourge. The first cases were recorded in the small Fyorian town of Tenuráen, on the south slopes of the Rohándal range. The horrors are told in a manuscript of the time; symptoms included high fever, itchy pustules on the skin, bleeding from the nose and ears, convulsions, and in the final stages, a rotting and sloughing off of the skin, exposing the skull. The death toll was appalling; nearly ninety percent of the town perished. From Tenuran it spread to nearby towns and then all of Rohándal; there have been periodic outbreaks to the present. (It must be noted that the disease has lost some of its virulence; now about fifty-percent who contract it survive, though they are often disfigured, and the final stages have become somewhat less horrific.)

The Karjans, more or less immune to the plague, took advantage of its outbreaks by moving north of the Rohándal range into Fyorian territory. The Fyorians responded to this by forming armies and devising *mechana*s for war.

A note of explanation is needed at this point. Fyorian science had developed to the point where they were using electronics, computerized systems, and some quantum effects. Much like industrialized societies in this world, the increases in the standard of living that this brought were enjoyed by all, though the use of some electronics (among other devices) was limited by manufacturing processes that were determined not to cause pollution or other environmental problems (the Fyorian respect for nature). However, with the threat of the Karjans, development of new machines became secretive, and they were generally made into small self-contained units which could not be easily taken apart. These were spread among the Fyorian people, but no one was told how they worked. In response to war with the Karjans, the Fyorian *ahíinor* scientists had become "wizards" or loremasters, their machines were "talismans" or *mechana*s. (I have chosen the latter two terms to avoid the associations with 'magic', which their science definitely is not, though it often appears so to the uninitiated. –Author's note.) So it remains.

The Fyorians devised ways to strike from a distance; these were probably some type of missiles or bombs. The Taennishmen, still influencing the Fyorian policies, were reluctant to let these weapons be used, but other forms – various forms of laser guns and exploding bullets – were also developed. The Karjans responded with their own mechanical artillery, not as technical as that of the Fyorians, but nearly as effective because of the Fyorian ban on long-range attacks. At first all that happened was a stockpiling of weapons, however; the Karjan leaders knew that they would be fighting a losing battle against the Fyorian technology if full-scale war were to break out. The turning point came when the Karjan king Roaghumtsuk coerced the

Fyorian *ahíinor* Sanral to steal several hundred *mechana*s for him; but before the results of this could be felt, there was a brief respite in the hostilities. Shar came to Tond.

The mythology and significance of Shar will probably always be debated. He is of course mentioned in some of the earlier legends recorded in the Tonílda, as a messenger of the Creator. The Taennishmen noted that in some time in the future he would become manifest as a human; though they did not record from where he would come. The confusion remains; some reports point clearly to him being a Taennishman himself (some claim to see him in Taennishland), others claim he is a Sherványa. At any rate he appears to have come from a small town near the great city of Lánnishar (which appears to bear his name); there are a number of half-legendary events surrounding his birth. Little is known for certain until he was an adult; he apparently made claims to be something more than just human, and prophesied that the Karjan rule was about to come to a sudden catastrophic end. This, as well as his powers of healing and "undoing the effects of destruction", of course made him popular with the Fyorians, Sherványa and Taennish. With a group of followers he rode into Hwatsats 'Ragezhi; he was almost immediately rounded up by the Karjans and thrown into prison. They brought him before Roaghumtsuk himself; it is said that on that day the forces of creation and destruction – the Fyorian Teilyándal' and Tralgor, or the Karjan *kaetark* and *linaen* – faced off, and there was not a skirmish in all of Tond. Though Shar apparently said or did nothing to defend himself, Roaghumtsuk killed him with a flaysword (a particularly fiendish Karjan contraption) and burned the body – and was in turn attacked by some rebel Karjans, bound, and thrown off of the roof of a high tower. What happened after that is a matter of conjecture. Shar had clearly been killed, yet (true his possible Taennish nature), "death could not hold him", and he returned to Tond within days. There are many accounts of him since then. Roaghumtsuk was of course dead. What effect all of this had on the Fyorian/Taennish religion is rather confusing (and out of proportion compared to the apparent smallness of the incident itself); generally five different versions of the religion appeared within about a hundred years. Two claimed that Shar was a messianic figure; in one form he was the leader of an ever-growing list of minor deities, all of whom had control over various aspects of life. In the other, Shar alone was a human form of the Creator, and humans, corrupted by the Sunderings, were to give their lives over to him to undo the corruption and gain a form of salvation. A third form of the religion rejected these 'new' kinds of ideas, and carried on much as before (with a few minor revisions later). The fourth form claimed that Shar was a prophet, one in a long line, which would eventually point the way back to Taennishland and the way things were before the Sunderings. The fifth, an obvious syncretism with the Karjan religion, claimed that Shar was a good twin; his evil twin was Trálgor or Roaghumtsuk, and they were doomed to battle throughout eternity. All of these forms of the religion are mentioned elsewhere in these volumes.

Several forms of this religion turned hostile towards others; a sort of "multiple inquisition" took place in Kondiláen and several other major cities of Fyorian culture. The details are unclear, but apparently several of these religions took hold in different cities, and made war on the cities that practiced other religions. The *mechana*s were used for warfare, and (again) the Taennishmen vanished out of Tondish history. This time they did not reappear. The Karjans took advantage of the weakened Fyorian empire by moving north into Rohándal and up the rivers to the Sherványa Lands. The Fyorian king countered with a threat of total annihilation; the Karjans replied by stepping up their effort to conquer; and the seeds for the Devastation were sown.

Like the Sword of Law, what exactly the Devastation was, will probably never be known. Certainly atomic (or thermonuclear) weapons were used; there may have also been biological and/or nanotech warfare. Manuscripts from the period mention an invasive "blue slime" that changed all matter it touched into more of itself; no one knows how it was stopped (there is apparently some of it left, covering a small island somewhere near the Drennic Lands). The skullpox was raging at the same time, and "the wrath of Kullándu" was unleashed in several places at once. Rohándal was blasted from a green land to a desert; there were virtually no survivors, and the Sword of Law disappeared in the ashes of Kondiláen (some say that, impervious to destruction, it was blown into the air and settled elsewhere). Borrogg, likewise, was devastated; the Fyorians had built a secret *mechana* factory there just before the cataclysm – apparently the Karjans knew about it. It is said that the fires burned for three years, and filled the air with choking smoke. The population of Tond shrunk to less than a quarter, after all the suffocation, diseases, starvation and destruction played out. Some areas have never recovered.

Several centuries passed before any Tondish

culture began to rebound. The only Fyorians that had survived were wanderers in other lands and the Grimborn in northern Rohándal; slowly the former began to trickle back into the south. They found a blasted land; it is said that thousands of square miles of vegetation had been instantly been fossilized in the fires. The ground – bare stone – was strewn with bones.

However, the returning Fyorians did find oases, in the same locations as the springs that had always watered Rohándal – though the familiar plants had been replaced by new, strange, and often poisonous varieties. The Fyorians were determined to rebuild their homeland, and they brought farm animals and plants from the nearby Sherványa Lands. Slowly, Rohándal was rebuilt, though Fyorian civilization was only a shadow of its former self.

The returning Fyorians divided up into three groups, each with a prefix attached to their surnames: *Ras-*, for those living in the farthest south; *Dar-*, for those in the west; and *Kun-* or *Kéwan-* for those in the east. These, along with the Grimborn of the north (whose surnames had always begun with *Ak-*), formed the "Four Tribes" which were to use the power of the Four Elements to rebuild Tond. The *ahíinor* became a priestly caste, secretive in their knowledge of the ways of the Four – the old science (which had crafted the *mechana*s) and religion (which had prevented it from doing harm) were mostly given lip service or forgotten entirely. As the power and bureaucracy of the loremaster-wizards grew, they began to see themselves as the "Guardians of Tond", using their power to prevent another Devastation. A blatant sexism (rare in Tond) entered their culture – an often-heard phrase was *"ahíinu ro fyányikan nel meyen xóndasen"* – "The ways of the *ahíinor* are not for the eyes of women". Thus Fyorian culture had assumed its (unfortunate) modern form.

The Karjans, likewise, suffered considerably in the Devastation, and rebuilt their culture afterwards, though again it was quite different. In the first place, the Imperium had only about a third of the destruction; most of the *Hwatsats* Towers and cities, for example, were only partially damaged. The main Karjan problem was disease; the river Cheihar was choked with filth, and its waters had become poisonous. About half of the Karjans died (and many more of ills that took longer to manifest themselves); but within about seventy years the water had become pure again. The Karjan leaders were also anxious to prevent another Devastation, and they began to negotiate with the Fyorians, although they apparently still believed that they had been called to purify the world for Gaejtark-Bad'hani – covertly, they continued to strike and lay waste to villages far from the centers of Fyorian civilization. Two political groups formed in the Imperium: the "New Peace" who wished to make lasting peace with the Fyorians, and the old *tsajuk* orders, who called for continuation of the violence needed to rid Tond of "imperfect" people such as the Fyorians and Sherványa. (One leader of a tsajuk order, Tseshk, actually insisted that the Devastation was a worthwhile price to pay for their goal of destruction.) In a century of conflicts, power seesawed between these two groups, and wars and battles broke out. Many of the remaining Ondish slaves took advantage of the turmoil and revolted; most were able to slay their overlords and return to Ond (thousands had escaped before them, during the Devastation itself). A few

Taennishmen wandered into the Imperium and set the remainder free – one of the last times Taennishmen were seen in Tond. Karjan slavery ended.

Around this time, Fyorians began to infiltrate Karjan leadership, placing selected rulers (from the New Peace) on the thrones of the various *Hwatsats*, and often slaying leaders of the *tsajuk* orders. Eventually Fyorians themselves began to appear as Karjan rulers, as well as Ondish (who were partially Fyorian by descent – see below). This was quelled by the Battle of Hwatsats Pfrentukch ("Battle of the Tower of the Rising Moon") about two-hundred years ago, but continued secretively. The Imperium became "Fyoricized", though Fyorians still considered the Karjans as their enemies. This fear was not unfounded – the last old *tsajuk* order, determined to restore "proper" Karjan rule, continued right up to the time that Tayon Dar-Táeminos found them in Hwatsats 'Ragezhi. That tale is told elsewhere in these volumes.

THE ONDISH

The island of Ond, located in the Great Lake known as Zéyiisíilan in Fyorian and Tsenwakh in Karjannic, was originally uninhabited. Both Fyorians and Sherványa began to settle there about a thousand years ago; the Fyorian capital was in the north in Gánuwein, the Sherványa lived in five city-states on the eastern shores. The two groups met, but due to their cultural similarities and Taennish-influenced belief in non-violence, they settled next to each other and intermingled, rather than fighting. When the Karjans found them during their initial raids up the river Chelhar, they took a large number of them as slaves; their labor helped to build the Karjan *Hwatsats* and roads. As non-Karjan, they were considered *dadrek*, the lowest of the lowest castes (see above – *dadrek* is plural of *tadrek*); some Karjan slaveholders began to "increase their worth" by breeding them with Karjan slaves. Thus when they regained freedom several centuries later, they were of thoroughly mixed Karjan and Tondish ancestry.

The Karjans built a city on the southern coastline of Ond, called Ts'hakreh, "Palace". This was a pleasure center for the Karjan rulers. Immediately following the Devastation it was taken by an uprising of returning refugees from the Imperium – these continued to call it Chakreh, as they pronounced the Karjan sounds. Karjans never returned to Ond until the last *tsajuk* order made a surprise raid (told elsewhere in these volumes) – by then the Ondish had become a people of their own, showing slight allegiance to the Sherványa (by claiming to be Sherványa and using Sherványa names) but generally not affiliated with any others. They developed the art of music to a high degree, as well as the culinary arts – Ondish food was considered the most delicious in Tond, though they began to guard their recipes. The old Fyorian/Taennish religion continued unaffected by the development of the *ahíinor* loremaster order elsewhere in Tond. Some Ondish settled in the Imperium, however, and accepted Karjan ways. Many of these returned to Ond later, and in a great effort to continue "improving" their gene pool with Karjan blood, set up brothels in Ond, to cater to Karjan men. These still exist (illegally), despite attempts by the Ondish leaders to stamp them out.

THE EMB

The Emb live south of the Fyorian and Karjan

territory, and thus are somewhat outside of "mainstream" Tondish culture, whatever that means. Like the Karjans, they originated outside of Tond; though in this case the origin was even farther, though, very mysterious; their origin story is that they entered Tond from another world. According to the story, they entered Tond *awem pod neng kayab, emfo tauz aniz* "through a doorway in a cave, one thousand years ago". This points out an interesting feature of Emb philosophy: no one knows where the cave is, and the "thousand years" is not relative. Apparently it has *always* been "a thousand years ago", regardless of when the statement was made. In Emb philosophy, the past, the world of memory and history, is a state of singularity, a timeless eternity; and the future and the world of speculation is another kind of stasis. The present exists as a split instant, a kind of dream, between the two realities of eternal past and eternal future. This rather Zen-like philosophy was bred from countless years of meditation and thought; but it was also influenced by Fyorian/Taennish thought – Fyorians wanderers have been in the Emb Lands for generations.

The Emb version of the Fyorian religion is complete devotion to Teilyándal'/Shar during the "point of time" (*mij ab toka*) that is the present. Of course this "point of time" stretches out into all points of time, so this state of complete devotion at any and all given instances is rather difficult to achieve; those who have reached it are known as *mayar*, and they generally retire into a monastery called a *klemon* (there are several in the Emb lands) and see no one. They are not like teachers, since they are not giving out any knowledge different from anyone else, and any students would distract them from their constant duties anyway.

Others strive to achieve this state, but there are certain parts of the Emb culture that are rather difficult to reconcile with it. One is the set of complex laws of retribution and repayment. Any act of violence must be avenged with the same kind of violence. This could lead to a cycle, but (in theory) it does not – the half-legendary king S'Chefik is credited with a series of laws that prevent the revenge from being meted out after justice is brought to the original criminal.

The Emb have left little written history. (One reason for this could be that their tendency to see time as a frozen instant, but a more practical reason could be that their writing was said to be quite unsatisfactory for the spoken language, and very difficult to learn. At some time in the past, they abandoned this "original" alphabet, and replaced it with the Tondish *talweheínnaa*. There may be some historical documents stored in a collection somewhere, but very little known material remains, and it is indeed very difficult to decipher.)

The general outline of Emb history, however, is not difficult to reconstruct. After their mysterious appearance, they first colonized the shores of the Green River, setting up a number of villages and a capital city at Sawarsh. From there they traded with the native Tondish living in the area, and intermarried with them. There was a period of tyrannical god-kings, *komak*s, who were (after about one hundred years) defeated by a rebel group called the *frim*s. Their leader was S'Ayal, who set up the S'Ayalik dynasty, which lasted for about three hundred years. The dynasty seems to have fallen victim to some kind of corruption, and their last ruler, Queen M'Nayan, was hanged by a mob of commoners.

A brief period of turmoil led to the establishment of the S'Kreyik dynasty (King S'Chefik lived during this period, and it is also the time when the Fyorians began appearing). This was the Emb golden age, apparently at roughly the same time as the Fyorian golden age far to the north. The Emb also began exploring during this period, moving southwards into the floodplain of the second large river, the Blue River. Here they set up several more towns and a second capital at Gómilar (a native Tondish name for the area). There was some conflict with local tribes called the Ren, the Jwaa, and the Tendh, which was settled by intermarrying and giving government positions to members of these tribes.

Emb history seems to be lacking in the kind of epic warfare that raged in the Imperium and the far north of Tond. Even the Karjans in their most warlike phase (just before the Devastation) posed little threat. The Emb are physically by far the largest people in Tond; the Karjans were intimidated by such "monsters" and never attacked in large numbers. Only one incident with the Karjans is mentioned in history: a Karjan ship voyaged out of the Imperium, down the coastline and up the Green River, with the intent of capturing Emb for slaves. They landed at night by the town of Eyarsh, and about twenty Karjans disembarked and went into the nearest house, tying up the people that they found. They returned to the ship with their captives, only to find that other Emb had boarded and were holding the remaining Karjan crewmembers hostage. Both groups were let go, with the promise that the Karjans, if they ever returned, would only do so for with peaceful intentions. There were some subsequent Karjan raids, met with the same results.

With no coordinated Karjan invasion, there was likewise no Devastation; only a few Emb in the far north of the Emb lands suffered the effects of the catastrophe (though there is some speculation that the Green River may have been poisoned for a short period of time). Thus Emb culture has survived to the present roughly the same as it always has been. There are several Emb kingdoms, the largest along on the Green River and the Blue River, each ruled by a king (*kanru*) or queen (*kuinru*) who delegates authority to a number of lesser rulers (*lodru*), one or more in each town. (S'Tam, Lord of Arsh, whose story is told elsewhere in these volumes, was a *lodru*.) There are also elected rulers (*piru*), roughly the same number for each town as the *lodru*; together, they make decisions regarding the town. It is a special privilege of both *lodru* and *piru*, however, to travel – and both often vanish out of their towns for months at a time.

Like the Karjans, the Emb are not native to Tond and are not of the native Tondish race. They are generally of dark skin and hair (as are many peoples of tropical climates); their eyes are brown or green, their hair is usually wavy, occasionally curly. Their features show a wide variety, though there is a tendency to have what the other Tondish call a "long-faced" look, with high foreheads and narrow cheeks. A lot is made of their style of dress, which consists of loose-fitting robes and trousers – the clothing is made by a process (a closely guarded secret) that renders vegetable fibers and tree bark into comfortable cloth which is waterproof *in one direction only*; thus the Emb are often seen to be comfortable walking in heavy rain and humidity. This cloth is sold throughout Tond, though it is very expensive everywhere except in the Emb lands.

Emb jewelry is also called unusual by the other Tondish, being made of found stones or seashells or animal teeth, rather than the gems and precious metals favored elsewhere. Equally strange is the Emb weaponry; spears made of wood but filled with a metal core are handled by a leather atlatl with extreme skill; these spears also have many practical uses (i.e. walking sticks, and, lashed together, storage racks). The Emb are also known for making equally "exotic" beverages such as *kahei* (coffee?) which is often drunk cold, sweetened with honey or fruit juices.

OTHER PEOPLES

Accounts of other peoples in Tond are seen from time to time, including the wandering Glephadhii (or Gleph), a secretive people of generally Karjan appearance, though their language appears to only be distantly related (though more so than to the "native" Tondish languages). Several times they have come under intense persecutions by the Karjans; by some accounts they are in fact ancient enemies. At any rate, at this time they are found mostly in scattered Sherványa and Kayántii towns in the north of Tond, and little else is known about them.

Other groups include the Tendhish and Ren-Jwaa, both of southern Tond and related to the Fyorians. Also the names of several peoples living on a smaller continent to the west of Tond are mentioned from time to time; these are said to be also related to the Fyorians, and have extraordinarily long names for ethnicities – the Andrish, Mientéilikhan, and Puhwóngesdátreh.

Among the "stone age" western peoples, the Dorren (noted for their ability to "blend in"), the Neffic, and the Chetosic peoples are the most numerous.

The Languages of Tond

As in any large land area, the many peoples of Tond speak an equally large number of languages. Most of these languages are fairly obscure, spoken by a small number of people in a small village or tribe, or on an island. Several others have expanded across enormous ranges (as some languages do everywhere), and are spoken by large percentages of the Tondish population. Among this latter group are Fyorian (the major *lingua franca* of nearly all of Tond); its close relatives Sherványa and Ondish, as well as Kayánti, Drennic, Karjannic, and Emb. The first five of these are "native" Tondish languages, members of the Tondic language family, while both Karjannic and Emb originated outside of Tond, in different parts of the world; they are related neither to the Tondic language family nor to each other.

The following are descriptions of the major languages spoken in Tond. This article is somewhat technical, though I have tried to avoid too much linguistic 'jargon' (and that which I use, I try to explain immediately). All of the pronunciations are the same as those referred to at the beginning of this book.

FYORIAN

Descended from the language of the Ancients, Kelsíima or Old Fyorian, the Fyorian language is today the most widely spoken of all Tondish languages. It is the language of the wandering *ahíinor* loremasters, one of the great literary languages of Tond, and the Tondish *lingua franca*. And, unlike another widely spoken *lingua franca* (namely American English), it is not considered difficult to learn.

SOUNDS MADE IN THE FYORIAN LANGUAGE

The general 'sound' of Fyorian is a melodious, polysyllabic language rich in vowels. This impression is partly because a large percentage of syllables (and words) end in vowels, and also because the ratio of vowels to consonants is greater than in English. The vowel sounds themselves are not unusual to speakers of English, though Fyorian linguists have theorized about them in somewhat unexpected ways. The inventory of consonant sounds is somewhat more exotic, containing two varieties of the German or Scottish CH, several varieties of R, and two clicks. The overall sound of the language is not as "foreign" as some other Tondish languages such as Drennic and Karjannic; it has been described as sounding like a cross between Hawaiian and French.

CONSONANTS

(Those with the star* cannot occur at the end of a syllable.)

- Sounds made with both lips: P*, B* (both of these are quite rare)
- Sounds made with the upper teeth and lower lip: F, V (there is a tendency to pronounce these with both lips, like the P and B)
- Sounds made with the tongue and teeth: T, TH, D*, DH (TH as in "them"), Q* (click)
- Sounds made with the back of the throat: K, KH (German CH), G*, GH (voiced KH), X* (click)

- Sounds made with the nose: M, N, NG (as in "singer")
- Hissing sounds: S, SH, Z, ZH (Z as in "azure")
- R's and L's: R (flapped), Ŕ* (rolled), Ṛ (back-rolled), L
- Others: H, Y, W

Notes:

1. Combinations: R, L, Y, and W can come after almost any consonant. The Fyorian script has letters for the combinations FY and LY, the latter of which carries a particular meaning in some words (see "consonant distribution", below). S and SH can come after T, the latter resulting in a sound very close to CH as in "church". Z and ZH can come after D, the latter resulting in a sound very close to J as in "judge". These latter two combinations are found mostly in Karjannic words "borrowed" into Fyorian. No consonant combinations can occur at the end of a syllable.

2. The Fyorian T and D are pronounced with the tongue between the teeth (in the same position as for the TH and DH), similar to the T and D in Spanish. The T is actually very different from its English counterpart; not only pronounced with the tongue between the teeth, but followed by an audible H-like puff of breath (almost like the T-sound in Mandarin Chinese). The K sound also has this puff of breath.

3. KH and GH are pronounced very smoothly, with no "rasp". Back-rolled Ṛ has an obvious friction, and carries a particular meaning in certain words (see "consonant distribution", below).

4. K can occur at the end of a syllable in some 'archaic' dialects, particularly the speech of the Grimborn.

5. Double consonants, like the NN in *áenn* "circles",

are actually pronounced double, i.e., drawn out twice as long as a "single" consonant (*áen*, with one N, is the singular form "circle"). These are actually always two sounds, in this case, a "nasal" vowel (see "vowels", below) and a consonant N. The only consonants that occur "doubled" are N, L, and R.

CONSONANT DISTRIBUTION and "COLORED WORDS"

Several of the Fyorian consonants are tied up in a phenomenon known as "consonant distribution", seen to some extent in most Tondish languages, but especially developed in Fyorian and Sherványa. Consonant distribution, put simply, is the fact that certain consonant sounds are found only in certain types of words. The combination LY, for example, is found only in words denoting pleasant or good things, and in adjectives denoting pleasantness (*lyánnas*, "nice"; *leilyáendas*, "beautiful"). It also appears in the words for one's own family members (*káelyor*, "my son"; *máelyika*, "my mother") as opposed to the words for another's family members, which have the "plain" L (*káelor*, "somebody else's son", *máelika*, "somebody else's mother", etc.). Certain LY sounds have become locked into the words into which they were originally added, as in *Teilyándal'*, the title of the greatest Tondish deity (but it is still said that one can tell if another is a believer in the Fyorian religion or not by whether he says *Teilyándal'* or *Teilándal'*). The back-rolled Ṛ is found only in "bad" words and expletives (*tṛákesándas*, "dung-eating", considered to be the worst insult in the language). (Both of these sounds can actually be inserted into a word containing a "plain" L, or a different type of R, to emphasize the speaker's feelings about the thing or person spoken of; for example, if

Rolan and Shillayne have a fight, she might back-roll the R in his name; after they make up he might call her *Shilyéin*.) The throaty GH and KH sounds are often also used in unpleasant words.

In poetry, the distribution of consonants is taken a step further. Words containing the LY are designated as "blue-green"; words containing the Ṛ (and sometimes the GH or KH) are designated as "red". These colors are not true synaesthesia because they are not fixed by perception but by convention. However, the poets using them have managed to add a subtle flavor to language that is quite difficult to translate without using entirely different words. Some poetic words are actually new inventions, with an infix to create the desired "color". The most frequently cited example is in three words for "big": *zhándas* (merely "big", with neutral emotional content); *zhalyándas* (a "blue-green" word for "big", with connotations such as ripe, plump, spacious, or impressive in a good way), and *zhaghándas* (a "red" word for "big", with connotations of swollen, bloated, or grossly distended).

VOWELS

A (as in "f<u>a</u>ther"), AE (as in "b<u>a</u>t"), AI or AY (as in "h<u>igh</u>"), E (as in "b<u>e</u>t"), EI or EY (as in "sl<u>eigh</u>"), I (as in "b<u>i</u>t"), II (as in "b<u>ee</u>t"), O (as in "b<u>o</u>ne"), U (as in "f<u>oo</u>d"), R (as in "h<u>er</u>"), L (as in "midd<u>le</u>"), N (as in "did<u>n</u>'t").

Notes:

1. Not all dialects distinguish between I and II, though there are separate letters in the script for these sounds.

2. All vowels except AI, EI, L and N can occur with the tongue curled back ("retroflex", written AR, AER,

etc.). These are reminiscent of American Midwest pronunciations.

3. All vowels except AI, EI, and L can occur pronounced through the nose ("nasal", written AN, AEN, etc.). These sound "French" to the American ear.

4. The Fyorian script also has letters for vowels + L: AL, AEL, etc.

5. All vowels can be pronounced with a high or low voice pitch. There is a similar feature in English, where, in a word of more than one syllable, one syllable is conspicuously higher pitched and louder than the others, e.g. *uniVERsity*. However, in Fyorian: a.) Two or more (or no) high-pitched vowels may occur in a given word, b.) Single-syllable words may have a high or low pitch, c.) The high-pitched vowels are not louder than others, and d.) Changing the pitch may result in a different form of a word or a different word entirely. High-pitched vowels are marked with an accent mark, Á, ÁE, etc.

6. Low-pitch U almost disappears at the end of a word, or changes to W before another vowel.

7. Any two vowels next to each other form a "diphthong"; the first slides smoothly into the second (an example of this in English is the O and I in 'boing'). If they have different voice-pitch, the pitch also slides, producing a rising or a falling intonation.

GRAMMAR AND SYNTAX

SENTENCE STRUCTURE

Fyorian syntax is of the familiar subject-verb-object variety, except that the preferred order is subject-object-verb. The subject, object, and objects of prepositions are all marked with a "postposition", a particle that comes after the word it modifies:

máu arn "cat (subject)": *íi ngas máu arn nggáras* "a cat is approaching"
máu yo "cat (object)": *an íi ngas máu yo zéyas* "I see a cat"
mau níi "to a cat": *an íilan zó máu níi yéidhum* "I gave the ball to a cat"
máu nahei "in the direction of a cat": *íilan nézmi arn máu nahei xámum* "The mouse ran towards the cat" (an unusual case!)
máu nó "of a cat": *arn máu nó ó* "this is the cat's ball"
fyórlaa nel "of me, my": *arn fyórlaa nel máu* "this is my cat".

etc.

As can be seen from these examples, the "postpositions" act essentially like prepositions in English. There are two main exceptions, one of which appeared in the example above.

a. "Directionals": postpositions indicating movement (and referring to inanimate objects) often have a prefix *na-* indicating movement into position, a suffix *-ka* indicating movement away from position, or both:

kwéli do "on the table"
kwéli nado "onto the table"
kwéli doka "off of the table, away from a position on the table"
kwéli nadoka "across the top surface of the table; onto then off of the table"

etc.

b. The "subject" postposition changes for first person ("I"), second ("you"), third ("he or she"), or fourth ("him or her over there") as well as whether the sentence is a statement, speculation, question, etc. This postposition actually evolved from a verb meaning "to be". In fact, if there is a subject in the sentence, marked with its usual postposition, a verb on the end is not necessary. (In this chart, "?" indicates a question.)

	Statement	?*	Request *	Maybe	And then…	causing …
1st person	aan	laan	ǩáan (rare)	waan	ẕhaan	shaan
2nd person	ein	lein	ǩéin	wein	ẕhein	shein
3rd person	arn, rn	larn, lrn	ǩárn ("let him")	warn	ẕharn	sharn
4th person	on	lon	ǩón ("let him")	won	ẕhon	shon

	If…	Therefore…	Because …	I doubt if…	I heard that…
1st person	ghaan	xáan	saan	traan	taan
2nd person	ghein	xéin	sein	trein	tein
3rd person	gharn	xárn	sarn	trarn	tarn
4th person	ghon	xón	son	tron	ton

*These usually move to the beginning of the sentence.

As can be seen by this chart, the forms are predictable. The first consonant changes for type of sentence, and the vowel changes predictably for first, second, third, or fourth person (this is called the "person vowel", and is a characteristic of the Tondic language family). The high or low voice pitch is not entirely predictable. Some examples of how they work in a sentence:

Ján arn fyór. "John is a man."
Ján aan fyór. "John (me) is a man."
Ján aan sháiras. "John (me) is writing."
Aan sháiras. "I am writing."
Larn Ján sháiras? "Is John writing?"
Kéin (kíilan) sháiras! "Please write (this)!"
Kárn Ján (kíilan) sháiras. "Let John write (this)."
Ghaan (áshmei) árukus, xáan (fyánléi) zéyus. "If I go there (tomorrow), I'll see (you)".
Ghaan (áshmei) árukus, láan (fyánléi) zéyus? "If I go there (tomorrow), will I see (you)?"
Ján arn (úr yo) sháirum, zharn (úr yo) vii léizum. "John wrote (it), and then he read (it) again."
Ján warn fyor. "Maybe John is a man." "I think John is a man."
Ján sein fyor,... "Because you, John, are a man,..."
Ján téin (úr yo) sháirum. "I heard that you, John, wrote (it)."

etc.

As can be seen, some of these provide information that would normally be supplied by an entire separate sentence or clause in English. For example, when stating the fact that "John is running", the Fyorian speaker would also indicate with a single word whether he observed this action first hand or whether he heard it from another source. Strikingly similar sentence constructions are found in some Native American languages.

Also, some of these function as conjunctions in English. Fyorian actually has only three true conjunctions: *zhen*, (obviously related to *zhaan*, *zhein*, etc.), meaning roughly "and" and simply linking sentences; and *ámréi* and *zóndrei*, both meaning "but" but with slightly different nuances (*zóndrei* implies contrast).

Fyorian sentences generally do not contain as many words as their English counterparts. Often, this is due to the fact that words are dropped if they are understood. For example, the sentence above, *Jan arn (úr yo) sháirum, zharn (úr yo) vii léizum.* "John wrote (it), and then he read (it) again." could be stated *Jan arn sháirum, zharn léizum.* "John wrote, and then read." This may make some utterances in Fyorian seem vague to the speaker of English, but of course if there is any ambiguity the "missing" words can be supplied again.

VERBS

Verbs in Fyorian come in pairs. One verb denotes something *doing* something; its paired form indicates something *being done* to something. These are called "active" and "receptive" verbs. The concept is similar to the active and passive verbs in English, though the range of meanings is much greater.

Active: *Aan zéyas.* "I see."
Receptive: *Aan duzéyas.* "I am seen."

Active: *Ur rn íisyánnas.* "It tastes good (gives off a good taste)."
Receptive: *Aan (ur yo) dusyánnas.* "I'm tasting (it)."

Active: *(Kálan tárni) arn éyas.* "(That tree) is green ('is giving off greenness')."
Receptive: *(Váná yo) aan déyas.* "I'm making (i.e. painting) (the wall) green."

Active: *Aan karishándas.* "I'm teaching."
Receptive: *Aan karíshandas.* "I'm learning ('being taught')."

etc.

The difference between the two forms is often predictable. The "active" verb is the basic root word, and the "receptive" is made by adding *d(u)-* (which changes to *n-* before t, d, k, g, n, m, or ng) to the beginning (if the verb consists of one or two syllables) or changing the voice-pitch (if the verb consists of three or more syllables). An exception shown above is *íisyánnas* "to taste good" and *dusyánnas* "to taste", but here obviously one has a prefix (*íi-* indicates "good", i.e. *íizéyas*, "to look good").

A small number of verbs consist of a single consonant or group of consonants, plus the tense ending (see below). These are from the oldest layer of vocabulary in the Fyorian language, and nearly all Tondic languages have related words. A few examples are:

k-, e.g. in present tense *kas* "to rule"
mr-, e.g. in present tense *mras* "to tend livestock"
x-, e.g. in present tense *xas* "to be true"

These are the active forms; the receptive always take *n-* on the beginning:

nkas "to be ruled over"
nmras "to be tended, shepherded" (pronounced *m'mras*)
nxas "to receive truth, to learn, to understand deeply"

These are invariably pronounced with the low voice pitch.

A small number of "active" verbs usually contain a built-in object. This type of compounding, known as polysynthesis, was very common in Old Fyorian but its use is dwindling. The most common polysynthetic verb is *esás*, "to eat", which may be stated alone but usually has a prefix indicating "to eat *what*". The prefix is a noun, stated in its singular form, and connected right to the verb stem. We already saw the expletive *tŗákesas*, above; more polite (and common!) examples include:

níikesas "to eat meat", i.e., *Aan (kínrei nel áven) ngá yo níikesas* "I ate meat, beef, (for dinner yesterday)." Notice that the word for "beef", *ngá*, has its object postposition.
omyesas "to eat vegetables"

etc.

Fyorian verbs may contain a "directional", indicating direction of movement or various other subtle shades of meaning. These also occur in English, i.e., "to dry out", "to dry up", "to dry off". Unlike English, however, Fyorian directionals are not separate words. They occur right after the main stem of the verb, and tend to influence voice intonation.

zéyas "to see"
zéidóas "to look at"
zéikádoas "to stare at"
zéyúmas "to look around, search for"
zéinádókas "to look through, look over, glance through, check out"

etc.

Directionals do not occur in the single-consonant verbs.

Fyorian verbs also may contain the "honorific" or "formalizer" *-ánd-*. This does not change the meaning but elevates the sense. Again, this occurs right after the main stem (just before a directional) and tends to influence voice intonation.

ésas "to eat"; *esándas* "to dine"
glendóas "to get"; *glenándoas* "to receive gratefully"

etc.

The Fyorian verb always ends with its tense ending. There are 7 basic tenses:

nggárras "to come, does come, comes" (present)
nggárrum "came" (past)
nggárrus "will come" (future)
nggárran "is coming, was coming, will be coming" (continuous)
nggárrerei "generally comes, habitually comes" (habitual) – this is quite rare, since the present and "repetitive" tenses is used for this meaning.
nggárruwei "repeatedly comes" (repetitive) – this is

much more common than the "habitual" and seems to be replacing it in many sentence forms.
nggárriis "always comes" ('always').

These are further modified by additional words at the end of the sentence which specify "past", "continuous action", etc., in reference to the tense of the verb ending (i.e., the verb *menálum* "to think", with the *-um* past tense ending and the additional word *káari* indicating "past", results in a "double past" meaning "had thought".) There are about fifteen of these; some of the most common are:

Past: *káari*
Remote past: *yúsi*
"Stop action" (a very short amount of time; suddenly completed action): *ái*
Continuous; incompleted action: *áareyaa*
"Already": *táami*
Future, yet: *kórei* (usually used with a negative verb)
For a long time: *tókaa*

In the present tense, these seven additional words result in the following meanings:

zéyas yúsi "has seen, a long time ago"
zéyas káari "has seen"
zéyas ái "sees right now, immediately!"
zéyas áreyaa "is seeing right now"
zéyas táami "has already seen"
zéyas tókaa "sees for a long time"
zéyasen kórei "hasn't seen yet, didn't see yet"

In the past tense, they would result in the following:

zéyum yúsi "used to see"
zéyum káari "had seen"
zéyum ái "saw right then, at that very moment"
zéyum áreyaa "was seeing"
zéyum táami "had already seen"
zéyum tókaa "saw for a long time"
zéyum kórei "hadn't seen yet, didn't see yet"

etc.

It is possible to stack these up: *Arn (ur yo) zéyan twényum táami áreyaa tókaa* "he saw (it) when he had already been running for a long time." There is no particular order in which they are stated. And, obviously, not all combinations of basic tense + additional word actually make sense.

Besides the basic tenses, there are two other tense endings which do not take the additional words. These are *-an*, indicating linking (without any specification of time) and *-ang*, indicating result.

Arn twényan (fyŕláa) zéyum. "Running, he saw (me)."
"He saw (me) while he was running."
...(wéiv ní) gáiran gímlum... "...did gyre and gimble (in the wabe)..." (a line from Lewis Carroll)
Arn (drí yo) sumáyum xávang. "He dropped (the glass) and it broke."
Arn (vána yo) túveyas éyang. "He is painting (the wall) green." "He is painting (the wall); it is becoming green."

A verb may also be stated with a high-pitched Á at the end instead of a tense-ending. This is a (often slightly rude) command: *gárrá!* ("Go!); *gárrausá!* (Go away!) Here, one could mention another form of *tṛákesándá!*

There are also a number of modal verbs, which attach to the end of the sentence, and take the basic tenses and the additional words. Like modal verbs in English, they indicate ideas like "can", "must", and so on. When a modal verb is present, the main verb takes the -*an* ending.

Aan gárran kŕnas. "I can (am able to) go."
Aan gárran túmas. "I am permitted to go."
Aan gárran túmum káari. "I could have gone…"

etc.

Certain verbs seem to be derived from others with different vowels. Usually one is more intense than the other. The example usually cited is *lúmas* "to shine" and *lámas* "to glow". The forms of these are not predictable.

Old Fyorian also had an "intensifier" verb form, in which the verb was repeated with the prefix *mi-* in between. These are the staple of the old loremasters' formulae, i.e., *trúmitii káva mi-káva ahíi kúlah* "Please 'open *mi*-open' lore-fire" (modern Fyorian *trúmii kéin ahíinukúlu kawándas* "Please (request) lore-fire open.") Although there are related forms found in most Tondic languages, it is extremely archaic in Fyorian and was probably old-fashioned even before the Devastation; thus it is an example (one of many) of the loremasters' deliberate obfuscation.

NOUNS
Many Fyorian nouns are derived from verbs.

Usually this is accomplished by means of endings. Typical endings include:

(verb) *karrishándas* "to teach"
karrishándor "teacher (male)"
karrishándika "teacher (female)"
karrishándala, karrishándal' "teacher, male or female (unspecified person)"
karrishándu "teachings, lessons" (abstract)
karrishándand(u) "a thing used for teaching" (the meaning in this case is rather vague)

etc.

    (Noteworthy is the fact that the "male" and "female" endings look rather Indo-European. Linguists have not overlooked this, and cite it as one reason to classify the Tondic language family as a member of the hypothetical Nostratic superfamily.)
    The single consonant verbs also can become nouns, with the same endings:

kas "to rule" → *kor* "ruler, king" (*kika*, "ruler, queen"; an archaic word; more common are *elénika* and *reyénika*, which are not related)
mras "to manage livestock" → *mror/mrika* "shepherd"

    Nouns for people groups, etc., are not derived from verbs, but have their own characteristic endings – some of which are identical to those on nouns from verbs.

Fyórándor "Fyorlan man"
Fyórándika "Fyorian woman"
Fyórándala, Fyórándal' "Fyorian person"

Fyóránya "Fyorian people, Fyorian ethnic group"
Fyórándal "Fyorian land"
Fyórándii "Fyorian language"

The "person (unspecifed gender)" and "land" ending sound nearly alike (they are spelled differently in the Fyorian alphabet). Usually context is enough to clarify; however, an alternate version of "Fyorian land" is *Fyóránduhand(u)*, actually a compound noun (see ADJECTIVES, below). Also, a verb can be constructed from the ending for "language", by dropping the *-ii* and adding the appropriate verb ending: *fyórándas* "to speak Fyorian", thus *ínglándas* "to speak English", etc. (Some speakers do not drop the *–ii*, but shorten it to a y: *fyorándyas* "to speak Fyorian".)

Most nouns do not derive from verbs. These include innumerable impliments (cookware, writing utensils, books, blankets, weapons, etc.), body parts, animals, plants, shapes, natural phenomena, places, etc.

qáví "cooking pot"
shendólakh "quill used for calligraphic writing"
dath "bedsheet"
ílda "book"
máltus "sword"
mé "eye"
íno "dog" (or *kyáu*, also "dog")
ásalan "lion"
ngolánka "mushroom"
áen "circle"
trillórn "sun"
tyóm "meadow"

etc.

A few animal names are derived from the sound the animal makes, i.e., *máu* "cat" and *kháa* "crow".

There are a small number of descriptive endings that can be placed on certain nouns. These include *-ís* "big", *-ím* "small", *-íisíilan* "the one and only", *-itón*, used to signify royalty, and *-iláen*, used to signify sacredness. There are several more of these, and they are from an extremely ancient layer of Fyorian vocabulary.

kámís "a large body of water"
kámím "a small body of water, a small lake or pond"
kámíisíilan "the Great Sea (on the west of Tond)"
tyéritón "a throne", from *tyér*, "a chair or stool"

etc.

Some nouns are compounds, though usually the first part is stated as an adjective (see ADJECTIVES).

Fyorian nouns come in singular, dual, plural, collective, and inclusive forms (the latter two are often interchanged and the distinction may be disappearing). These are made by endings; there are slight differences in the endings depending whether the singular form ends in a consonant, a vowel (including N, L, and R), or a final U (which is barely sounded).

ENDING IN A CONSONANT
tyóm "meadow"
tyómar "two meadows"
tyómis "meadows"
tyómáalis "a group of meadows"
tyóméinnaa "all meadows"

ENDING IN A VOWEL
mé "eye"
mér "two eyes"
mén "eyes"
méáalis "a group of eyes"
mééinnaa "all eyes"

ENDING IN A FINAL –U
tlándu "country"
tlánd(w)ar "two countries"
tlánd(w)is "countries"
tlándáalis "a group of
    countries"
tlándéinnaa "all countries"

Nouns ending in the final –OR (masculine ending) are also slightly irregular, as the –OR vowel changes to a consonant R for the dual, collective, and exclusice forms.

ENDING IN A FINAL –OR
ahíinor "loremaster"
ahíinrar "two loremasters"
ahíinorn "loremasters"
ahíinráalis "a group of loremasters"
ahíinréinnaa "all loremasters"

Some of the collective nouns end in –*áaris* and some in –*áalis*. There is no particular rule which is which, though in general, if the word contains a consonant R, the collective ending contains and L and vice-versa. For all words with final –ND, the collective is –*áalis*.

Depending on context, the "inclusive" form may indicate all of the ones present, all of the ones in a particular group or list, or all of the ones that exist.

In colloquial Fyorian, it is possible to invent words with two plural endings, i.e., *tlándáalisar* "two groups of countries". These are considered clever wordplay, but are not the "correct" forms (though they exist in several related languages).

There are no non-count or mass nouns. Liquids are usually stated in a singular, collective, or inclusive form; powders (like sand) and grains (like rice) are plurals: *shéman* "sand", from *shéma* "a grain of sand".

ARTICLES

There are two articles in Fyorian, but these do not correspond exactly to "a" and "the" in English. "The" (the definite article) is expressed by *íilan*: *íilan zhánika* "the girl", *íilan ílda* "the book". This, however, is not used as often as its English counterpart, and usually denotes something for which there is only one, or one at a time: *íilan Móna Líisa* ("The Mona Lisa") or *íilan Íngutland no Kór* "The King of England". The other article, *áman*, corresponds to places in English where there are usually <u>no</u> articles, and indicates "that type of thing in general", i.e., *áman tyóméinaa on éyas* "(all) meadows are green". (Do not confuse *áman* with *amán*, which means "many"!) The indefinite article, "a" or "an" in English, is indicated by *íi ngas* "one of" (see numbers, below): *íi ngas zhánika* "a girl, one girl", *íi ngas ílda* "a book, one book". Sometimes *íisang* is also used as an indefinite article; this word has appeared relatively recently (from *íi* "one" and *sángu* "thing") and its use appears to be spreading.

It must be noted, however, that all articles are

optional in Fyorian...!

ADJECTIVES

"Adjective" as a semantic category does not technically exist in Fyorian. All descriptive attributes are expressed as verbs or as compound nouns.

An example of a verb-adjective appeared above: *éyas* "to be green". Other examples are *súas* "to be small, short", *kólmas* "to be long", *omómas* "to be interesting", *mórdhas* "to be bad", *kírikas* "to be noisy, chatty", *lánggas* "to be boring", and *dlánggas* "to be bored". As can be seen from the latter two examples, the active/receptive duality appears in these words as well. They also take all of the basic tenses and additional tense endings:

súas "is small"
súum "was small"
súerei táami "is generally already small"

etc.

As predicates, these function exactly as other verbs.

Ján arn súas. "John is short."
Ján arn (kóyor la) súum. "John was short (as a child)."

When combining with a noun, they are linked with the postposition *ke*:

súas ke fyor "a short man"
éyum ke tárni "a tree which was green" (literally "a was-green tree")

(*Ke* changes to *'e* if the noun begins with a K, KH, G, GH, or X.)

Ke also has four other forms, which modify the meaning of the adjective and correspond quite closely to the comparative and superlative forms in English:

rúas ke fyor "a tall man"
rúas kás fyor "a taller man"
rúas káa fyor "the tallest man"
rúas ko fyor "a less tall man"
rúas kói fyor "the least tall man"

These are added on the end of the sentence (i.e., after the verb), for comparatives:

Kálan fyor arn fyŕlaa tá rúas kás. "That man is taller than me." (*tá* is a postposition meaning "than".)

It is possible of course to combine these with the tenses into complexes with very subtle meaning, which can only be approximated in English.

Kálan tarn súerei tókaa kás tárni (nél xámu). "That is (the type of) tree which I've heard generally remains the shortest for a long time (i.e., as it grows)."

Ke can be combined in any of its forms with verbs of action as well.

xávum ke nádyó "a broken window"
xávas ke nádyó "a window which is breaking (now)"

Phrases with *ke* also make adverbs; all five forms may be used in this case as well. Some speakers use *te* instead of *ke* for adverbs, particularly in western areas of the Fyorian lands. The origin of this alternate form is uncertain.

The other way to combine "adjectives" with nouns is to make compound nouns. This is much simpler than by using verbs, though the meanings are not as subtle. Basically, these are the "abstract" forms of nouns, ending in *-u* (see above). Most of these have the same root words as the forms with *ke*, but are used when the "adjective" is considered to be an intrinsic part of the noun being described. Examples from the story of Rolan Ras-Erkéltis include *éyuhand*, "oasis" (as opposed to *éyas ke hánd*, which would only mean "green place") and *ahíinukúllu*, "lore-fire" (as opposed to *ahíinas 'e kúllu*).

RELATIVE CLAUSES

These function as adjectives: "the man whom I saw" is rendered as "the I-saw man" (*an zéyum ke fyor*).

PRONOUNS

Fyorian inherited its unique pronoun system from its language family. For the subject of the sentence, most pronouns do not indicate first, second, third (or fourth) person; this is done by the subject particle (see above). This is completely different from English, where "I" is first person, "you" is second, and so on. Fyorian subject pronouns are merely gender and number indicators (with two exceptions).

fyor "masculine pronoun"
fyán "feminine pronoun"
fyándis "plural pronoun"
kála "masculine or feminine, unknown or unspecified

person"
ur "pronoun for an inanimate object, 'it' "
layá "I (used by adult to child)"
lyáa "You (used to a beloved person)"

All of these may take particles indicating plurals:

fyán támii "dual feminine pronoun, 'we, you, or they' for two women"

fyán ánii "plural feminine pronoun, "we, you, or they' for three or more women"

fyán anáaris "inclusive plural feminine pronoun, 'all of us, all of you, or all of them' concerning women" or "distributive plural feminine pronoun, 'the group of us, you, or them' concerning women"

Notice that the "inclusive" and "distributive" plural forms have merged. Context makes it clear.

These can make interesting syntactical constructions. Note, for example, that *fyándis támii* must mean two people, one of each gender, so it almost always means a courting or married couple.

If these are used as objects in the sentence, obviously the subject postposition cannot be of help. Here, they attach a suffix: *-l-*, plus the "person vowel" (see above).

fyŕlaa "me (masculine)"
fyŕlei "you (object, masculine)"
fyŕlar "him"
fyŕlo "him over there"
fyándislei támii "you two people whom I am addressing (object)"

etc.

These suffixes are used elsewhere in the language (see POSSESSIVES, below).

When used as an object of a sentence, these do not take postpositions, although *níi* may be used for indirect object ("to me", "to him", etc.) if there is a chance of confusion. In other parts of the sentence, the normal postpositions are used.

POSSESSIVES

There are two ways to indicate "my", "your", etc. The simplest is simply to add the same suffix as the object pronoun (see above) to the thing in question.

íldalaa "my book"
íldalei "your book"
íldalar "his / her book"
íldalo "book belonging to him / her over there"

etc.

The other way is to use the object pronoun and a postposition, either *nó* or *nel*. *Nel* is used for possession by a human; *no* is for possession by something else (or for a general genitive case).

ahíinor nel árukand "loremaster's walking-staff"
máu no táv "cat's food"
mordhándu no tókaa "the Devastation ('great-destruction's time')"
fyŕlaa nel táv "my food" is also possible, though this longer form is considered rather bossy. "Mine!"

DEMONSTRATIVES
kíilan "this (here by me)"

kéilan "that (there by you)"
kálan "that (there by him / her)"
kólan "that (over there)"

These can be used in either of the same two senses as in English, i.e., "this book" or "this is a book". For plurals, they take the same particles as the pronouns.

kíilan támii "these two things"
Kéilan ánii "those things (there by you)"

etc.

These are obviously related to a set of locatives:

kíi "here (near me)"
kéi "there (near you)"
káa "there (near him/her)"
kó "over there"
i.e., *máu arn kó* "the cat is over there"

NEGATION
Negatives are expressed by adding *-en* on the verb, just after the main tense ending.

aan gárrum "I went"
aan gárrumen "I didn't go"
aan gárrasen táami "I won't have already gone"

etc.

If a specific word or phrase in the sentence is being negated, *ro* precedes it:

aan pái yo ésum "I ate the pie"
aan ro pái yo ésumen "I didn't eat the <u>pie.</u>"
aan pái yo ro ésumen "I didn't <u>eat</u> the pie."
ro fyŕ aan pái yo ésumen "<u>I</u> didn't eat the pie."

etc.

Ro can also mean "without" as in two compounds commonly used in this book, *Rohándal* (=*ro hándu dal*, "place without any place", desert) and *Tairánda* (= *tái ro ánda*, "evil without name", nameless evil). *Ro* drops its *-o* when the word being negated begins with a vowel.

"AND", "EITHER / OR" etc.
These are expressed by bracketing:

zén máun kyánn zn "dogs and cats"
zén máun kyánn zúu "cats and/or dogs"
zén máun kyánn zúyaa "either cats or dogs"
sú máun kyánn su "neither cats nor dogs" (the final U in *su* is barely sounded).

"And" may also be expressed by *te*: *máun te ínon* "cats and dogs" – this is used primarily while listing things.
(NOTE: Fyorian has two words for "dog": *íno* is a loanward from Karjannic.)

EMPHASIS
Any word may be emphasized by putting *ka(h)* before it:

fyŕ arn rúas "he is tall"
ka fyŕ arn rúas "now, HE is tall"

fyŕ kah arn rúas "he IS tall"
fyŕ arn ka rúas "he is very tall"
fyŕ arn ka ro rúasen "he is NOT tall"

etc.

QUESTIONS

To form questions, move the subject particle to the front of the sentence (see above). There is also a question word *nán* "what", which compounds with other words:

nánkala "what person?" = who?
nánhandu (pronounced *náhand*) "what place?" = where?
nánmen "what reason? (literally 'what think')" = why?

etc.

Nán always has a high voice pitch, and all syllables following it in the compound have low pitch. This question compound appears in the sentence where the word is that it replaces:

Ján arn gárrum "John went" → *Nánkal' larn gárrum?* "Who went?"
Ján arn Línda yo zéyum "John saw Linda" → *Ján larn nánkala yo zéyum?* "Who(m) did John see?"

(For the appearance of the L- prefix, see SENTENCE STRUCTURE, above.)

Any of these may also be stated with the subject marker at the beginning of the sentence:

Larn Ján nánkala yo zéyum? "Who(m) did John see?"

NUMBERS

1 *íi,* 2 *ter,* 3 *rén,* 4 *fyer,* 5 *gó,* 6 *shín,* 7 *shándi,* 8 *há,* 9 *qer,* 10 *íi-ngé* ("one-zero", used in mathematics), 10 *des* (used in counting), 11 *des-íi,* 12 *des-ter,* 20 *ter-des,* 21 *ter-des-íi,* 100 *hyáa,* 1000 *sár,* 0 *ngé*

These are joined to nouns by means of postpositions. When simply counting, *ngas* is used: *íi ngas ílda* "one book", *ter ngas íldar* "two books". When counting in a series (ordinal numbers), *yam* is used: *íi yam ílda* "first book", *ter yam ílda* "second book", etc. When counting attributes, *lin* is used: *íi lin ílda* "single book", *ter lin ílda* "double book", etc. It is possible to use plurals with the latter two: *ter yam íldar* "second (group of) two books"; *ter lin íldan* "three or more double books", etc., though these are obviously fairly rare.

NAMES

(Names are given here in their anglicized spellings.) Fyorian names are an ancient part of the vocabulary and thus (like names in English) have lost most of their meanings. There are some patterns: masculine names tend to be two syllables, high then low voice pitch, and end in *-an* (Rolan, Teyan), *-ar* (Keldar, Qenvar), *-ul* (Arnul, Sendul) *-oy* (Hanroy, Kelnoy) or *-ath* (Elrath, Sendath). Feminine names tend to be two syllables (low then high voice pitch) or three syllables (low, high, low) and end in *-éin* (Shilein, Kelein), *-áen* (Zhulaen, Krisaen), *-rí* (Andri, Tulri), *-éyaa* (Andréyaa, Larqéyaa) or *-áena* (Kelaena, Toraena). Very small children are sometimes given cute nicknames by adults, which denote some adorable feature or personality trait, such as *Ríntáldar* "Apple Cheeks". At least one of these appeared in this tale: Ranti, Hanroy's young son – *rántyas* means "cuddly". These of course fall out of use by the time the child is nine or ten years old.

Fyorian family names also are very old and the meanings are lost in prehistory. However, those returning to Rohandal from the Devastation divided up into three groups, living in the east, west, and south of Rohandal respectively (the borders to these areas are rather vague), and attached a prefix to their surnames. Those in the east used *kun-* or *kéwan-* (from *kewándii*, "water", there is more water in the east than elsewhere in the desert of Rohandal; *kun* is a shortened 'eroded' form used if the surname is three or more syllables); those in the south used *ras-* (meaning unknown; "south" is *mmú*, older form *mbu*, the origin of the word "Emb"...!); those in the west used *dar-* (*dáru* means "west").

It is customary in formal settings to introduce a person by his or her full name, with the prefix, and the place where he or she was born (followed by a postposition meaning "from that place"). Thus, Rolan's full name (seen several times in these stories) is *Rólan ras-Erkéltis mmú Rohándal, Xóa Éyuhánd karáa*, literally "Rolan Ras-Erkeltis (of) South Rohandal, Xóa Éyuhánd from".

WRITING

The Fyorian alphabet, the *talwehéinnaa*, is the most often-used writing system in all of Tond. Originally it was devised for Fyorian alone (and based on several earlier systems) but it was spread by the wandering *ahíinor* both before and after the Devastation and came to be used for many other Tondish languages. The *ahíinor*, when coming across a foreign sound that could not be represented with the existing *talwehéinnaa* letters, would simply invent a new letter and add it into the alphabet. Eventually all of these added letters were standardized, and the result is a kind of Tondish "International Phonetic Alphabet". It is now used for nine out of ten written Tondish languages, but no single language uses all of its symbols.

Consonants are represented with looped characters with (like the familiar Roman alphabet) ascenders and descenders. Descenders which occur on the right of a symbol have a characteristic "hook". A symbol (called *onér*, "strong") placed over the loop means denotes the sharply pronounced, breathy, or aspirated consonants (i.e., T is pronounced in the same place as the mouth as D, but is much louder). The other consonants are voiced. Doubling the loop originally meant "smooth" (i.e., TH is pronounced in the same place as the mouth as T, but is made by smoothly breathing the sound as opposed to 'spitting' it); some letters were switched and changed, and this system is no longer systematic. Consonant letters have names all ending in *-a*, for example, *ta* sounds like a T, *sa* sounds like an S. Vowels are represented with shorter characters, but these have a number of forms indicating the R, L, and N modifications as well as the high tone. The script overall is quite calligraphic (but not as much as the Karjannic Imperial writing) and has been said to superficially resemble a mix of Greek and Arabic.

Symbol	Value	Symbol	Value
	(begin sentence)		
	H		
	X		
	Q		
	D		T
	DH		TH
	G		K
	GH		KH
	B (rare in Fyorian)		P (rare in Fyorian)
	V		F
			FY
			HL (not used in Fyorian)
	L		
	L at beginning of sentence		
	R		HR (not used in Fyorian)
	Z		S
	ZH		SH
	N		HN (not used in Fyorian)
	NG		HNG (not used in Fyorian)
	M		HM (not used in Fyorian)
	(pause)		
	(indicates a name)		
	(indicates a place)		
	(end of sentence)		

This chart represents the consonants (and punctuation) used in the *tálwehéinnaa*, with their English values. Note that there are several letters which are not actually used in Fyorian. Those with the *onér* symbol are in the column on the right. The "pause" is used like either a comma or an apostrophe (in place of a dropped letter). The "Q" letter, usually standing for the click with the teeth, is also used to stand for the prefixes on the "receptive" verbs, regardless of how they sound. It has also often been used in place of the "D" letter on the end of words like "Tond" and *"ahíinand"* (mechana); this is a shortcut (the Q letter can be written more quickly) that is never used in formal writing.   The "colored" consonant sounds (besides the GH and KH) are written with digraphs: the back-rolled Ŗ is written with the letters for RG; the "blue-green" sounds are written with the letters for LY and NY.

	A		AR		AL		AN
	A (at end)		R		L		N
	AE		AER		AEL		AEN
	I				IL		IN
	Y						
	O		OR		OL		ON
	E		ER		EL		EN
	EI						EIN
	II		IIR				IIN
	OI (rare)						
	A (rare)						
	U		W				
	W						

The *tálwehéinaa* vowels have modifications: curly ascenders or descenders to indicate the vowel plus R, L, or N. Y and W are included in the vowels because they are derived from the letters for II and U respectively; the extra letter for W (at the bottom) is a recent addition to the alphabet and used interchangeably with the other one.

Not shown is the indication of the high tone. This is achieved with a looped symbol (called the *tŕn*) which is added over the vowels (though not over the modified vowels with the R). The following example shows how *á*, *ál*, and *án* are written.

SOME FYORIAN WORDS USED IN THE "TOND" SERIES OF BOOKS

("Receptive" forms are given the familiar designation of "passive")

adéras: to live, to dwell

adérhand: a house or home (literally "dwelling place") [plurals: *adérhandar, adérhandis, adérhandáalis, adérhandéinna*]

adérlaa: (my) home

ádhel: a Fyorian robe [plurals: *ádhelar, ádheln, ádheláaris, ádheléinna*]

ádhelhand: a closet or wardrobe [plurals: *ádhelhandar, ádhelhandis, ádhelhandáaris, ádhelhandéinna*]

áen: a circle, a bracelet [plurals: *áenar, áenn, áenáalis, áenéinna*]

áen: a year [plurals – irregular and literary: *áenwar, áenwis, áendwáalis, áendwéinna*]

ahrénnu: magic, enchantment (does not have a supernatural connotation)

áilyas: to love

áindas: to stand [used as a transitive verb in the idiom *arn áindas* "it stands" = there is or there are]

amarn [= amrei arn]: but (it is)

amrei: but

anáarislau: all of us (a great many people)

anáarislar: all of them (a great many people)

anáarislei: all of you (a great many people)

anáarislo: all of them over there (a great many people)

ánda: a name [plurals: *ándar, ándan, ándáalis, ándéinna*]

árgh: a fly [plurals: *árghar, árghis, árgháalis, árghéinna*]

arn áindas: "it stands (transitive)" = "there is" or "there are"

arn: (he, she, it) is; (they) are

árras: to arrive

árrendas: to be caught up in something, carried away, deeply involved [passive of *arréndas*]

arréndas: to catch up someone in a story, carry away someone in an activity (compare *azúrghas*)

árrum: past tense of *árras*

árukand: a walking-staff [plurals: *árukandar, árukandis, árukandáalis, árukandéinna*]

árukas: to walk

árukor: a (Fyorian) wanderer

árukráalis: collective plural of *árukor*

átau: heat, warmth

átawas: (to be) warm

atánwas: to give off heat or warmth

au: [reflexive prefix]

áu: blue-green(ness)

áukaghándu: self-destruction, suicide

áusyas: (to be) foreign

áwas: (to be) blue-green

ázurghas: to be caught up in something, carried away by something [passive of *azúrghas*] (has a distinctly negative feel, with connotations of "addicted" or "enslaved")

azúrghas: to enthrall, enslave, bewitch

cháimas: to be cut [passive of *sháimas*]

cháimum: past tense of *cháimas*

chánkas: (to be) guarded (passive of *shánkas*)

chŕ: a bird [plurals: *chŕar, chŕis, chŕáalis, chŕéinna*]

dáa: only (adv.)

dáestu: darkness

dal: same as *ndal*

dálei: (dá'lei) only [used after a verb to indicate "only that was happening, and nothing else"]

dánkal: one's sibling or relative [plurals: *dánkalar, dánkaln, dánkaláaris, dánkaléinna*]

dánkalnlar: his or her siblings or relatives

dar: surname prefix for the western Fyorians

des: ten

devrákas: to invade

dhárvas: to leave something in its present state

díng: a bell (onomatopoeic) [plurals: *díngar, díngis, díngáalis, díngéinna*]

dláamvas: to be afraid (passive of *láamvas*)

do: inside of

doka: out from inside of

dolághu: sorrow, (mental) pain

dúndas: to find something

dúndum: past tense of *dúndas*

'e: [same as *ke*, used if following word, described, begins with K of G]

éikyu: eternity

éikyusalándu: celestial music, music of the spheres

émras: most of

erkándas: (to be) heroic

érkas: (to be) strong

esándas: to dine [transitive verb]

ésas: to eat

estráahas: to expect something, wait for something

cstráhas [irregular passive of *estráahas*]*:* to be expected

estráu: something which is expected

étaghas: (to be) broken apart [passive of *etághas*]

etághas: to break apart

étaghu: a case of being broken apart [plurals *étaghar,*
   étaghun, étagháalis, étaghéinna]

étaghwis: the Sunderings [irregular literary plural of
   étaghu]

eténnas: to hold or contain something

éyas: (to be) green

eyn: (you) are

éyu: green(ness)

éyuhand: an oasis

fa: after

fódoskwas: to step on something vigorously, to stomp
   (onomatopoeic)

fyer: four

Fyoránya: Fyorian people

fyórlo: they, them (over there)

Fyoryal: a year in the Fyorian calendar

fyúras: archaic

gám: a mango [plurals: *gámar, gámis, gámáalis,*
   gáméinna]

gán: an oak tree [plurals: *gánar, gánn, gánáalis,*
   gánéinna]

gáng: a gong (onomatopoeic) [plurals: *gángar, gángis,*
   gángáalis, gángéinna]

gántas: (to be) angry

gántu: anger

gárnyas = gár-ni-as: to go in, enter

gárras: to go

géidhala: bringer, giver [plurals: *géidhalar, géidhalan,*
   géidhaláaris, géidhaléinna]

géidhalan: plural of *géidhala*

géidhas: to bring or give something

ghaan: would (1st-person form)

ghánt' [=ghántu, "red" variant of *gántu*]: destructive

wrath

gharn: would (3rd-person form)

gheyn: would (2nd-person form)

ghráas: to harm, do damage

ghráu: harm, damage

go: five

grásku: deformity

gréfandas: (to be) forgotten [passive of *grefándas*].

grefándas: to forget

grefándum: past tense of *grefándas*

grefándumen: not forgotten

gréshas: to sow, scatter about

gréshum: past tense of *gréshas*

grímvor: a survivor from the Devastation (origin obscure)

gyárndas: to ask

gyárndu: a question

ha: eight

háhas: to laugh (onomatopoeic)

hákhas [irregular "red" variant of *háhas*]: to laugh, especially in an evil manner

hákhum: past tense of *hákhas*

hálya: a game [plurals: *hályar, hályan, hályáaris, hályéinna*]

hánd: place [often used as an ending to indicate "place of"]

hándis: plural of *hand*

háras: to make war

hárf: a harp [plurals: *hárfar, hárfun, hárfáalis, hárféinna*]

háru: war

hin: behind

hinka: out from behind

hisíyas: to whisper (onomatopoeic)

hisíyum: past tense of *hisíyas*

hyá: hundred

hyálnáaris: centuries [collective of *hyálnu*]

hyálnu: a century [plurals: *hyálnar, hyálnun , hyálnáaris, hyálnéinna*]

ii lin: single

ii ngas: one (when counting objects), a, an

ii yam: first

ii: one

íilaka: alone

íilan ter: "the two" = both

íilan: the [indicates items belonging to a class of one, i.e., "The King of Kaii", "The Sword of Law"]

íilyas: (to be) good, beneficial

íilyu: good, benefit

ii-nge: ten, when used in mathematics (literally "one-zero")

ílda: tale, story, book [plurals: *íldar, íldan, ildáaris, ildéinnaa*]

íldawal': storyteller, author [plurals: *íldawalar, íldawalan, íldawaláaris, íldawaléinaa*]

imarn [ima arn]: now (it is)

íno: a dog [plurals: *ínar, ínon, ínáalis, ínéinna*]

ínyas: humble

iyen: first (before doing something else)

káa: (the) most

káa: a face [plurals: *káár, káan, kááalis, káaéinna*]

káari: [indicates action which began an indefinite time in the past and may be continuing – a "perfective" tense in English, i.e. "I have seen it" or "She has been reading".]

kágas: to kill

kághan: killing, murdering

kághas: ["red" variant of *kágas,* to kill] to slay, murder *kághu:* murder, death by foul play

Kálalyar: He (special 3rd-person pronoun for God)
["blue-green" variant of *kálalar* or *kállar* "he or she"]

kám: a sea, ocean [plurals: *kámar, kámis, kámáalis, káméinna*]

kámiin: a road of path [plurals: *kámiinar, kámiinn, kámiináalis, kámiinéinna*]

kánd: a kingdom, empire [plurals: *kándar, kándis, kándáalis, kándéinna*]

kántas: (to be) easy

kár: there (near him or near her)

kará: from, out of, away from

Karjanánya: Karjan people

kárlan: that (near him or near her)

kásu: social unrest

kavezán: a tower [plurals: *kaveznár, kavezánn, kaveznáalis, kaveznéinna*]

ke: [indicates previous word is to be used as an adjective]

kéi: there (near you)

kéilan: that (near you)

Kelsíima: the old Fyorian language

Kelsíimutánd: the old Fyorian empire

kémmas: to establish

kémmu: establishment

kewan: surname prefix for the eastern Fyorians

kewándii: elemental water

keyn: (you), please [indicates polite request]

kháa ["red" variant of *káa*]: an ugly face, a grimace [plurals: *kháár, kháan, khááalis, kháaéinna*]

kháagas: to grimace

khástu: aggression

khásu ["red" variant of *kásu*]: civil war

khétas: to maraud, plunder

khór ["red" variant of *kór*]: a tyrant [plurals: *khrár,*
    khórn, khráalis, khréinna]

khóru: (physical) pain

khrásaghal' ["red" variants of *krása* and *gála*]: "belly-
   crawler", a snake (implies poison and deceit)

kíi: here (near me)

kíilan: this (near me)

kitál: a dulcimer-like instrument [plurals: *kitálar, kitáln,*
    kitáláaris, kitáléinna]

klénnas: (to be) exact(ly)

kó: over there

kó: that which, a thing which (nominalizing pronoun)

kó'lan: that (over there)

kó'lin: such a thing

kólyas: to find something

kólyum: past tense of *kólyas*

kóntru: a difference

kór: a king [plurals: *krár, kórn, kráalis, kréinna]*

krása: belly

krém: a skull [plurals: *krémar, krémis, krémáalis,*
   kréméinna]

kullándu: elemental fire

kúllu: fire

kúmyal

kun: same as *kewan*

kwán: water

kwénas: (to be) possible

kwénu: a possibility

kwénum: past tense of *kwénas*

kyémas: to choose or decide (to do something)

kyémum: past tense of *kyémas*

kyémuwei: to make a general choice about something
   (habitual of *kyémas)*

láamvas: to cause fear

laghálas: to moan, make unpleasant sounds ["red"
    variant of *lálas*]
láina: silence
lálas: to sing, chant
lályas ["blue-green" variant of *lálas*]*:* to sing beautifully
lámas: to glow
leilyáendas: (to be) beautiful (physically)
lén: a star [plurals: *lénar, lénn, lénáaris, lénéinna*]
lor: above (does not imply movement)
lór: air
lornáalis: elemental air
lortélas: to prophecy
lortélu: a prophecy [plurals: *lortélar, lortélun, lortéláaris,*
    lortéléinna]
lúmas: to shine
lúmu: light
lúsu: a flute (onomatapoeic) [plurals: *lúsuar , lúsuan ,*
    lúsuáaris , lúsuéinna]
máelika: mother [plurals: *máelikar, máelikan,*
    máelikáalis, máelikéinna]
maellórn: 1. poetic name for the moon; 2. month
máelyika ["blue-green" variant of *málika*]: (one's own)
    mother
máino: same as *urmáino*
máltus: a sword [plurals: *máltusar, máltuis, máltusáaris,*
    máltuséinna]
máu: a cat [plurals: *máwar, máun, máwáalis,*
    máwéinna]
mázas: (to be) difficult
mé: an eye [plurals: *myár, mén, myáalis, myéinaa*]
médhras: to throw something in a straight direction
    (comparc *nagéras*)
melándas: to know (a fact)
ménnas: to think (about)

méi: a day [plurals: *méyar, méyn, méyáalis, méyéinna*]

méyeináalis: a week, group of several days

mi: with

mordhándalan: that which brings destruction

mordhándu tókaa: the Devastation

mordhándu: (great) destruction, evil, sorcery

mŕ: metal

mŕqemor: a metalsmith [plurals (irregular): *mŕndrar, mŕndorn, mŕndráalis, mŕndréinna*]

mú: nothing(ness)

múas: must, have to

múnggas: to swallow (onomatopoeic)

myár: (two) eyes [dual of *mé*]

na: before

nado: into

nadoka: through

nagéras: to throw, scatter, or broadcast something (compare *médhras*)

náhand: where? (literally "what place?")

nalaka: around

nalorka: over (implies movement)

námmen: why? What reason (do you have)? (literally "what think?")

nani: onto

nanika: across

nánkal' [=*nankala*] who? (literally "what person?")

nánxai: why? What cause? (literally "what cause"?)

ndal: archaic ending for place-names, i.e. Rohándal, Éyundal

ndhárvas: to be left in a current state (passive of *dhárvas*)

nel: 's (indicates possession by humans)

nélyas: (to be) kind (refers to doing something kind) [see *nnélyas*] *nemándas:* causing sleep

némang: [resultative of *némas*]

némas: to sleep

nému: sleep

nésmi: a rodent [plurals: *nésmyar, nésmin, nésmyáalis:, nésmyéinna*]

ngáa: a cow [plurals: *ngáár, ngáan, ngááalis, ngáaéinna*]

ngas: (used with a numeral to indicate counting, as in *ren ngas máun* "three cats")

nge: zero

nggárras: to come, approach

nggéidhas: to receive, get [passive of *géidhas*]

nggréshas: to be sown, scattered about [passive of *gréshas*]

ngís: an apple [plurals: *ngísar, ngísis, ngísáalis, ngíséinna*]

ni: in, at, on the surface of

níimas: (to be) significant

níimu: significance

nika: off of

nkémmas: to be established [passive of *kémmas*]

nnélyas: (to be) kind (refers to the kind action itself, i.e. kind words) [passive of *nélyas*]

no: 's (indicates possession, not by humans)

nol: rare variant of *nel*, sometimes used for body parts, i.e. *fyal nol mér* "his eyes"

noshéi: night [poetic form of *shéi*]

nqémum: to forge (metal)

ntófyas: to be hidden by something [passive of *tófyas*]

nyau: meow

ó: a ball, sphere [plurals: *ór, ón, óáalis, óéinna*]

olándu: an idea

olyandándu: a very good idea ("blue-green" honorific

form of *olándu*)

on téluwei: "they say..." or "it is said..." (see *on, télas*)

on: (that over there) is, or (that person over there) is

on: (the generic "they" or "one", as in "that's what they say" or "one should be careful")

ós: (to be) the same (often used before another adj. to indicate "quite" or "exactly")

ósh: a bone [plurals: *óshar, óshis, óshάalis, óshéinna*]

qámangas: (to be) histrionic, affected

qamángas: to affect, cause to be overblown, [back-formed active of *qámangas*]

qámellas: to be burnt [passive of *qaméllas*]

qaméllas: to burn

qaméllum: past tense of *qaméllas*

qámngas: to change into something

qémor: same as *mŕqemor*

qer: nine

qóghas: to doubt

r'estráu [=ro restráu] something which is unexpected

ra: during

raharn [=ra arn]: before and/or during [indicates preventative or preemptive action]

ras: (surname prefix for the southern Fyorians)

raságh: poison

ráth: herb, (herbal) tea

ren: three

rénthas: to stop or cease doing something

rényas: to begin

reyénika: a queen [plurals: *reyénikar, reyénikan, reyénikάalis, reyénikéinna*]

ro: no, not, without [negates following word]

rós: [= ro ós] not quite as, not quite so much

rowéikas [= ro wéikas]: unaware

ŕras: to hear

sáalu: a sound [plurals: *sáalar, sáalun, sáaláaris, sáaléinna*]

sáfas: to pass something down through generations

saghóalyas ["red" variant of *sáalyas*]: to make an unpleasant sound

sáalas: to make a sound

sáalyas ["blue-green" variant of *sáalyas*]: to make a pleasant sound

sáldas: to use

sálu: a song

sáluaa: music

sályuaa ["blue-green" variant of *sáluaa*]: (one's favorite) music

samáglas: to give off cold(ness), cause something else to be cold

sámas: (to be) cold

sámu: cold(ness)

sánatu: a berry [plurals: *sánatar, sánatun, sánatáalis, sánatéinna*]

séllan: even I (am)

sellarn: even it (is)

sémnang: crushed [resultative of s*émnas*]

sémnas: to crush

sén: thousand

shaghándas ["red" variant of *shándas*]: (to be) inflated, bloated, grossly exaggerated

sháimas: to cut

sháimum: past tense of *sháimas*

shalyándas ["blue-green" variant of *shándas*]: (to be) ripe, ample, plump

shán: same as *shándii*

shándas: (to be) big

shándii: seven

shánkan: combining form of *shánkas*

shánkas: to guard something

shéi: night

shigáyas: (to be) wrong

shin: six

shíras: to know

shíru: knowing, knowledge

shírum: past tense of *shíras*

siinón: a cave [plurals: *siinónar, siinónn, siinónáalis, siinónéinaa*]

siinónthwas: (to be) cavernous

sólas: to lose something

sólum: past tense of *sólas*

súas: (to be) small

sughúndas ["red" variant of *súas*]: (to be) puny, weak, grossly inadequate

sulyúndas ["blue-green" variant of *súas*]: (to be) petite, or (said of children) cute

súran: detail [plurals: *súranar, súrann, súranáalis, súranéinaa*]

sútas: to remain in one place

súwas: to sit

sya: because

syélnas: to depend (on) for a result, be regulated (by), be the result (of)

ta: more than (refers to time, i.e., more than three months)

táekom: a mountain [plurals: *táekomar, táekomis, táekomáalis, táekoméinna*]

táelor: father [plurals: *táelorar, táelorn, táeloráalis, táeloréinna*]

táelyor ["blue-green" variant of *táelor*]: (one's own) father

tamóskas: to attack

tán: stone (substance, or individual rocks) [plurals:

tánar, tánn, tánáalis, tánéinaa]

Tánd(u): the continent of Tond

tánd: earth, land, country

tánei ngís: a pomegranate (literally "seed apple")

tánei: seed, stone, pit [plurals: *táneyar, tánein,*
táneyáalis, táneyéinaa]

tánein: plural of *tánei*

tármas: to plan

tármu: a plan [plurals: *tármar, tármun, tármáalis,*
tárméinaa]

tárn: a tree, also, a wooded place [plurals: *tárnar, tárnn,*
tárnáalis, tárnéinna]

táv: food, foodstuff [plurals: *távar, távis, táváalis,*
távéinna]

táyu: evil, an evil thing or act [plurals: *táyar, táyun,*
táyáalis, táyéinna]

te: (indicates an adverb)

te: and

té: hand [plurals: *tyár, tén, tyáalis, tyéinna*]

teghámmas ["red" variant of *témas*] (to be)
undistinguished, boring, banal

téilas: to exist

téilandas: to make, cause to be [related to *teilándas* as
a standard active/passive verb form, though here
the meaning is causative.]

teilándas: honorific form of *téilas*

teilándumen: did not exist [negative past tense of
teilándas]

Teilyándal': (=*Teilyándala*) "He Who Is" or "That Person
(unspecified gender) Who Is", God (capital G).
[Honorific "blue-green" variant noun form of *téilas*.]

tél: word (individually, as in a dictionary) [plurals: *télar,*
téln, teláaris, teléinaa]

télas: to say

téllas ke: known as

telyámmas ["blue-green" variant of *témas*] (to be) just right, not too this or too that

témas: (to be) medium (size)

ténggas: to have, contain

ter: two

tléngas: to require

tlíiki: finger [plurals: *tlíikyar, tlíikin, tlíikyáaris, tlíikyéinna*]

tóa: often

tófyas: to hide

toká: sometimes

tóka: time

tókaa: time (of), age

tókáali: a cultural period or age (i.e. bronze age, modern period, etc.)

tómal': friend (gender unspecified) [plurals: *tómalar, tómalan, tómaláaris, tómaléinna*]

tómika: (female) friend [plurals: *tómikar, tómikan, tómikáalis, tómikéinna*]

tómor: (male) friend [plurals: *tómrar, tómorn, tómráalis, tómréinna*]

tráku: (a piece of) dung, (a piece of) shit [plurals: *trákar, trákun, trákáalis, trákéinna*]

trálgas: to deceive

tregánnas: to have holes or gaps, be ragged

trillórn: 1. poetic name for the sun; 2. same as *méi*

trúmitii: please (polite word)

tsáalal': one who listens

tsáalas: to listen [passive of *sáalas*]

tsáfas: (to be) passed down through generations [passive of *sáfas*]

tsáfum: (was) passed down through generations [passive of *sáfum*] *tsólas:* (to be) lost [passive of *sólas*]

tsólum: (was) lost [passive of *sólum*]

túas ke máltus: the Sword of Law (one of the *mechanas*)

túas: to cause order

túlas: to lose something (with a temporary connotation, i.e., I lost my keys)

túlum: past tense of *túlas*

túu: order, peace, lawfulness

tyáu: (one's) life

tyáular: his/her life

ún: a cloud [plurals: *únar, únn, únáalis, únéinna*]

ur: it, they (things)

urmáino: that thing or those things which were mentioned before (subject of previous sentence)

várka: a snake [plurals: *várkar, várkan, várkáalis, várkéinna*]

vii: again

vór: word, proverb, wise saying [plurals: *vŕar, vórn, voráalis, voréinaa*]

voráalis: (collective plural of vór)

vrénnu: a fraction, small piece of something

wághtas: [irregular "red" variant of *wártas,* to wait] to lurk

wártas: to wait

wéikas: (to be) aware

xáelika: daughter [plurals: *xáelikar, xáelikan, xáelikáalis, xáelikéinna*]

xáelor: son [plurals: *xáelorar, xáelorn, xáeloráalis, xáeloréinna*]

xáelyalan: (one's own) sons and daughters

xáelyika ["blue-green" variant of *xáelika*]: (one's own) daughter

xáelyor ["blue-green" variant of *xáelor*]: (one's own) son

xáinas: to cause

xáláaris: a family

xáláarislar: his or her family

xavándas: to weave, twine together

xenarn [=xen arn]: (it) may be

xéndadhas: to be carved

xendádhas: to carve

xérandas: to be unleashed, be let free

xerándas: to set something free

xerándum: past tense of *xerándas*

xóa: the sound of wind [plurals: *xóar, xón, xóáalis, xóéinaa*]

xontráavas: to deter, stave off

xóthaa: several (used with *ngas* as a counting word)

yálas: (to be) whole, complete

yam: (used with numerals to indicate ordinal numbers, i.e. *fyer yam ilda* "the fourth book")

yásh: a plague [plurals: *yáshar, yáshis, yásháalis, yáshéinna]*

yo: (indicates the direct object of a sentence, particularly in an unexpected place in the sentence)

za... : in that way,...

zéyas: to see

zhánika: a girl [plurals: *zhánikar, zhánikan, zhánikáalis, zhánikéinna]*

zhánor: a boy [plurals: *zhánrar, zhánorn, zhánráalis, zhánréinna]*

zhen: (and) then

zn... zn: and [used to bracket items thought to belong together]

zondrei: but, rather

THE BEGINNING OF THE "SONG OF ORIGINS" IN ITS
ORIGINAL FYORIAN
(here, the apostrophe indicates the final low-pitch U,
which is barely sounded or not sounded at all.)

*Lúmu ro arn téilandumen, su trillórn máellorn s'
nagérum.*
Dáestu ro arn téilandumen, su noshéi siinón s' eténnum.
Átau ro arn téilandumen, su trillórn kullánd' s' nagérum.
Sámu ro arn téilandumen, su noshéi kám s' eténnum.
Teilyándal' arn téilandum dálei,
Mú arn Kálalyar na téilandum.
Ro na arn Kálalyar na téilandumen.
Zhen Kálalyar arn zéyum, sálu karn teilándum.

Teilyándal' arn engkéilii yo téilandum,
Kaláarislar arn zn menálular téllular zn no xáelyalan,
Kaláaris arn Kálalyar nii éikyusalándis súlum.

SHERVÁNYA

Sherványa and Ondish are Fyorian's closest
relatives in Tond. They also descended from the
language of the Ancients before the Devastation.
Sherványa, spoken in a large region east of Rohándal, is
noted as being a very musical language.

It is very similar to Fyorian, as Rolan Ras-Erkéltis
noted on several occasions. About fifty percent of its
vocabulary is intelligible to Fyorian speakers, and more
can be understood once they "get used to" the accent.
The syntax is nearly identical, except for a series of
"redundant" pronouns that contain two "person"
references, indicating that the first of these is aware of

the latter, but is not necessarily a part of the action of the sentence. For example, *áarei* is a redundant pronoun with the first person marker (*aa-*) and a second person marker (*-ei*), indicating that "I am aware of you...". These pronouns are separated from the rest of the sentence by a postposition (usually *na*), and then the next word is a regular pronoun, the subject of the sentence. For example, *áarei na rei návan ng'gáyaye* is "I am aware of you, that you were going there". Other differences are a slight variance in the tense structure (Sherványa does have "continuous" tenses, those with -*ing* in English, which Fyorian lacks), "ownership" prefixes instead of suffixes, two-syllable subject particles (*návan*, above), and different endings, both on verbs (Sherványa verb-endings often end in -*usei* or -*l*) and on postpositions (the ending "vowel + *tdii*" is used on all postpositions of motion).

In phonology, Sherványa is somewhat simpler than Fyorian, having completely lost the clicked sounds and the back- and front-rolled R-sounds. All words must end in a vowel, a liquid (L or R), or a fricative (TH, S, F, DH, Z, V, SH, ZH). Syllables in the middle of a word, however, can end with a "hard" consonant (T, D, K, G, P, B), which they cannot in Fyorian. In Sherványa, these "hard" consonants are stopped off rather abruptly if they come at the end of a syllable, like the C in "act" in English. "Consonant distribution" and "colored words" are as active in Sherványa as in Fyorian (a famous Sherványa poem uses the phrase *líina wei-líinya* "silence, your beloved silence" with the NY indicating "beloved"). Vowels in Sherványa are pronounced with the same R, L, and N-modifications as in Fyorian.

Sherványa is written with the Fyorian *talwehéinnaa* alphabet, although it is called *taluéinnaa*. The alphabet appears simpler than in Fyorian, because Sherványa uses fewer "modified" vowel symbols – the vowels with R, L, and N are written with the regular vowel plus a consonant. Several of the consonants are also written differently.

ʃ⁊ ᵽʃ̃ᵐ⁊ ᵑ⁊ʰ⁊ ᵽᵑ⁊ᵽ⁊ᵐ̃ᵹ⁊
ƒ⁊ʃ⁊ ᵑ⁊ᵑᵐ⁊ ᵽᵑ⁊ᵽᵤ⁊⁊ ʰᵤᵽᵐ̃ᵽᵑᵤᵐ̃ᵑ⁊ ʃᵤᵑ̃ᵐ⁊ ᵑ⁊ᵑ⁊²

Sherványa inscription, the beginning of Shani's poem in chapter 18. The letters with the curly descenders correspond to the Fyorian letters with a small loop inside the larger loop.

ONDISH

Spoken on the island of Ond (*Ánd*) in the middle of the inland sea of Tsenwakh, Ondish (*Ándánla*) is another close relative of Fyorian and Sherványa. It resembles these languages in both pronunciation and grammar. The nouns and pronouns function closest to Sherványa, the verbs and verb tenses are closer to Fyorian. In another way, however, it is quite different – the island of Ond is deep within Karjan territory, and the two cultures, native Tondish and Karjan, have intermingled there for centuries. At times the truce has been uneasy, at times there has been outright war, but at other times the two cultures have blended and learned from one another. The result of this has been felt on the spoken language of the island – Ondish is a thoroughly mixed idiom, obviously Tondic in its structure but full of Karjannic words, many thousand by some estimates. This mixture is even obvious in the place names: the largest city is Gánuwein, a Tondic word referring to oak trees (i.e., 'oak' in Fyorian is *gánwu*), while the second largest (and home of the Ondish royal palace) is Chakreh, from *ts'hakreh*, the Karjannic word for 'palace'.

The sounds used to speak Ondish are perhaps closest to Sherványa, sounding rather like Fyorian but allowing more consonants at the end of syllables. However, Ondish has added a CH and a J sound (as in 'church' and 'judge'), neither or which exists in Sherványa. This is undoubtedly the result of Karjannic influence, as these sounds are common in Karjannic (see below).

The most interesting part of the mix comes in the nouns. Karjannic nouns make plurals by changing their first consonant (see below); Ondish plurals follow the Sherványa patterns. However, in the many 'borrowed' Karjannic words in Ondish, *both* plurals are used, sometimes separately with different shades of meaning, sometimes together.

chim "a word" (Karjannic -*chim*, a noun ending)
chimal "two words, separately, as in a list" (Sherványa dual)
chimm "words, separately, as in a list" (Sherványa plural)
jim "words in general" (Karjannic plural)
jimal "two words together, as in a speech, or written" (Karjannic plural, Sherványa dual)
jimm "words, together, as in a speech, or written" (Karjannic and Sherványa plurals)
jimuwein "All words, or a group of words regarded as a unit" (Karjannic plural, Sherványa collective)

etc. (Not all words have all of these plural forms.)

Karjannic verbs in Ondish do not go through their complex Karjannic changes (see below), but add the verb *réilas* "to do", (related to the Fyorian *rélyas*), i.e. *rakézhréilas* "to rule in a tyrannical manner" (from *hrakezh*, the Karjannic royalty).

Ondish is written with the *talwehéinaa*, though Ondish scholars can write Ondish in the Karjannic imperial script as well, with certain modifications (i.e., letters for the Tondish 'click' sounds, and several more symbols for vowels).

KAYÁNTII

Spoken in the north of Tond, Kayántii is another relative of Fyorian, though not as close as Sherványa or Ondish. It is generally considered to be a difficult language to learn.

Its difficulty cannot be in its pronunciation. Kayántii has the simplest system of sounds of any Tondish language. There are only 9 consonants in all. The original Tondic languages had a "fivefold" system (five sounds for one place in the mouth, i.e., K, KH, G, GH, X). In Kayántii, this has been reduced to two, "strong" and "nasal", giving, for example, T and N for one series; thus there are K, NG (as in "singer"), T, N, P, and M; the sounds W, Y, L, and R complete the inventory. The consonants T and P become D and B between vowels, but the Kayántii speakers themselves are not aware of this change. As for vowels, the system is similar to Fyorian but does not have the end modifications; Kayántii speakers say that their vowels are "pure". The system of voice pitch is like Fyorian except that the "high" pitch dips, resulting in something of a "Scandinavian" melody to some Kayántii words (for example, in the word *Kayántii* itself, the middle syllable *yán* is pronounced lower, not higher, than the others).

Kayántii is a subject-verb-object language, the same word order as in English. An interesting feature (also found in Drennic to the west) is that the verb "to be", which became the subject postposition in Fyorian and Sherványa, has remained a verb, and changes for tense, mood, and person, as well as for modal forms such as "can" and "want to". For example, *watá ka* is "I am", *watá ka kéyaa* is "I am going", *watá kan kéyaa* is "I want to go", *watá kan ka kéyaa* is "I want to be going". The verb endings are extremely complex, having a much finer division of time than is found in other Tondish languages; there are about thirty different tenses, some similar to Fyorian, many completely different, and some having meanings as subtle as "not later than tomorrow" and "early in the morning yesterday". Kayántii nouns also have endings; the "gender" endings are related to Fyorian (including *-oru* for male and *-ika* for female), but the "case" endings (used in place of the "object" particles) are not. Examples of the latter are *kenáe*, hill (subject), *kenáeli* hill (object), *kenáeku*, to a hill, *kenáepu*, of a hill, *kenáekai*, inside of a hill.

Kayántii is written with the *kántán*, an angular version of the Fyorian *talwehéinnaa* alphabet (but readable to the Fyorians). The name of this script comes from *kan* and *tan*, the first two letters.

Kayántii inscription, *Kenáekikabérika kuo léntu* "It happened at that time in Kenáekikabérika".

DRENNIC

Another member of the Tondic family, to which Fyorian belongs, is the large chain of dialects (collectively called Drennic) spoken in the northwest islands. Since this is not one language but many, any descriptions of it will have to be generalizations and/or descriptions of the "standard" Drennic, as spoken on the island of Kwi-So and the other Drennic States.

Drennic and its cousins, although also distantly related to Fyorian, are a different *type* of language. They are what linguists call "monosyllabic tonal languages". In languages of this type, most words consist of one syllable, and each syllable has a distinct pitch-pattern. Unrelated words often differ in this pitch pattern only. In standard Drennic there are five pitch-patterns, known in linguistic jargon as "tones": high, low, medium, falling, and rising. In other Drennic dialects there are also dipping and "humped" tones that start low, rise, and fall again, as well as "combination" tones such as high falling and high rising, or "drop" tones, where the voice noticeably changes pitch downward without a slide in the middle. The number of tones found in any given Drennic dialect ranges from three to ten.

Like all tonal languages of this type, Drennic tends to be monosyllabic; however, it is also "inflected", where words can change forms (as many tonal languages are not). Most of the changes are in the endings and tones, both of which are related to changes found in Fyorian. For example, *nàtk* (akin to Fyorian *lyánnas ke*) means "beautiful", *nàtx* (Fyorian *lyánnas kaa*) is "most beautiful", and *nát* (Fyorian *dlyánnas*) is "to make beautiful". (The different accent marks in

Drennic indicate approximations of the tone patterns, and the X indicates a back click. The Fyorian word also means "nice" or "friendly", not "beautiful".)

Drennic sentences are constructed subject-object-verb, finally ending with the verb "to be", similar to the Fyorian subject postposition. The "to be" is quite complex, consisting of a person-vowel (see Fyorian, above) and a final consonant indicating tense. The most common form is *àt*, indicating "he/she did", as in *Jan Meri í tsè àt*, "John saw Mary". Other forms correspond to more complex tenses. Drennic adjectives usually occur after the noun they modify, but they can also come before it, indicating that they are modifying something else but referring to some quality of the noun; for example: *mák srég* is "strong horse", but *srég mák* is "strong, like a horse" and is in fact a common Drennic masculine name. (In these two examples, *mák* means "horse".)

Drennic is noted in Tond for its strange sound; partially this is due to the tone system, but it is also due to the consonants. Drennic is unique in the Tondic language family for being able to end, not only with a "hard" consonant (see Sherványa, above), but with two (as in *nàtk*, above). This may be a feature "borrowed" from the two Karjannic-like languages, Tashkrian and Chashk, which are also spoken in the northwest islands. Most Drennic dialects have lost all of their fricatives (soft consonants, i.e., SH, ZH, F, V), an opposite deveploment to Sherványa. Drennic has also retained all three of the original Tondic clicks; in fact, the number of clicks is actually six because in standard Drennic they can be voiced or unvoiced. Nasal sounds (M, N, NG) at the end have all become "hard" consonants, but some nasals have been re-introduced from Fyorian and

Kayántii. The vowels are roughly like elsewhere in Tond, though some Drennic dialects also have umlauts. Drennic is written with the *talwehéinnaa* (which is called *pyō kàip* "Fyorian writing") or with one of two indigenous systems: far in the north a syllabary is used (an alphabet where each letter stands for a syllable), apparently a very old system; and in the Drennic States an angular "vertical line" alphabet is used. The name "vertical line" refers to the fact that every syllable is written as a cluster of symbols affixed to a vertical line (resulting in the "stick figures" mentioned by Tayon), though the scripts itself runs horizontally, left to right.

Inscription in the "vertical line" script (the vertical lines are often printed first). This is actually the first stanza of Lewis Carroll's poem "Jabberwocky" in Fyorian, written with the Drennic characters. No suitable Drennic texts were available at the time of publication.

KARJANNIC

Karjannic is spoken in the Karjan Imperium, immediately south of Rohandal across the South Rohandal Mountains (Prapfkts Mountains in Karjannic); thus it is a neighbor of Fyorian. The two languages have "swapped" a few words, but other than that they are quite different; in fact, few languages anywhere are as dissimilar as Fyorian and Karjannic.

Karjannic is a member of the Karjic language family, which originated on a continent to the west of Tond. Tashkrian and Chashk, spoken in northwestern Tond, are other members of this family. All Karjic languages are 'classifier' languages, which group ideas (particularly nouns) into categories, each category with its own grammatical and syntactical features (other 'classifier' languages include Navajo and Zulu). These languages are extremely difficult for adult non-natives to learn, and tend to have complicated constructions that make Fyorian (and English!) look like checkers as opposed to chess. Karjans traditionally view this complexity as superiority, and insist that their language is in fact the most perfect of all, having been invented sometime in the past by a committee. Fyorians poke fun at this, noting the (to them) rough sound of spoken Karjannic, and admitting that only a committee would have invented *that*. Probably, however, there was no such committee, unless it was a group that agreed on certain standard forms.

SOUNDS MADE IN THE KARJANNIC LANGUAGE

CONSONANTS

- Sounds made with both lips: PH (F with both lips), BH (V with both lips), P, B
- Sounds made with the upper teeth and lower lip: F, V, PF, BV
- Sounds made with the tongue and teeth: T, TH, D, DH (TH as in "them") -- the TH sound seems to be becoming rarer, and is merging with the HL sound.

- Sounds made with the back of the throat: K, KH (German CH), G, GH ('voiced' KH)
- Sounds made with the nose: M, N, NG (as in "singer"),
- Sounds made with breath through the nose: HM, NH, HNG (nothing like these occur in English)
- Hissing sounds: S, SH, Z, ZH (Z as in "azure")
- "Ejective" sounds with sharp breath: TS (as in "cats"), DZ (as in "adz"), CH (as in "church"), J (as in "judge")
- R's and L's: R, L, HL (Navajo Ł, Welsh LL)
- Others: H, Y, W, ' (apostrophe indicates a glottal stop, or "catch" in the throat; sometimes, however, the apostrophe is also used to avoid confusion in combinations, for example, TH is as in "thin" but T'H is as in two words in English, e.g. "white hen" (and the Karjannic word *krat'huk* "a sailor").

Any consonant can occur in any place in a syllable, even in the middle where a vowel would be expected. The consonants F, S, SH, TS, and CH regularly function as vowels. There is no distinction between consonants which are pronounced sharply and loudly, or those which are "unreleased" (where the mouth moves into position to pronounce the consonant, but then moves on to the next sound before actually enunciating it). For example, a typical vowel-less Karjannic syllable, *pgt*, could be pronounced as (with the vowels silent or whispered) *pug-ta*, *up'g-ta*, or *p'gut*. A similar process occurs in English: for example, the C in "act".

GH is as in Fyorian; KH is a little rougher, with a bit of a "rasp" and close the Fyorian back-rolled Ṛ.

Karjannic linguists traditionally arrange the consonants in a grid of 14 "sets" (*bvrek*) of 4 "permutations" (*dksh*) each. These sets include some combinations; the Y is always a consonant. The sets are important to the grammar of the language, and will be discussed in detail below.

	Permutations:			
	1	2	3	4
Set 1	K	KH	G	GH
Set 2	T	TH	D	DH
Set 3	PF	F	BV	V
Set 4	P	PH	B	BH
Set 5	TS	S	DZ	Z
Set 6	CH	SH	J	ZH
Set 7	HNG	NGY	NG	NGW
Set 8	HN	NY	N	NW
Set 9	HM	MY	M	MW
Set 10	H	HY	'	HW
Set 11	HL	LY	L	LW
Set 12	HR	RY (ri)	R	RW (ro)
Set 13	HW		W	
Set 14	HY		Y	

(The last three sets are irregular. In set 12, two of the varieties of R are followed by vowels; and in sets 13 and 14, there are only two permutations – with sounds found in other sets.)

VOWELS

A (as in "f<u>a</u>ther"), AE (as in "b<u>a</u>t"), AI or AR (indistinct; variably as in "p<u>ie</u>" or "p<u>ar</u>"), E (as in "b<u>e</u>t"), I (as in "b<u>i</u>t"), O (indistinct, variably as in "b<u>oa</u>t" or as in "t<u>o</u>"), OO (as in "c<u>oo</u>k"), U (as in "d<u>u</u>ck").

The Karjannic scripts arrange six of these in pairs of

"long/short": A/U, AE/E, O/OO. The short pronunciations are far more common.

Because Karjannic has so few distinct vowel sounds, it is often difficult for the Karjan to learn correct pronunciation in Fyorian.

ASSIMILATION

In spoken Karjannic, many of the sounds "assimilate" into neighboring sounds, producing a word of phrase that is pronounced differently than expected. (This phenomenon is common in languages; an example in American English is "didn't you" pronounced as "did'n choo".) Medial CH and J sounds in particular are altered: *tsech'ehna* "I see" is pronounced *tse''ehna* (the two apostrophes indicate a glottal stop that is longer than usual); *krichpfanga* "I greet (you)" is pronounced *krippfanga*; *tsajjukka* "he is fighting" is pronounced *tsaijukka*. The rules governing these changes are regular though complex, but in writing (and in the rest of this description of the language), the words are spelled etymologically, not by pronunciation.

GRAMMAR AND SYNTAX

SENTENCE STRUCTURE

The standard Karjannic sentence is nearly a mirror image of its Fyorian counterpart, since the usual order is verb – subject – object. The verb is really a cluster of words, frequently called the "verb complex".

THE VERB COMPLEX

The verb complex has the verb at its core (see below); before and after it are optional modifiers. The first modifier, which always begins the sentence if it is used, is the 'mood indicator'. This functions a little like the 'subject postposition' in Fyorian, further indicating the way in which the verb 'controls' the rest of the sentence. The mood indicator breaks into two parts: the first indicates whether the sentence is a statement, speculation, command or request, question, etc.

statement	*ta-*
speculation	*ri-*
polite request	*ke-*
command	*ka-*
question	*li-*
counterfactual (would...)	*wa-*
other (i.e., "if...",	*pa-*

This is joined to its second component with a Y, W, or glottal stop. The second component indicates type of action or state:

completed action	*-'ach*
incompleted action	*-'ash*
state: 'becoming'	*-'as*
state: 'is'	*-yas*
state: 'becoming not'	*-'ak*
state: 'is not'	*-yak*
possibility of --ing	*-to*
possibility of not --ing	*-tok*
other process	*-yef*

The following examples show how these function with a verb (the example verb is *tsegala* "to write"; the changes within this word are explained in "verbs", below).

ta'ach tsechgahla "I am writing"
ta'ash tsechgala "I wrote"
ta'ash sechgala "I had written"
tayas tsechkahla "I am a writer"
ta'ak tsechkahla "I am no longer writing; I am becoming
     a non-writer, etc."
tayak tsekkahla "I am not a writer"
keyef tseshgahla "Could you write, please?"
kayef tseshgahla "Write!"
wa'ach tsechgala "I would have written"
wa'ach sechgala "Had I been in the process of writing"
pa'as tsechkalwa "If I were to become a writer"

etc.

If used with a first person pronoun (see below), the 'request' and 'command' forms take on the meaning of 'I or we have been asked to...". Thus, *keyef tsechgala wak* "I have been asked to write".

As can be seen from these examples, these are quite complex and sometimes the meanings can only be approximated in English. However, there is a certain amount or redundancy between these and the verb itself. Therefore, unless the intended meaning is very subtle or cannot be deduced from context, these 'mood indicators' are seldom used in conversational speech. In writing, however, they are used very frequently.

The 'mood indicator' is followed by the verb itself, which in turn may be followed by a subject pronoun. See "verbs" and "pronouns" below.

VERBS

It is useful in Karjannic to distinguish between

"animate" and "inanimate" root words. Animate roots can become verbs (all verbs are in fact from animate roots) and thus are part of the verb complex. An animate root word consists of two vowels and at least three consonants (from the grid of sets and permutations, above), arranged in a pattern of C-V-C-V-C. In the examples here, the main three consonants are in caps:

PeHNuHN "runner / to run"
TSeKaHL "writer / to write"
HraKeCH "king, queen / to rule"

These are the citation forms of the words, the form in which the word is listed in a dictionary. From this citation form, two verbs can be derived.

1.) stative verb, "to be a ____". Add -*a* on the end.
    pehnuhna "to be a runner"
    tsekahla "to be a writer"
    hrakecha "to be a ruler"
2.) active verb, "to do ____". Add -*a* on the end, change second consonant to "third permutation".
    penuhna "to run"
    tsegahla "to write"
    hragecha "to rule"

These two form the backbone of the Karjannic verbal system. From these, the various tense and person forms are derived.

There are four basic tenses, most of which can occur in all four verbs from a single root. (From now on, only one sample animate root will be given, *tsekal* "to write / writer"). The four basic tenses are present, future, past, and "always", and are made by changing the third main consonant.

1.) present, as in citation form.
2.) future; third main consonant in second permutation form:
   tsekalya, "will be a writer"
   tsegalya "will write"
3.) past; third main consonant in third permutation form:
   tsekala "was a writer"
   tsegala "wrote"
4.) "always" (or "never" in the negative form); third main consonant in fourth permutation form.
   tsekalwa "always is a writer"
   tsegalwa "always writes"

Doubling the last consonant (that is, pronouncing it twice as long as usual) results in a continuous verb, rather like adding -ing in English.

tsegahlla "is writing"
tsegallya "was writing"

etc.

In addition, each verb has several "person" forms. The four basic forms are made with an added -*ch*- immediately after the first vowel; this goes through its four permutations.
1.) first person: -*ch*-: *tsechkahla* "I am a writer",
   tsechgahla "I write", etc.
2.) second person: -*sh*-: *tseshkahla* "You are a writer",
   tseshgahla "you write", etc.

3.) third person: *-j-*: *tsejkahla* "He/she is a writer",
   tsejgahla "He/she writes", etc.
4.) impersonal: *-zh-*: *tsezhkahla* "one (a person) is a
   writer", *tsezhgahla* "one (a person) writes", etc.

A negative person form is made with *-k-* in the same
manner.

1.) first person: *-k-*: *tsekkahla* "I am not a writer",
   tsekgahla "I don't write", etc.
2.) second person: *-kh-*: *tsekhkahla* "You are not a
   writer", *tsekhgahla* "you don't write", etc.
3.) third person: *-g-*: *tsegkahla* "He/she isn't a writer",
   tseggahla "He/she doesn't write", etc.
4.) impersonal: *-gh-*: *tseghkahla* "one isn't a writer",
   tseghgahla "one doesn't write", etc.

There is a passive form made with *-n-*, and a
negative passive made with *-kn-* (the *k* changes through
the permutations, the *n* does not change in this form.)
In the case of the verb "to write", obviously some of
these are nonsensical and thus not in use.

tsen'gahla "it is being written".
tsegn'gahla (third person, third permutation *g*) "it is not
   being written".
(In both of the above examples, the apostrophe is used
   to separate confusing consonants, which do not
   appear in the Karjannic script.)

The passive can be used with stative verbs. The
result is a noun, not a verb (see nouns, below).

LINKING VERBS

Two verbs may be linked, indicating that one takes place at the same time, or as a result of the other (context usually makes this clear; if not, two sentences may be stated). In this case, the -*a* on the end changes to -*ne*.

garjragne gijmbola wiweyb"...(they) did gyre and gimble in the wabe" (Lewis Carroll)
tooshgapne to'on'gaphtsash "Give, and it shall be given unto you." (Luke 6:38) (See 'transitive verbs, below, for more explanation on the endings on these examples.)

PHRASAL VERBS

Another use of the -*n*- form is to create a 'phrasal verb'; that is, a verb which subsumes an entire noun phrase. There are several types of phrasal verbs in Tashkrian and Chashk; Karjannic has only one. It consists of the stative verb in its -*n*- form without its final -*a*. The stative verb here functions more properly as a noun, and the meaning of the 'phrase' is that the thing in question is approaching the speaker (or the speaker is approaching it). With the stative verb *tsekal* "to be a writer", the result is *tsenkahl* "a writer is approaching", which is rather nonsensical though understandable. A better use of the phrase would be something like *tsech'ehnj tsenkal* "I went to see a writer" because the direction of which party approached whom is not specified (*tsech'ehna* "I went to see", from *tsehen*, "to go and see". The apostrophe here means a glottal stop.). An even better example is *karnchaen* "someone is approaching", from the stative verb *karchaen*, "to be a person". This type of phrasal verb appears often in place names, such as Hwatsats

Hondrakch "Tower of Dawn, Tower of Sunrise, Tower of the Rising Sun", where *hondrakch* = "the sun (is) approaching us". The second consonant in its third permutation form is not a passive (or a mistake!); the sun is not an animate noun and thus does not change in that manner (see nouns, below). Idiomatically, "the sun approaching us" means "sunrise" and "the moon approaching us" (*pfentrukch*) means "moonrise". (In Karjannic cosmology, "approaching [the Karjan lands] means moving upwards.) A negative form of this same construction is possible, indicating that the thing in question is going away; this uses a *-we-* directly after the main verb: *hondrakwech* "the sun (is) going away from us", hence, sunset. In the far western dialect of Karjannic, this negative form is pronounced the same as the positive, but has a distinct and quite dramatic drop in voice pitch in the first syllable: *hòndrakch*. This is the only example of voice pitch carrying such a degree of meaning within a single word in Karjannic; there are a great many more of these in Chashk. In all of these, the *-ch* functions as it would in a transitive verb (see below).

PLURAL VERBS

The verb can be singular (the forms discussed so far) or plural. The plural refers to the number of people or things performing the action, not the action itself, i.e., the plural of "I go" is "we go", not "I go more than once". The plural is made by voicing the first consonant, that is, changing a first-permutation consonant to a third, and changing a second-permutation consonant to a fourth.

tsechkala "I am a writer" → *dzechkala* "we are writers"

etc.

REFLEXIVE VERBS

A verb can be made 'reflexive' (the subject doing it to him/herself) by adding *km-* to the beginning, i.e., *tsech'en* "I see" → *kmtsech'en* "I see myself", *kmtsesh'en* "you see yourself". In the plural, this means "to each other" or "among one another": *kmdzech'en* "we see each other".

TRANSITIVE VERBS

A large number of verbs do not exist just by themselves or with only a subject. With the verb 'to write', for example, it is obvious to ask 'to write *what*?' These verbs with objects are transitive verbs, which in Karjannic take particular forms.

In transitive verbs, the *-a* on the end drops off of all the verbs which have it. It is replaced by a set of classifiers, which refer to the nouns that make up the object(s) of the sentence. These classifiers will be discussed in depth under 'nouns', below.

The transitive verb may have up to three objects. The following example has two:

tsechgahlltaesh 'I am writing (a letter) to you'.

This can be broken apart into three parts:
tsechgahll 'I am writing'
ta 'classifier for flat objects, such as (in this case) a letter'
sh 'classifier for animate roots, in this case, changed to second permutation form, you'

The verb 'I am writing a book to you (i.e., for you to

read)' would take a slightly different form:

tsechgahllsash "I am writing a book for you (to read)', where *sa* is the classifier for books.

The three possible object classifiers are direct object, indirect object, and auxiliary, always in that order (which is the same order in which the nouns will occur in the rest of the sentence). The indirect object has several forms, which can be illustrated best with the verb *paprak* "to throw" (and *ok* is the classifier for round objects, such as a ball):

prajbaga "he threw"
prajbagok "he threw a ball"
prajbagokch "he threw a ball to me" (plain sense)
prajbagokoch "he threw a ball for (the benefit of) me"
     (-*o*-, benifactive sense)
prajbagokich "he threw a ball at me" (-*i*-, linear
     direction)
prajbagokench "he threw a ball for (instead of) me"
     (-*en*-, surrogate object)
prajbagokkoch "he threw a ball for (the harm of) me"
     (-*k*- negative + benefactive = detrimental)
Thus: *Ta'ach prajbagokich prajbagokkach!* "He threw
     they ball at me and tried to hurt me with it!"

The classifier for animate nouns (and for pronouns) is *ch*, which changes according to whether it is first, second, or third person, or impersonal: *ch, sh, j, zh*; as the same marker changes when it occurs as the subject. The classifiers for inanimate nouns (see nouns, below) do not change.

An example of a transitive verb with all three

objects (including the auxiliary) is *prajbagokichmt* "he threw the ball at me over (the wall)", where *-mt* is the classifier for large vertical surfaces. The auxiliary thus takes the place of a prepositional phrase in English, though only one is permitted in a Karjannic transitive verb.

MODAL VERBS

There are several words in Karjannic that function as auxiliary verbs, and which do not change. These include *prk* "to like to", *gsh* "must, to have to", *drf* "must not", *shok* "should", *knelg* "can, to be able to", and so on. These are attached to the beginning of the main verb: *shok-tsechgahla* "I should write".

PARTICLE ENDINGS

There are a few 'particles' that can occur on the end of a verb, which are similar to the 'particles' for objects (see nouns, below) but do not refer to a specific thing stated later in the sentence. These include *chuk* "that", *sko* "a little bit", etc., i.e., *chlarchhnagchuk* "I learned that", *chlarchhnagsko* "I learned a little bit" (*chlarhnaka*, "to learn").

"COLLAPSED" VERBS

Certain verbs have "collapsed" forms. These are without vowels, with the second consonant in the second permutation form (for consonant sets 3, 4, and 6) or in first permutation form (for the other consonant classes). They are attached to the end of regular animate verbs, resulting in two distinct forms, both which function essentially as adjectives.

1.) passive subject form: the word *gruntagkshk*, used in this book, is an example, "manufactured creatures". *Gruntag* is the plural passive past tense of the stative verb *krutaka* "to be a creature, to be alive (not used for humans)." *Kshk* is the collapsed form of *kojoka* "to manufacture", telling what the creatures had done to them.

2.) adjectival form: two examples occur in this book: *kargoortstk* "killer man-lizards" and *dzokra-krtsng* "dwellings at the edge of wandering". In the first example, *kargoor* is a 'false stative verb', a coined word from *kar-* "man" and *koor* "lizard"; *tstk* is the collapsed form of *tsataka* "to be dead" or *tsadaka* "to kill" ("to die" has a different form). There is a particular sense of horror to this word, not translatable into English: since the collapsed verbs have no directionality; the 'man-lizards' are both killers and dead zombies. *Dzokra* are dwellings (animate root *tsogala* "to dwell"), *krtsng* in the collapsed form of *kratsang* 'to wander to the edge of known territory, to explore", telling in this case where the dwellings are (right at the edge of Karjan land).

Collapsed verbs are used sparingly, mostly in set phrases and coined words, as they can sometimes be confused with the endings of transitive verbs. A form of humor in Karjannic is to invent collapsed forms of nouns that happen to have three consonants, and use them like collapsed verbs; an example is deliberately reading *Dzokra-Krtsng* to mean "dwellings of the fruit fly" because *krootsarng* "fruit fly" can be jokingly collapsed into *krtsng* as well. Of course this example works even better in the plural: *Dzokra-Grtsng* "dwellings of the fruit flies" (see nouns, below).

TRANSFORMING VERBS TO NOUNS

Animate roots can be either nouns or verbs; their

use as verbs was discussed above. As nouns, the most common form is the animate-class noun, which means "a person who does ___". For example, *tsegahla* means "to write" and *tsekahla* means "to be a writer"; its noun form is *tsekahl*, "a person who writes", or simply "a writer". These nouns are made by simply stating the animate root in its citation form, or with the second consonant in third permutation form, without any further endings or consonant changes. This is usually considered the basic root word (though in these words, too, the consonants can undergo the 'permutations', see below). Another form is made by reversing the last consonant and vowel; these mean something like "a thing that is involved in doing ___". Their meanings can be rather vague, but many of them have specific meanings that are common objects in Karjan culture, i.e., *tsajka* "sword", from *tsajuk* "Karjan warrior". (This is anglicized with an A on the end for purpose of pronunciation.)

NOUNS

Karjannic nouns fall into twenty-five classes and some sub-classes, each with its specific forms and grammatical features. In the case of animate roots, it is possible to say that there is little distinction between nouns and verbs; these change in the same manner as verbs (the only difference is the part of the sentence in which they are used, and the fact that animate nouns do not have the -*a* or other endings, see above).

The second main consonant changes to indicate part of the sentence (see below); the third main consonant changes, in the same manner as in a verb, to further specify the tense (which here must be rendered as an entire phrase in English):

tsekahl "writer"
tsekaly "one who will be a writer"
tsekal "one who was a writer"
hmejdagch tsekal "A person who had been a writer met me" (*hmedaka* "to meet")

etc.

The other noun classes do not have such complex metamorphoses, and cannot take perfectives or tenses.

Each noun class has a characteristic verb ending (as above), definite and indefinite article (both optional), pronoun ("it"), relative pronoun, and ending for adjectives and numerals. For example, animate nouns use the consonant from the ch-series (as above) for all forms, with the articles being *cha* and *chel*, and the relative pronoun being *ach*. Nouns denoting animals have *–wa* for the verb and adjective endings, *wak* and *wa* for the articles, *wam* for the pronoun, and *wahan* for the relative pronoun; nouns denoting places have *–l* for the verb ending, *-la* for the adjective ending, *la* and *al* for the articles, *elak* for the pronoun and *lak* for the relative pronoun. (*Tsech'enwal chanwa wa ino wahan tsomgla al kiwarn* "I saw a big dog which was in a colorful garden"). There are about forty noun classes, and the words associated with them are not predictable from those for other noun classes. If the exact noun is known or can be inferred, it does not need to be stated; the verb and adjective endings, pronouns, etc., fill in where necessary.

Almost all nouns are made plural by voicing the first consonant, as in the case of verbs, i.e., *tsekahl* "writer", *dzekahl* "writers", *kyamtsk* "mountain", *gyamtsk* "mountains". If the noun begins with a vowel (i.e. *ino*, "dog"), then the singular and plural are alike; or, if confusion may arise, the plural may be marked with *es* "some": *tsech'ehnwa ino* "I see dogs", *tsech'enwa es ino* "I see some dogs". The plural can be further modified by adding e- to the beginning, this means "many": *egyamtsk* "many mountains". Noun classes for powders, liquids, "dots" and grains, and measurements have no plural form.

ROOTS OF ANIMATE NOUNS

A curious feature of many animates is that they seem to consist of two smaller, single-syllable roots. The word *Karjan* itself is one of these, consisting of *kar* 'man' and *chaen* 'woman'; thus the word could be said to simply mean 'people'. The root *kar* appears again in the coined word *kargoortstk*, the "lizard men" manufactured by Gaeshug-Tairánda; here, it also means 'man', while the *goor* is another root meaning 'lizard', and *tstk* is the collapsed form [see above] of *tsatak* 'to kill'. The word *tsatak* itself contains a shorter root, since both it and *tsachuk* 'warrior' begin with *tsa-*, as does *tsamook* 'hunter' and *tsapfeng* 'murderer'. *Tsachuk* is also said to mean 'tooth'; the warriors of the Old Imperium were often called *Gaejtark-Bad'hanani dzachuk*, the 'Teeth of Gaejtark-Bad'hani', and the words *chukat* 'to chew' and *chuktsa* 'ivory' appear to be related. Curiously, none of these roots are found alone, separated from the other parts of larger words; for example, *kar* means 'man' in a larger word, but no one speaks of one *kar* (a word for a man is *katsan*), and there is another unrelated word *kar* which means 'silt in a river', and is never found in a larger word. However, all of these single-syllable roots have individual characters when written in the ancient hieroglyphics [see below], and thus probably represent another layer of vocabulary, functioning the same way in Karjannic as the Latin and Greek elements in English or the Chinese elements in Japanese and Korean. Its origins are unknown; similar words appear in Tashkrian but not in Chashk.

PRONOUNS

All nouns have their pronouns; the pronouns of most classes (which are always third person) were discussed above. Animate nouns have their own set of pronouns, and since animate nouns are usually humans, they can be "I", "you", "he or she", etc. Each of the pronouns comes in three grades, 'normal' (used in conversation among friends), 'rising' (used to one's social superior), and 'falling' (used to an employee, a child, or to anyone 'below' you in a social stratum). The 'exclusive' forms mean 'not including you (the person spoken to)', whereas the plural forms always include the person spoken to. For example, *ali* means "you and I", *jawa* means "I, not you guys", *wajala* means "you guys and us", *a* means "you and him or her", *aki* means "they and not you", and *yap* means "they and you guys".

When used as a subject, these immediately follow the verb in the verb complex, and then are linked to rest of the sentence by a slight pause or the preposition *ta*:

tsechgahlla wak "I am writing"
tsechgahllj wak (ta) ya "I am writing to him / her"
tsechgahlltaej wak (ta) ya "I am writing a letter to him / her"

tsechgahllj iwak (ta) ch'hlaghat "I am writing to my boss" (*ch'hlaghat* "to my boss", from *hlakat* "boss". Here, the first-person subject 'falling' form is used, as 'my boss' is 'above' me in a social stratum. If this subject were not used, then the 'rising' form of "him/her", *ehl* or *eth*, would be inserted as an "extra" object.)

etc.

One infamous utterance with these pronouns appears several times in the Tond story, the old battle cry of the Imperium under Tarshkn: *Kayef grechdaemwsh arjala!* *Grechdaemwsh* is the plural first-person 'always' form of *kretam* "to conquer, destroy" with the *-sh-* ending indicating 'you'; *arjala* is the rising form or "we (exclusive)". Thus, "we who are above you (are commanded to) always conquer and/or destroy you (who are below us)". The meaning is obviously much stronger than its usual English translation "we come to conquer" indicates. (For the meaning of *kayef*, see sentence structure, above.)

ADJECTIVES

Adjectives can be made from animate nouns by adding *-i* on the end (the second consonant is always in the third permutation form). Like the Fyorian adjectival verbs, these behave like verbs, having the verb endings; unlike their Fyorian counterparts, however, they can only take two tenses, present and past (this is actually similar to English – we can speak of a 'broken' window and perhaps a 'breaking' window, but other tenses have to be expressed in more elaborate ways, i.e., 'a window which will be broken').

chanaka "to be big"
chanaki "big"
chanakiwa ino "a big dog"
tsajuka "to fight"
tsajuki "fighting (adjective)"
tsajukiwa ino "a fighting dog"
mredehngim tsyawi "a window which is breaking"
(*mredehnga* "to break")
mredengim tsyawi "a broken window"

Other adjectives are not derived from animate roots and cannot take tenses (again, like English – we can speak of a 'small' rock but not a 'was-small rock'). These also have -*i* on the end and a verb ending.

fsti "quick, fast"
fstiwa ino "a quick (i.e. running) dog"
fstil kretam "a quick attack"

Adjectives of both types may take a number of prefixes indicating "becoming" (*aj-*), "becoming not" (*kaj-*), possibility of being (*an-*), etc.

PREPOSITIONS
These function as in English, with one exception (see below).

ta kyamtsk "on the mountain"
kok kyamtsk "towards the mountain"
hwajdahnnkf kok po kyamtsk "He is walking towards the mountain."

etc.

The one exception is the preposition meaning "inside of", which graphically illustrates its meaning by being inside of the noun it modifies. It consists of the sounds *-iw-*, inserted immediately after the first consonant of the noun. One example of this is the name Ai-Leena gave to one of her pets in the Tower of Dawn: *Prk-Hwiwandzaz* "Always like(s) to stay in the Tower" (*prk* is a modal verb meaning "like to", *hwiwandzaz* is a phrasal verb derived from *hwatsats* "tower", including the preposition *-iw-* and the "always" tense with the third consonant in its fourth permutation.)

POSSESSIVES

Add *ch-* for first person, *sh-* for second, *j-* for third, and *zh-* for impersonal, and the vowel *o* if the result is unpronounceable:

tohmohn "friend"
chotohmohn "my friend"

The relationship 'belonging to' is expressed by a number of methods, depending on noun class. Some nouns duplicate the last syllable, others add a suffix (based on the possessed items' noun class!), others add the suffix *–i* for all items possessed, others and a prefix, and still others add the infix *-aw-* in the last syllable.

tsekal "a writer"
tsegalal shkrat "a writer's pen"
ino "a dog"
inoya yeb "a dog's bone"
inoj ksatsan "a dog's man (owner)"
plitska "storm"

eplitska tswok "a storm's lightning; the lightning in a storm"

kyal "bush"

kyawal laep "a bush's leaves; the leaves of the bush"

DEMONSTRATIVES

fi means "this", *fa* means "that".

QUESTIONS

Karjannic has a number of question words, i.e. *vak* "who", *phal* "where", *tslk* "how much". These are used at the beginning of the sentence. There are also question adjectives, with *ak-* at the beginning, i.e. *ak-tolka* "how long?"; these are used by themselves, or as regular adjectives in a sentence (but require an answer). Simple yes/no questions are made with the *li-* prefix on the mood indicator (see above).

NUMBERS

1 el, 2 hla, 3 ching (or) *chng, 4 gaech* (or) *gch, 5 gwok, 6 kael, 7 ruk, 8 tsaek* (or) *ts'k, 9 pfra, 10 tom* (or) *kfagwok* "two (times) five", *11tom s el* "ten and one", *12 tom s hla, 13 tom s ching, 20 hlatom* (or) *gaechgwok* "four (times) five", *21 hlatom s el, 25 kfatom s gwok* (or) *kmgwok* "five of itself", *100 tyak* (or) *kmtom* "ten of itself", *1000 shek* (or) *tomtyak, 0 nyar.*

As can be seen, many of these have alternate forms made by multiplying; for example, ten has an alternate form "two (times) five", *hlagwok*. Mostly these are done with multiples of five (i.e., fifteen is *chnggwok*) and ten, though it is possible with other numbers. (The multiples of five are used very commonly, and related forms are found in Tashkrian and Chashk as well, indicating that Karjic languages may at one time have had a base-5 number system.) When the number is squared, the "reflexive" verb (!) prefix is used, as in 25 "five of itself" or *kmgwok*. Interestingly, the alternate form for 100, "ten of itself", or *kmtom*, is the same word that linguists have reconstructed for the ancestor of all of the Indo-European languages.

Karjannic numerals are not stated alone except in mathematics. When used for counting, each must have an ending specified by the noun class (see above). For example, counting people (animates), the numbers 1, 2, 3 would be *elch, hlach, ch'ngch*. For counting cows (animals), they would be *elwa, hlawa, ch'ngwa*. For counting the horns on the cows' heads (if they had varying numbers), 1, 2, 3 would be *elpn, hlapn, chngpn*. Tayon Dar-Taeminos noted this at one point, noting that the horns on the heads of the 'unicorn deer' actually varied in number and so the animals should be called '*elpn chrak*', '*hlapn jrak*', and so on (*chrak*, plural *jrak*, "horn").

NAMES

Personal names are a matter of confusion in Karjannic, particularly when attempting to use them in another language that does not share the Karjannic naming customs.

Karjannic given names, known as *karaz*, are (like their Fyorian counterparts) from a stock of ancient names, many of legendary characters, most of which have lost all their meanings and are simply 'name words'. All given names have a long form and a short form; the short form usually consists of the first one or two syllables of the long form. Examples include (for men) the several members of the last old-tsajuk order that wanted to overthrow Ai-Leena's; they all had relatively common Karjannic names. Their short forms, given in the text, were Roagh, Beyn, Yarch, Rech, Grogd, and Bregg. Their long forms are Roaghrumtsuk, Beindaestaemk, Yarchkichkenik, Rechtanggwok, Grogdmkhrotsk, and Breggzdmgarshk. (By puns, some of these are not entirely meaningless. Roaghrumtsuk, for example, sounds like hro'akhrum-tsuk "Son of a Fire Spirit". See below for the –tsuk ending.) As can be seen from these examples, long forms of men's names usually end in K, though there are a couple of exceptions such as Rendugzgarm and Kyochtarnoogt (shot forms Rend and Kyoch). Women's names follow the same pattern, though tend to end in a vowel: Tyomarkintsha, Shreghantstavi, Jalmooktangi are common; their short names are Tyo, Shre, and Jal (Tyomarkintsha was one of Ai-Leena's Karjannic names).

But except among the upper castes of Karjan society, the given names, long or short, are seldom used. Instead, each person has a *karats* "name for the time being" (notice that *karaz* "given name" is a verb-like noun with its third consonant in its fourth permutation, that is, in its "always" tense!). A *karats* is selected by the person whose name it is, and indicates something about that person. It may be a phrasal verb, a noun, or some combination (including a noun and a 'collapsed' verb), and may be quite creative and complex. Some examples include Prk-Kontonriktl for someone who likes to play the *kital* (a popular stringed instrument) (modal verb *prk* "like to", + *kontohnri*, a phrasal verb "to play a musical instrument" + *ktl*, 'collapsed' form of *kital*), Karhwatsats "Man tower" for a particularly tall or strong man, Tsenkalwts'hrkch for someone who prides themselves on their "lordly" calligraphy (a high art to the Karjans), (*tsenkalwts*, phrasal verb "to write something such as handwriting", + hrkch, collapsed form of *hrakech*, "royalty"). *Karats* names for women can be even more creative, usually indicating something of beauty. The simplest are flowers (the idea is not unusual to speakers of English, where women often have names like Heather, Rose, or Jasmine) but more complex examples include Hondrakchi-Dyalk "Clouds at Sunrise", Twandzekt'hsp "Sea Spray" (*twandzek*, phrasal verb "to spray" + *t'hsp*, 'collapsed form of *t'hatsap* "sea" – a coined 'collapsed' form of a noun) and even Choph-Ob-Peshtikf-Tsenwak "Rainbow over the Great Lake filled with Fish". Ai-Leena actually kept the custom of the *karats* name; though Ai-Leena is a Sherványa name, it means "beautiful stars" (its Karjannic counterpart is Tngp'hl, which she uses on occasion; -p'hl is the adjective suffix for the noun class of stars).

Karats names are not fixed. They can be changed, and most Karjans adopt at least four during their lifetime.   For example, a boy might call himself Kfiwandzatstmk "Play in the Tower"; as a teenager he might change it to Tfach'ahla "I am an adventurer"). As an adult he might call himself by an occupation, though usually with some manner of indication that he was particularly good at said job (i.e. Kshlwa-ino-trgch "Trainer/raiser of loyal dogs".)

Karjans do not use "family names" in the way speakers of English are familiar with. Rather, men use -*tsuk* "son of (father's name)" and women use -*chul* "daughter of (mother's name)". Ai-Leena's full Karjan name is *Tyomarkintsha Tngp'hl Yathknchul (Ai-Liina) Hrakezh*; the middle two names mean "Beautiful Stars, Daughter of Shimmering River" (and of course *hrakezh* is her title as a queen).

WRITING

There is a confusing multiplicity of ways to write Karjannic. Oldest are the hieroglyphs, each of which stands for a word; combinations of glyphs within a square frame are used to represent the complex word-aggregates common to the language (see the example of Hwatsats Hondrakch, as explained by Teyan Dar-Taeminos). Other styles of writing (there are about ten) are alphabetic; most were invented separately over several centuries, often originally as codes for secret communications. Like all codes, they are quite regular and have few unusual or archaic spellings. The best known, and the most commonly used, is the *hragezhi tsekaltsekk*, the Imperial Script, a vertical writing with long slashing lines, described as "an elegant and angry script" by the Fyorian historian Renyar. The script is read top to bottom, left to right. The main consonants are written with large characters occurring in four forms indicating their four permutations; these are further modified to show that they are the first (or middle) and last consonant, the latter has a long 'tail' drawn downwards and to the left. Secondary consonants, those that come between the main consonants and vowels (such as the 'W' in *hwatsats*) are written with another character to the left, with a long 'tail' drawn upwards and to the left. (Thus the 'tails' often cross each other; this is not confusing and is actually thought to be a beautiful part of the calligraphic script.) Vowels are written with a smaller character to the right; vowel-like consonants are written with the usual "tailed" secondary consonants (to the left) and a special "vowel marker" (to the right). Other systems of writing Karjannic are written vertically (in the same manner), or horizontally left to right, and have related or unrelated symbols for the various consonant permutations; some scripts, such as the *grohlati tsekaltsekk*, the Merchants' Script, are based on the Imperial Script.

"Imperial Script" consonants (part one)

Beginning or middle	End	Additional		Beginning or Middle	End	Additional	
			K				KH
			G				GH
			T				TH
			D				DH
			PF				F
			BV				V
			P				PH
			B				BH
			TS				S
			DZ				Z
			CH				SH
			J				ZH

143

Beginning or Middle	End	Additional		Beginning or Middle	End	Additional	
			HM				MY
			M				MW
			HN				NY
			N				NW
			HNG				NGY
			NG				NGW
			HL				LY
			L				LW
			HR				RY (ri)
			R				RW (ru)
			H				HY
			' (glottal)				HW
			Y				
			W				
			(silent)				

The consonants of the Imperial Script. Included are the forms for the beginning (and middle), end, and the "additionals" – the latter are the consonants that occur between another consonant and a vowel. They are written to the left of the main consonant letter; for example, in *hwatsats*, the W is an "additional" written to the left of the H.

As in the Fyorian *tálwehéinnaa*, punctuation is derived from the consonants. There are a couple of different "end of text" symbols: the curl on the bottom indicates "end of sentence", another slashing line acts like a comma, and the curl with two slashes indicates

144

the end of the entire text. The following show how the K letter would look by itself, at the end of a word, and with these three punctuation marks.

	✓	E		⌣	AE
	o	OO		o	O
	e	U (uh)		e	A
	(	!			
	6	AR (ai)			
⦂ (or)	>	(indicates vowel)			

Imperial Script vowels, written to the right of the main consonant, are extremely simple. The dot indicates the "long" sound; the "U" (or "uh") is the schwa sound. The letter that "indicates vowel" functions as a regular vowel but indicates that an "additional" consonant (written to the left of the same main consonant) is to be treated as a vowel. For example, in *kmtom* ("hundred"), the first M is written as an "additional" to the left of the K, and the three dots are written to the right of the same K (the second M in *kmtom* is a regular consonant). The three dots is the standard form of this letter; the "sideways V" is a simplified form.

SOME KARJANNIC WORDS FOUND IN THE "TOND" BOOKS

'ahhinor: Fyorian loremasters (plural of *hahhinor*; noun
    class 25: foreign words)

Ach: at the time of; once upon a time (conventional
    beginning of a story; has no grammatical
    information)

al: (indicates a gerund)

Arjala: we, us, not including you (used by social
    superiors)

Ash: and (conjunction)

bad'hanini: "of war(s)" (genitive plural of *pad'han*
    "war"; noun class 23: abstract)

bizhulg: "these mountains" (*bi* "these" + *zhulg*
    "mountains"; noun class 8: places).

bohrazhulg: (name for) the South Barrier Mountains.
    (*pohra,* "south" + *shulg* "mountain"; the plurals
    form are *bohra* and *zhulg*; noun class 8: places)

Bvolaha: to follow

ch'nanok: our universe (1st person possessive prefix; *na*
    "everything"; *nok* "place"; noun class 8: places)

chachkuhma: "I feel pain" (1st person form of *chukahma*
    "to feel pain")

chig: different

chigtl: "it (the air) is different" (true adjective, suffix for
    noun class 20: ethereal)

chiweyhar: next to the Great River Cheyhar (name of
    the river; infix for location)

Chng: three

chohrakech: "my (fellow) member of royalty" (a term of
    endearment among the *Hrakezh*)

Chol: our place (1st person possessive pronoun; suffix
    for noun class 8: places – compare *wil'l.*)

Chomikak: "my friends" (1st person possessive prefix +
plural of hmikak "friends". This is a special broad
word for "friend" that may include those who are
not human, i.e. pets, imaginary beings, etc.)

Chopartaktfk: "my brother is wounded" (1st person
possessive prefix; *partak* "brother"; *tfk* "collapsed"
form or *tapfark* "to wound, to injure")

chugahm: one who feels pain

Chuhlmo: meanwhile

chukahma: to feel pain

Chul: (ending indicating "daughter of")

Dilarng: more

Dyichdaza: we always twist (plural 1st person tenseless
form of *tyidadza* "to twist")

Dzajdaka: they stand there, they are located there (3rd
person plural of *tsadaka* "to be located at")

dzepalbts: "these (places) are a barrier, separating
this/these other place(s)" (stative verb; 3rd person
plural subject, distributive plural object for noun
class 8: places; derived form of *tsebala*, to break
apart or separate)

Dzi: words (plural of tsi – noun class 23: abstract)

Dziwobek: "in the language of __" or "as speakers of __"
(locative form of animate noun *dzibek* "speaker of
__ language"; derived from verb *tsipek* "to speak __
language"). This is a plural form; the word was
spoken by Rolan (not a native speaker of Karjannic),
and he may have confused it with *dzi* "words",
which is a related morpheme.

dzn'raenksh: "the counterparts of these places" (*dzn*,
plural possessive for noun class 8: places + *raenksh*,
plural of *hraenksh*, a counterpart, similar thing of a
different type – noun class 24: abstract).

El: one

el-pejkana: it was the beginning of (nominalizing prefix; 3rd person singular past tense form of stative verb *pekahna* "to be the beginning of something")

Eth: (nominalizing prefix)

Eth-garkchaena: "those who are not Karjan" (nominalizing animate prefix; negative plural of *karchaen* "Karjan")

fot: often

Fsti: quick

Gaejtark :"they are makers" (3rd-person plural of *kaetark* "maker", stative verb form of noun class 1: animate – this is the title of the 'creative' deities in the Karjaenic pantheon, with the 'royal plural')

Gaetark: the Karjan creator deities (plural of *kaetark*)

Garchaen: Karjans (plural of Karchaen)

Garnchaen: Karjans (used as a passive object)

Gch: four

Grask (gras'k): archaic word for servants (plural noun class 1: animate, derived from obsolete *krazaka* "to serve")

Grdzajuk: armies of tsajuk warriors (collective prefix; plural of *tsajuk* "warrior")

Grechdaemwa: we always conquer (plural 1st person tenseless form of *kredahma* "to conquer")

grechdaemwsh: "we will destroy you" (active verb; 1st person plural future tense, 2nd person object of noun class 1: animate; derived form of *kretaema* "to destroy, conquer")

Grechdaemwsh: we always conquer you (first person plural tenseless form of kretahma "to conquer"; 2nd person suffix)

Greshtaemwopwa: "you will always be the destroyers of those vermin, for their own good" (stative verb; 2nd person plural tenseless form, benefactive object of

noun class 7b: vermin; derived form of *kretaema*
"to destroy, conquer" – see *grechdaemwsh*

Greshtaemyopwa: "You will be the ones who (for
benefit) destroy the vermin" (2nd person plural
future tense stative verb *kretahma* "to be
destroyers", akin to *kedahma* "to destroy";
benefactive object of noun class 7b: vermin)

Grichpfangsh: "many greetings to you" (literally "we
have greeted you" even if spoken by a single
person. First person plural of *kripfahnga* "to greet"
+ 2nd person object suffix.)

Gruntagkshk: "manufactured creatures"; one of
Gaeshug-Tairanda's armies. (plural past-tense
passive form of stative verb *krutaka* "to be a
creature; to be a monster"; irregular "collapsed"
form of *kochok* "to manufacture; to make in a
deliberate process", here functioning as an
adjective)

Gruntagtmka: "creatures (taken forth from) earth",
"earth creatures" (plural passive object form of
krutak "creature or monster"; irregular collapsed
form of *toomka* "earth")

Gwejlanicha: they dwell in each, they live in each (3rd
person plural locative distributive form of *kwelahna*
"to dwell")

Gwok: five

Gzadanwa: "to always exist" (plural tenseless form of
ksadahna "to exist")

Hannok: a section of a larger place

Hehlat: a captive, hostage

Hek: additional

Helapha: to assist

Hitsajuk: an army

Hla: two

Hlishhnahna!: "You are a demon!" – a common insult. (2nd person present tense stative verb *hlihnahna*, referring to one of the destructive deities in Karjan mythology – see *lihnahn*)

Hmag: big, great

Hmagkf: (referring to a natural phenomenon) great, big (*hmag*, big; ending for natural phenomenon)

Hmahrak: to become

Hmikak [see note at *chomikak*]

Hnaduka: to win

Hnatjtuka: he/she/it wins (3rd person form of *hnatuk* "to win")

Hnatuk: winner

Hngarshk: an army (same as *hitsajuk*)

Hnom: good

Hnum: several

Hondrakch: sunrise, dawn (idiomatic stative form of active verb "sun approaching us, moving upward", from *hatrak* "sun")

Hondrakkwech: sunset, dusk (idiomatic stative form of active verb "sun leaving us, moving downward", from *hatrak* "sun")

Hotrak: the sun

Hradzang: one who is at fault

Hraenksh: a similar thing of a different type

hragezhnok: the Imperium ("place of royalty", from *hrakezh*, the Karjaen royalty; noun class 8: places).

Hrajgezhkna: he rules over all others (1st person singular tenseless form of *hragecha* "to rule", derived from *hrakezh* "ruler"; exclusive suffix)

Hrajgezhnok: He or she rules over that place (3rd person singular locative form of *hragezha*, "to rule")

Hrakezh: (a member of) the Karjan royal caste

Hrakezhnok: The Imperium ("place of *hrakezh*"); see

Hragezhnok

hwatsats: tower (noun class 2: miscellaneous nouns structured as noun class 1)

Hwekh: time or age (i.e. Bronze Age, Marchine Age, etc.)

Hwiwatsats: "In the tower" (locative of *hwatsats* "tower")

Hwiwatsats: in the tower (hwatsats "tower"; locative infix)

Hyahngaki: young

Hyajngaga: It was a young person or young thing (3rd person singular past tense of stative verb *hyangaka* "to be something young", derived from adjective *hyahngaki* "young")

Hyotsak: to use

Jolinan: "their destructive powers" (3rd person prefix; plural of hlihnan "destructive power" – see *lihnahn*)

K'ha: not

Kachlakksh: "I am calling you forth!" (1st person present continuous form of *kahlaka* "to call forth"; 2nd person object suffix)

kachlakksh: "I am calling you forth" (active verb; 1st person singular, present tense continuous, 2nd person object of noun class 1: animate; derived form of *kahlaka* "to call forth, call out to, give a mission to"

Kael: six

Kaelchkf: six (buildings) are there (*kael* "six"; endings for buildings and location next to a natural phenomenon)

Kaetark: one who makes, is creative

Kajdzangwjl: "It is always the fault of" (3rd person, tenseless form of *kadzang* "to be at fault", "to cause (with negative connotations; 3rd person

object suffix of noun class 1: animate; object suffix
for noun class 23: abstract)

Kalaka: to call out, call forth

Karjaeni: Karjannic (adjective derived from *karjaen*)

Kayef: (indicates imperative to continue a process)

Ke tsak: even that which is ___.

Kejarka: to be in a particular class or order of things

Kep: from (genitive preposition used with names and
pronouns)

kiwarjaennok: "into the Karjaens' land" (indirect object
form of *karjaennok*, place of Karjaens; noun class 8:
places)

Kmpfoojkach: "power is used against itself" (reflexive
prefix; 3rd person present stative verb of *pfookach*
"a state of power")

Kmt: midnight

Kodehna: to hold something

kodlahna: to descend

kotlanwawits: "he/she goes down into (a place) from a
higher elevation" (3rd person singular, tenseless
form, directional object form for noun class 8:
places; derived form of *kodlan*, to descend from a
higher location)

Kraektks: strategy

Kratsahnga: to dwell

kratsang: traveler (noun class 1: animate)

Krazaka: [obsolete] to serve

Kre: to dare to (modal verb)

Kredahma: to conquer, destroy

Krichpfangsh: Hello (literally "I have greeted you". 1st
person singular of *kripfahnga* "to greet" + 2nd
person object suffix.)

Kripfahnga: to greet someone

Krtak: [obsolete] a force in nature

Krtakak: "of the forces of nature", used only in the
name of the Karjannic deities of nature.
(Genetive/possessive form of obsolete *krtak*, "the
force of nature")

Krutak: a creature or monster

Ksadahna: to exist

Ksep: expected

Kth: can, be able to (modal verb)

Kwatsihl: a counsil, meeting

Kwedehna: to go

Kwehlahna: to dwell [same as *kratsahnga*]

Kwehlaki: well

Kwezhhlekka: "they are being well; one is being well;
one is well" (impersonal present continuous form of
kwehleka "to be well")

Kyatsohla: to rescue

kyeth: (indicates two things happening at the same
time)

Le wa: "concerning you"

Le yan: "concerning others" (*yan*, plural of *hyan*
"other")

Letak: to be ready

Lihnahn: The Karjan destructive deities (plural of
hlihnahn)

Lihnahna: to destroy

Madzata: to collect or amass something

maha: air (noun class 20: ethereal)

Mebahla: to meet

Mejpalikfa: They met there in that building (3rd person
plural past tense of *mepahla* "to meet"; locative
form; suffix for buildings)

mok: far

moktsrenk: "farther north" (*mok*, far + *tsrenk*, north)

na: all

Ngsh: (preposition meaning "over", with the connotation of superiority – as in one thing beating out another in a contest)

Nyekshk: "those that are not ___" (plural negating prefix; "collapsed" form of *kechark* "to be a particular thing or class of things")

Oja: you (singular, respectful)

Ont: noon

Ot: resulting in ___.

P'sh: therefore

Pad'han: a war (noun class 23: abstract)

Pajpfookazhopwa: "power used beneficently against the vermin" (prefix indicating force or violence against an object; tenseless form or pfookach "power"; benefactive suffix; suffix for noun class 7b, vermin)

Partak: brother

pegahna: to begin

pehnuhna: to run

pekahna: to be the beginning [see *pegahna*]

Pfanata: to find

Pfookach: power

pfooksh: power (noun class 24: abstract derived from true adjective; *pfookishi* "powerful")

Pfra: nine

Pfrendukch: moonrise (idiomatic stative form of active verb "moon approaching us, moving upward", from *pfretuk* "moon")

Pfrendukkwech: setting moon (idiomatic stative form of active verb "moon leaving us, moving downward", from *pfretuk* "moon")

Pfretuk: moon

pohra: south

Pran: east

Prihngaka: to bring something

Prk: to want to, to like to (modal verb)

pyacham: to cross, go across a region or area.

Pyajahma: one who goes across a particular region

Ragezhi: "of royalty" (genitive adjective plural form of *hrakezh* "royalty")

rek ___ rak: less ___ than.

Ri'ek: (indicates reflexive or distributive action in a sentence)

Ruk: seven

Rukkf: Seven (buildings) or seventh (building), depending on form of word indicated

s': and

sh': 2nd person prefix attached to a noun of any class to indicate an often metaphorical "you are ___" (derived from the 2nd person copula infix)

Sh'pfooksh: "yours is the power" (2nd person prefixed irregular stative form of *pfookach* "power")

Shren: friend [same as *tohmohn*]

shulg: a mountain

T'senahnga: to happen

Ta'ach: (indicates indicative, active sentence)

Tabvarka: to wound

Taksan: many

Tapfark: one wounds another

Tarshknun: belonging to Tarshkn

Tayas: (indicates indicative, stative sentence)

Tehlehna: to respond

Teluhla: to return

Tigopa: to discover

Tinaka: to think, reason out

tk: although

tkau-: to help (modal verb)

Tkau: you (pl. exclusive respectful)

Tm: from this to that (i.e. *pran tm tsol* "from east to west")

Tmajhrag: it had become (3rd person singular past tense of *hmahrak* "to become"; perfective prefix)

Togapa: to be in a particular location

Tom: ten

Toomka: earth, soil

tremach: a foreigner (noun class 1: animate)

tremachkrtsng: a foreign traveler *(tremach,* a foreigner + *krtsng,* "collapsed" form of *kratsang,* to wander or travel; noun class 1: animate)

Truchtsakne: "I hope that ___" (1st person present tense of *trutsaka* "to hope" + link)

Trudzak: to hope

Truttsakne: (phonologically assimilated form of *truchtsakne*)

Tsa'eth: (indicates an indicative sentence referring to distribution of objects or classes of objects; links to previous sentence)

Tsadaka: to be located in a particular place

Tsajgardne: he battled and ___ (1st person singular past tense of *tsakart* "to battle", akin to *tsatak* "to fight"; link ending to other verbs)

tsajka: sword (noun class 5: implement, derived from *tsajuka* "to fight")

tsajuk: 1. warrior (noun class 1: animate, derived from *tsajuka* "to fight"); 2. tooth (noun class 4: body part)

Tsajuka: to fight

Tsakya: one's enemy (noun class 1B: animate with modifications for feelings of the speaker)

tsakyats: "(that place is) formidable or intimidating" (true adjective with ending for noun class 8: places)

Tsatak: one who is located at a particular place

tsatak: to fight, to struggle

Tsatka: a struggle (noun class 23: abstract; derived from
   tsatak "to struggle, to fight", akin to *tsajuk*
   "warrior")

tsebahla: to break apart or separate

Tsedahma: to say, report

Tsehnat: to send

tsepahl: one who breaks apart or seperates something

Tsezhdamle: "It has been said that ___; it was said that
   ___" (impersonal past tense form of *tsedahma* "to
   say, to report"; link suffix to next sentence. The
   exact meaning is "One said that ___.")

Tsibeka: to speak a particular language

Tsipek: one who speaks a particular language

Tsk: eight

Tsl: (definite article for noun class 9: buildings)

Tsobvrak: to surprise

Tsol: west

Tsom: (and) then

tsopfraghtl: "he/she is surprised by it (the air,
   atmpsphere)" (active verb, 3rd person singular,
   tenseless form, 3rd person object of noun class 20:
   ethereal; derived form of *tsopfrak*, to be surprised).

tsrenk: north

tstk: "collapsed" form of *tsatak* (to fight, to struggle),
   used as an adjective suffix in *kargoortstk* "lizard
   man")

Tsuk: (ending indicating "son of")

Tyidatsa: to twist

Tyitatsa: one who twists

Vyoran: Fyorians (plural of *Fyoran*)

vyorannok: the Fyorians' lands ("place of Fyorians",
   from *vyoran*, plural of *fyoran*, a Fyorian – noun class
   8: places).

Wadzadza: "things (i.e. ruins) that used to be a tower"

(plural past tense form of stative verb *hwadzatsa* "to be a tower")

Watsats: towers (plural of *hwatsats*)

Wekhl: of (many) ages (genitive plural form of *hwekh* "age")

Wil'l: our place (1st person plural respectful possessive pronoun; suffix for noun class 8: places – compare *chol.*)

TRANSLITERATION OF AI-LEENA'S LETTER IN BOOK FOUR, WITH EXPLANATIONS

(Compare this with the English translation found on Page 35 of Book Four.)

Gwechhleka arjala. Gwechdena (we went) Beworroggne techlula (we returned); t'sezhnanga ("this happened) k'ha (not) kseptil (expected situation – adj + ending) kyatslo (rescue) kep Rolan jomikak le taksan (many) 'ahiinor. Tayas lochkapa arjala (we are in) tiwawak (in the town) fo kwatsihl (of council) Riwohandal.

Ach Biworrogg, ta'ach bvachhnadne (we found) gyach[u]tsolj (we rescued them) Rolanpak Arnul, le hnum (several) le dzarjaen (other people) akik (rel.) 'ejlada (captives). Tayas lojkapoch (they are located with us) Arnul tach (and others) ak (rel.) kyachutsola. Ta'as kwejhleka ya.

Ta'ach aukh (also) tichgobvutsuj (we discovered facts about it) Gaeshug-Tarranda. Ile (here) tsm-lechbvottsish tugnits: ta'ach majdzattsya (it is amassing) wak krutak idzajuk (armies), tayas fstil krejthaemt rosh (all of) Tond. Kth (of course) brichbvenyul. Ta'ach tsong (soon) pajhralwal (they will have a council about it) wach 'ahiinor chokraetks (our strategy). Chulhmo (meanwhile), kichbvakkshl ahinoror pfooghach. Kojntehnko (it contains an object) pag (bag) kos (rel.) Kwaa prijngagko (he brought it) ahiinand; bvojloh (they will follow) dilarng (things to do further; more instructions). Ka'ach mishtakj awa (you ris. meet with them) le raghezh akik dishnak (you think) tl-'ejlaphch (they could help us); pfoojkachnel hmoojpfakm (it has power, it moves) jodzajuk ngarshk (their tsajuk armies) ya Rewohandal wits (rel.) mishtakj awa lomokor tach ahiinor. Prijngakhshtaesh (he will bring you another text) Kwaa gwokpl (five days); tsom (then) prijngakhko nam (many) sartiko (of a certain type, adj.) ahiinand. Ml-'yoshtsakhko, (you may use them), ka'ach dzeshnathkoj (send them to them) 'ekko (extra ones) S'Lansek kep ahiinor Terol Shriwen Hiwembnok. Ka'ach leshtakne (you are ready to) teshlehlne (to respond to) awa tach Hriwakezhnok ye ra (yes no) wiwts pewahral.

Imaya twachbvakts hragezhi shojopfang bvook'welwsh, k neh kayef trejrakhjts Chwandokhratk michtakpf jogayashi.

EMB

Spoken by another people in the far south of Tond, Emb is (unfortunately for the present text) not well studied. Most of the travelling Emb are rather secretive about their language and learn Fyorian to communicate with others. From what little material is available, Emb appears to be an inflected language with strong isolating tendencies. There are three main verb forms (a present or citation form, a past, and a participle); these differ mainly in vowels (many forms are irregular), while in the present tense there are endings denoting first, second, or third person. Gerunds are created with a suffix; additional tenses are made with combinations of the three standard verb forms plus auxiliary verbs. There are a number of common expressions consisting of a verb plus one or more prepositions, and prepositions are used with nouns rather than case endings or particles. Phonology includes fairly common consonants and vowels, with a tendency to include vocalic nasals (such as the M as the prefix to feminine names); clicks and the unusual Karjannic consonants are not found. Word order appears to be subject, verb, object (the same order as in English). In an Emb dictionary, many words have been noted that are similar to languages from outside of Tond. Several Emb words have gained currency throughout Tond: for example, *autóm* means "travelling, on a journey" (used as an adjective) and is frequently heard in the conversations of Fyorian loremasters.

This description is rather vague, and further studies will follow.

The Arts of Tond

Tond is a highly literate culture, and like all cultures, it is also artistic. Of course the visitor from this world is likely to be stumped by some aspects of its "foreignness", though he could find a lot that is familiar too. The same visitor might also be confused by its plurality; Tond is not a single culture but an interaction of many.

LITERATURE

The non-written oral literature of Tond goes back millennia, and the traditions are still very much alive in the northern regions, particularly Kaii, the Drennlands, and the northern Sherványa Lands. In all of these places, large audiences gather to hear master storytellers (such as the Drennic *Chelloi*) recite epic tales that often last for hours over several consecutive nights. These tales are ancient, based on historical incidents, contain sections both memorized by rote and sections of ad-lib, and recited in a half-chanted *profundo* style of verse that makes a sheer delight from the sounds of the spoken language. Rhyming is used in the tonal languages of the Drennic Islands (and some of the tales rhyme in tones as well as sounds); but complex patterns of consonant repetition are more commonly used in the Kayántil world, where rhyming is unsuitable for the language. Nearly half of these tales belong to a sub-genre of "Location Histories", which begin with a long description of a certain place and then describe its entire history from the Sunderings to the present (such a tale is that of Kenáekikabérika, mentioned elsewhere in these volumes). Other sub-genres include histories of vanished kingdoms, tragic love stories, lives of ancient semi-mythical heroes (from their birth to their death), and ribald comic tales (which derive much of their humor from parodies of other tales, and are usually told during New Year's festivities). A curious feature of some of these stories is that they have several alternate endings, following, for example, the lives of a different character or the incidents that occurred in a slightly different region – but comparisons of the alternate endings (and with other related tales) reveal that they are actually all interconnected and rarely, if ever, contradict each other. (A tale with an alternate ending, the legend of Keilátia, is discussed elsewhere in these volumes.) In recent centuries, (after the Devastation), storytellers have increasingly been Fyorian *ahíinor*, and Fyorian-style tales of wanderers and their *mechana*s have been added to the repertoire, but they are not considered as interesting since they are much newer and have not had their verse refined over countless generations.

Some storytellers tell their tales with just their voice, and some use an improvised accompaniment on the *kital*, an instrument very much like a hammered dulcimer without the hammers – this accompaniment is not considered music in the usual sense, but consists mostly of sound effects (including literal renditions of birdsongs, and rapping on the wooden side of the instrument for battle sounds). All storytellers adopt different voices for the speech of different characters in the tale, often using imitation archaic forms of speech for the older characters (one is reminded of the Grimborn, who use archaic speech when addressing others, and are far enough north to be influenced by this tradition.)

In contrast to this oral literature, book-writing is more prized in the literate south of Tond (the Fyorians, Emb and Karjans are all highly lettered, with mandatory schooling for most people – until the age of fifteen in Rohándal). Much of the book writing is, of course, based on the older oral tradition; there are vast collections of (originally oral) tales that have only relatively recently been codified into book form (within the last thousand years or so, or since about five centuries before the devastation). The Fyorian *Tonílda* (the source of the Song of Origins) is similar to these, though it is very much older, perhaps by three millennia. Other tales such as the Fyorian legends of Ésrathan and North Rohándal (the latter is an example of a "Location History"), the Karjannic "Chonggor and the Lizard-Men" epics, and the Emb legends of S'Remik and S'Chim, were also originally oral but are best known in book form. As with the northern oral literature, rhyming is an intrinsic part of the verse, especially in the Emb legends; though Fyorian adds the idea of recurrent verse-forms, such as the repeating descriptions of the Four in the Song of Origins Appended Verses. Karjannic verse (of this type) often rhymes in vowels only – including some of the "vowel-like" consonants unique to the language (see Languages of Tond) – thus, *handrakch* is said to rhyme with *kwakrapch*.

The book has of course created some of its own genres; the novel and the poetry collection are both familiar to all southern Tondish. Improvised poetry is also popular among the Karjans and the Emb, often in the form of contests.

MUSIC

As any foreign culture, the music is the most "foreign" and the most difficult to appreciate. Tondish music is also extremely varied (more so than the literature or visual arts) but quite a rewarding art form.

There is no music industry, so "popular music" (comparable to rock or rap) doesn't exist, and the basis for much of the music is the folk song. Tondish folk songs are of the same sorts as anywhere: lyrical love-ballads, tales of heroes, laments. Shillayne Ras-Maruthaen sang two of these elsewhere in these volumes; one of them came from Dandwo (western Tond) and one from the Drennic Lands -- the fact that Rolan Ras-Erkéltis did not find them difficult to listen to shows their universal appeal. Such songs are usually pentatonic (five-note, approximately the black-notes on the piano) with one or two added notes (sometimes called the 'enemy tones', see below), accompanied by repetitive patterns on the kital or any of several other pan-Tondish instruments such as the guitar-like toral, the harp (small enough to set on one's lap while playing), the koto-like chetak (of Karjannic origin), or percussion such as the ketatang or the senten. These latter two have very onomatopoeic names. Wind instruments include various flutes and shawms (including the raucous suníihaa, whose tone is described variously as "goosey" or "like a singing mule") and a double-flute called the tér-lúsu ("two-flute" in Fyorian). There are no bowed instruments except in the Emb lands; other Tondish musicians have described these as excruciating.

Folk dances are also plentiful; the rhythms are

somewhat more complex than the four-sets-of-four used in much American dance music. In Fyorian dance music, the rhythms are often played steadily by one or two percussion instruments such as drums, but the melody (played on a kital or tér-lúsu) often includes phrases that are longer or shorter than the repeated rhythm – often bringing the melody and the rhythm into conflict. If the musicians can navigate successfully through such a piece and then wind up together again, they are considered to be masters.

Classical music genres have grown up in various places in Tond, usually in the royal courts but often spreading out to the surrounding towns and countryside. There are many of these, most not related to others; of particular interest are the Karjan and Ondish court music, the Emb bolsã songs, and the Sherványa Nocturnal Music.

The Karjannic and Ondish court music is an orchestral form, similar in some ways to European symphonic music. The orchestra consists of various percussion and plucked string instruments, including very large bass marimbas, metal slabs, and 'gongs' made of glass; these are struck with very soft mallets and do not break as easily as it might seem. The compositions are generally written down (and have been for several centuries), though the performers often choose to omit, move, repeat, or add sections. Several set forms of Karjannic music are based on the idea of more than one section with exactly the same number of beats; these are then combined in various ways. The tuning is extremely complex, using a microtonal scale (set according to mathematical formulae by the composer of the piece) with up to forty distinct pitches per octave. Ondish court music does not use such a complex scale (it tends to be pentatonic, like Tondish folk music), and it seems simpler on the surface, but with more contrapuntal details. It also adds wind instruments such as the *shúwaa*, a very soft shawm, and flutes.

In contrast, Emb *bolsã* songs are an improvised chamber music, comparable in some ways to the various East Asian and Indian styles of 'traditional' chamber music, or American traditional (acoustic) blues playing. The songs, which are based on folk music and have lyrics encompassing the whole range of emotions (but generally tell of only one incident, not an entire epic), are sung by a single musician who accompanies himself on the *kitál* or *toral*. Other instrumentalists play along, their parts either improvised or worked out in advance (or some of both). These parts may relate to the sung melody (which usually consists of three-to-eight bar repeated patterns but is elaborated and decorated almost to being unrecognizable) or they may be based on another melody entirely, often clashing with the repeated accompaniment. The songs may begin simply, but grow in complexity for an hour or more, and often the instrumentalists begin a series of ever-lengthening "follow the leader". Master musicians can 'keep this going' for most of the song, with the repeated phrases growing to five minutes or more.

The Sherványa Nocturnal Music is arguably the most interesting musical form in Tond. Originally it was begun (centuries ago) as simple *kitál* concerts played very quietly at night for the sleeping Sherványa royalty; but as the ensemble grew, the music spread to nearly every city in the Sherványa lands. The music consists of a single theme, varied in a pre-determined way which is always the same, extended into a sleep-inducing piece that lasts the entire night. The piece always begins with more-or-less random soft strokes of large bells; this introductory section may last up to an hour. The other musicians join in with the melody as soon as a regular beat has been established – the "beat" may not be recognizable as such because of its extreme slowness. The melody is played by various flutes, plucked strings, and metal percussion instruments; played very softly. The melody consists of even notes; that is, if the melody contains longer or shorter notes, these are 'smoothed out' with extra pulses. Also, the melody is always played in a mode consisting (roughly) of the notes C, D, F, G, B, and a microtonal shimmer introduced by eighth-tones. If the melody originally uses any notes not found in this scale, they are moved to match. The players repeat the melody over and over, at their own speeds, but always related to the underlying slow 'beat'. Some players eventually break off and improvise; and slowly begin to add (after about two hours of playing) the 'enemy tone' E, which establishes a major triad and is not necessarily a clash. Eventually the D is dropped, resulting in a new mode. Again the players repeat and improvise, shifting again about an hour later, not by introducing another note but (after a change in the tone of the lowest gong-bells of the slow pulse) by moving the tonic to E. This establishes a 'sub-mode', which is minor again, and, after another hour, introduces another 'enemy tone', F#, this time a real clash. The F is dropped. This is the mysterious 'beautiful stars' mode, which lasts the longest, up to three hours, again with the players repeating and improvising. Another 'enemy tone', C# is eventually added, and the C is dropped; the resulting mode sounds pungent and 'bluesy' to the American ear. Finally, as the first rays of dawn appear, the last 'enemy tone', G#, fades in, defeating the G, leading to a 'triumphal' pentatonic. As the sun rises, the melody is played in unison, then the players stop, leaving the bells to resume their quasi-random tolling. Often a solo flute continues the melody for another fifteen minutes of so above this accompaniment.

Various travelers through cities which have the nocturnal music have reported that it helps to chase away any nightmares or dark dreams; in fact it seems to lull (or even hypnotize) the listener into sleep, and some unsuspecting travelers have been caught unaware by its spell and have (reportedly) slept for several days straight. One is to wonder whether or not this has ever actually occurred outside of legend.

Before leaving the topic of music, it must be reported that, unlike many of the other Tondish arts, the Tondish musical sound has occasionally been nearly duplicated here, though of course by accident. The Karjannic court music sounds similar to microtonal music by Harry Partch (there was a good recording on vinyl in the 70's, not yet reissued, so one has to be content with some older 1950's recordings reissued on CD, CRI Records Inc. There is also a partially Partch recording by NewBand, also including arrangements of Thelonius Monk, among others, on Mode Records.). The piece "Pleiades" by Xenakis is also remarkably similar to the Karjan court piece described by Rolan (when he was in the Tower of Dawn) if the movements are played with "Melanges" third. The Ondish court music has a similar sound with a touch of the European Renaissance and Indonesian gamelan thrown in, and superficially resembles the Orff-Shulwerk music (again, there was a good recording on vinyl in the 70's, "Streetsong", on the BASF label, more recent recordings tend to sound too European.). Emb *bolsã* songs are rather like Indian *raga*, if played without the accompanying drone – any record store with "World Music" should have several decent recordings of the style. The Sherványa Nocturnal Music is the most unique, but again is approximated here, by a mix (the reader will have to imagine it) of the experimental songs by Stefan Mikus (ECM Records) and the Javanese court gamelan music (not the Balinese gamelan, which is much more dynamic). Fyorian music has been semi-duplicated by Lou Harrison, particularly his music for classical guitar and Celtic harp (sounding like the *torál* and *kitál*, respectively) on Bridge records, a CD called "Just West Coast". Tondish folk music can be compared to a mix of Celtic (without the fiddles), Chinese (without the er-hu), Bolivian, and Ethiopian traditional music; that is, folk music of a rather 'smooth' variety, as opposed to the more strident sounds found is Balkan and Japanese traditional music, for example. (For dissonance lovers, there is considerable dissonance in the Karjan and Emb classical musics).

VISUAL ARTS

Visual arts are of course hard to describe, and without examples are even more abstract than the description of music just mentioned. So what follows will be a very brief overview of some of the more interesting styles.

In Kaii, stained glass is considered the highest visual art, used for the beautification of the monumental Kayántii buildings (see below). Apprentice artists study for twelve years before making their own first piece. The technique is very different from what is familiar to us – rather than cutting pieces of pre-stained glass and arranging them in wire frames, the Kayántii stained-glass artist works on clear glass, painting on the stains with a small brush. There are two methods; one is to simply add the stain; the other is to, with the help of clear glue derived from the pitch of an evergreen tree, add powders made from glass mixed with the stain, then cover the result with another pane of clear glass. The latter method is the most time-consuming (and dangerous – there is always the possibility of inhaling the powder), but the results are by far the most beautiful and subtle in color. The pictorial style used is vaguely "impressionist", with hazy washes of color, although with elongated and stylized figures.

Painting is esteemed mostly in Northern Tond, where it has achieved a high level. There are several styles; some are realistic, some with the characteristic elongated figures found in other Tondish art. Popular subjects are animals and plants, and scenes from legends. A form of symbolic abstract is known in the Drennic Lands; ill-defined horizontal lines and patches are blended into a hazy "landscape" whose colors and composition denote emotions or philosophical concepts.

Elsewhere in Tond, woodworking is very popular. Lifelike figurines of people and animals are found all over Tond, often painted or with jewels for eyes. Tables and chairs are often carved with a stylized foliage pattern that resemble *art nouveau*. These are probably related to the style of depicting figures in Kayántii stained glass, though this style is never used for human or animal figures in Fyorian or Sherványa art. Karjan woodworking has more abstract and geometrical patterns, often with a curious mix of chaos and order – for example; a carefully carved pattern of squares might enclose a scribble of lines burned on the wood at random. Some Karjan pictures for wall hanging, and tabletops, are "wood art", where the grain of the wood is colored in without any attempts at representation. Depending on the type of wood used, the details of the grain, and the colors chosen by the artist, an amazing variety of moods can be achieved by this simple manner of abstract painting. Sometimes "wood art" is combined with realistic painted figures, and/or a Karjan style of stylized figures that look rather "Indonesian" to the visitor from this world.

Tapestries are also popular throughout Tond, usually of several more-or-less realistic figures against a background of plain colors.

ARCHITECTURE

The great builders of Tond are the Karjans and the Kayántii. The monumental architecture of each will be discussed here, along with more mundane types of structures.

Karjan architecture shows an interesting paradox. The homes and buildings for common use are usually made of wood, and are generally spacious and open. The public buildings, plazas, and royal *hwatsats* towers, however, are monumental stone structures, often deliberately attempting to intimidate (rather than inspire) with their massiveness and claustrophobic interiors.

The towers are the most impressive, and the most expensive to build. Stone was quarried from several areas in the Imperium, and blocks were shipped up the river Cheihar or other waterways, or across Lake Twenwakh, on special wide ships designed for this purpose – regular Karjan boats would sink under the weight of the stone. Arriving at the selected lot (usually on a hill), the stone blocks were hoisted into place using logs as pulleys. The ground floors were built in this manner, and the spaces between the rather rough-hewn stone blocks were filled in with mortar. The second, third, fourth, and fifth stories were also made from the same types of stone blocks – first, an elaborate system of pulleys, winches, and counterbalances was constructed (often of the same blocks), and was used to pull the blocks up to their destination. The Towers usually had several more stories yet; these were built of wood, and then the outside was smeared with a light coating of the same mortar as below. This waterproofed the wooden part of the structure and gave the illusion that it was entirely built of stone. The Towers achieved their amazing height also because of architectural features familiar to the cathedral builders of Europe: flying buttresses to support the weight, as well as arches and vaulted ceilings (also used in Rohándal).

The bottom floor of the Tower was usually the throne room, where the *hrakezh* saw visitors. This was always the largest single room, usually covering the entire story; the ceiling was supported by wide stone pillars. The floor of this story (only) was made of marble, and it was often subtly sloped upwards to make the *hrakezh* appear larger than life (this was apparently not done in the Tower of Dawn). The ceiling of this room was always domed and painted with colors and symbols of the city where the tower was built (the Tower of Dawn, for example, had the image of a rising sun over mountains, painted where the far wall met the dome, and the dome itself was dark orange and pink – sunrise colors).

The upper stories usually did not correspond exactly to where they appeared to be from the outside. There was often a spiral staircase running around just inside of the tower, leading to all of the floors, though it usually bypassed the throne room (which had other, secret, entrances). In at least one case, the Tower of Kings (now ruined), it continued down to a large basement built by Fyorians, long before the Karjan tower was made.

One feature of the Towers that is not completely understood is how they were waterproofed and fireproofed. The mortar of course filled this function from the outside; but it was not used in the wooden interior. However, each Tower had at least one bath, heated by a primitive method of using stones heated by a fire; and there are no records of either the water leaking or the fires getting out of control. A least, in the Tower of Dawn and the Tower of the Setting Moon, the bath rooms were made of stone and located just above the center of the dome of the throne room (!); the rest of the floor was wood (to smooth out the top of the dome and make it flat), far enough away from the fire (which was kept in a stone oven) to avoid problems. It is not known if the other Towers were made on the same (rather impractical!) plan.

In contrast to the Towers, Karjan homes were made of wood, usually boards bound together with clay mixed with pitch, much like plywood. This material was flammable, so cooking fires were not used indoors (awnings were erected outside). The houses were built on stilts (rain and flooding were frequent in the tropical Imperium) and made in square and rectangular sections. Often they were taller than they were wide, giving (to the visitor from the north) a rather clumsy appearance; this feature is to create indoor areas that were permanently in shadow and thus cooler than the sweltering outside air. The roofs were usually thatched, as everywhere in Tond (except in Rohándal, see below).

Moving north, one can see that the stone buildings of the Kayántii represent a world truly different from that of the Karjans, and from our own. These monumental structures were actually seldom used except as public meeting places; thus, they did not need to be practical. Several times in Tondish history the various Kayántii cities were involved in contests to outdo each other in capricious monuments, which often appear to be more gigantic sculptures than buildings.

The forests of Kaii are full of tall pines, firs, and redwoods. Such lofty trees tended to obscure villages and towns, though there was a well-kept system of dirt roads linking them. Huge buildings were thus a way to attract attention from a distance.

The general tendency seems to be that the buildings should look organic, as if they sprouted out of the ground itself. Stone generally conveyed this ideal; it was often stained blue, pink or yellow, but its texture showed through the stain and the rough edges were deliberately left unpolished. Sometimes extra rocks were plastered on the surface with mortar to make it look even rougher.

One of the few shared features is a wide base, and a small arched doorway that was often made to look inconsequential when compared with the rest of the structure. One famous example is the Hall of Kílimetágilalamei, (right) a town hall in the town of the same name ("Forest on the Slopes of Mount Alamei"): there are four doorways, each about four feet wide and slightly less than six feet high, yet each opens into a tunnel cut through about twenty feet of rock (before one comes to the main room); the base of the building, which appears from the outside like bluish granite slabs leaning together in a vaguely floral shape, is about a hundred feet across. Similarly, the otherwise wholly dissimilar "fortress pool" (*tuolámika*) of Kenáekikabérika (Hill of the Horn Blower), (left), mentioned by Teyan Dar-Taeminos elsewhere in these volumes, has two entrances, accessible only by boat across an artificial pool; each entrance has little more space than for a single person to walk through. The lower part of the building itself is an impractical-looking sphere of blue-stained stone just under fifty feet high. It is nearly solid, with only a staircase and a couple of small dark rooms in the center. The main use of this building was to keep several valuable items safe during one a Kaii's many wars. As such it worked admirably; the small doorway was hard to get through (or even find), and the sphere proved impossible to climb.

The other shared feature of these buildings is the decoration, which often appears incongruous to uses such as the fortress, described above. Both the town hall of Kílimetágilalamei and the "fortress pool" of Kenáekikabérika are topped with elaborate constructions that appear all-too-flimsy, but are actually structurally sound. Lighter stone, or stone cut more thinly, and some wood, was used, to construct vaguely "Gothic" filigrees and arches and spirals, often their impossible-looking height was supported by building the entire structure around one or more still-standing redwoods or Douglas-fir trees. Glass was also used to lighten the load and add beauty; the Kayántii perfected the use of glass in Tond (see 'visual art', above), and they made both stained glass and clear windows.

175

Neither of these were set flat into the building, but bulged out in conspicuous domes and curves; various types of ribbing supported even the clear windows. Another unique feature was the sculpture of lifelike features from nature, made giant by the Kayántii imagination. The Hall of Kílimetágilalamei, for example, appears to have a forked tree-branch sticking through the stained-glass tower, and a lifelike heron perched on a wooden arch. Both are hollow wooden sculptures; the branch is as large as a small tree, and the heron is twenty feet tall. The hall of Kiligámeka has even more elaborate sculpture, including a giant thistle, mushroom, human figure (standing on her head, atop the mushroom), several glass "tubes", as well as an oversized spiked shield. Of course such sculptures often need to be repaired, as do the buildings themselves; it is a matter of Kayántii civic pride to keep these improbable structures as beautiful as possible.

Of course with such monuments, it is the outside that is the most important. But they are buildings too, and each does have several interior rooms. The wide base is usually a single large room, supported by pillars (or the rooted trunk of a tree, see above). This was much like the throne rooms in the Karjan towers, except in the case of spherical structures like the "fortress pool" building, which were mostly solid, see above. These rooms were used as meeting places of some type, depending on the building itself. The rooms above, in the lighter, decorated areas, were sometimes the residences of local dignitaries; or during times of war, they were used mostly as lookouts.

Before leaving the subject of monumental architecture, it must be noted that several of the Kayántii structures appear in the center panel of the painting "The Garden of Earthly Delights" by the early 16th-century Dutch artist Hieronymus Bosch. Apparently he visited Tond through one of the natural wormholes that open up from time to time.

Of course, most architecture in Tond is of the domestic, non-monumental, type. Houses are built of the materials that occur naturally in the area, and show a number of different types of floor plans. In the north, they tend to be longish "halls" built of logs lashed together; inside, they are single long rooms that can be divided by folding wooden screens, or, in some Drenn houses, by detachable curtains that are suspended from hooks to beams in the ceiling.

The north tends to be rather impoverished compared with elsewhere; the poorest northern houses (in the eastern part of Kaii and the northernmost Sherványa lands) have simple dirt floors with a fire-pit in the center; the houses are generally round, made of logs lashed together, and have wooden roofs with a hole in the center to let out the smoke from the fire. Due to air pressure from the inside of the house because of the fire, rain does not come in the hole. More southerly Sherványa homes are built on a similar plan but square or rectangular, with more than one room, and sometimes wooden floors (in the rooms without the fire-pit). With their thatched roofs, these houses look much like the country "cottages" found in many parts of the world.

Fyorian houses, made for the harsh conditions of the desert of Rohándal, are more distinctive. They tend to be very large, creating open (and ventilated) dark spaces inside which shut out much of the desert heat. There are often several rooms underground, further helping to lower the temperature (at least in the underground rooms). The frame of the house is made of wood, but this is layered inside and out with a form of adobe, which is fireproof – it also smooths out the square edges of the wooden buildings and gives them irregular shapes, so that no large surfaces are constantly in the heat of the sun (though there is often an upward-facing bowl-shaped area to collect water from the rare rains). This "smoothing out" is also used *inside*, so that a soft curve, rather than a sharp angle, often separates the floor from the wall (and the wall from the ceiling). Some floors (especially in hallways) are made to slope gently in the same manner. Tradition holds that this design is from the ancient Fyorian custom of living in caves called *siinónderand*s; practically, it is to make sure that some rooms are always higher than others, safer in the rare but sudden floods that occur in the area. It must also be noted that the Fyorians care little about the appearance of the *outside* of a building; they often appear run-down and the adobe is often cracked; this is of little consequence because there are as many as twenty layers. The insides, however, are where one spends the most time, and so they are almost always well repaired and made to appear beautiful.

The large Fyorian public buildings must also be mentioned. Fyorian towns usually contain a central plaza surrounded by open-sided wooden shelters; these are used for marketplaces, town meetings, etc. Another landmark in any Fyorian town is the inn; these of course sprung up as a result of the wandering of the *ahíinor* loremasters, and are found in towns far outside of Fyorian territory. The typical Fyorian inn consists of one or two large, often domed, central rooms (with a kitchen off to one side) – here there are tables, chairs, and usually a large assortment of amusements, such as game-tables and curios from various regions of Tond. One or more hallways lead off from the main rooms, these are usually straight and not gently curved like other Fyorian buildings. Doors in the hallways go to guest rooms, up to twenty in each hallway, and constructed much like rooms in Fyorian houses but a little smaller. Often hallways branch off from other hallways in a rather haphazard manner; inns are usually built small and added to over many years (this type of construction is taken to its illogical extreme in Fyorian inns built in the Sherványa lands, where rambling buildings cover entire hillsides and seem to have no plan at all).

In the south of Tond, Ondish and Emb homes are much like those of the Karjans, discussed above.

Some Notes on Ahíinu

Besides the "normal" Tondish arts, those familiar to us, there is the ubiquitous (but seldom seen) Fyorian "art" of *ahíinu*. Some explanations on it follow, others are found elsewhere in the Tond book series.

Nothing is more inexplicable to the person from this world than *ahíinu*. And yet nothing more colors the Tondish world and worldview, despite the fact that the vast majority of the people in Tond never see any *ahíinu* performed, and hear about it only through stories and rumors – the Fyorian *ahíinor* are an elite caste, and they keep their "secrets" well hidden.

It is perhaps wise to begin by stating what *ahíinu* is *not*. Although sometimes translated as "magic", it is not sleight-of-hand tricks and circus performances, though some of these are taught at the very lowest level and there is a certain amount of showmanship in all of the *ahíinor*'s art. Neither is it "magic" in the old pagan sense of casting spells, conjuring spirits, and fortune telling; this type of magic is known in Tond but is frowned upon by the *ahíinor* and the Taennishmen (who use an entirely different word for it, calling it *mordhándu*, the same type of works done by mordhs, and they expressly forbid it). There are too many traps, says the *ahíinor* lore; spirits can deceive; it is difficult to tell a well-meaning *enkéilii* from a demon or a vengeful ghost. The lore is full of spooky tales of the fates of those who disobeyed the ban. On a more subtle level, the *ahíinor* are not like C.S. Lewis' "materialist magician" either, dealing with "forces" but refusing to believe in spirits.

Ahíinu does not deal with anything beyond the realm of the purely physical, and thus it can be explained by (and as) science. This may seem to be a surprise, since the majority of the "art" consists of doing the seemingly impossible by saying strange words in Old Fyorian to equally strange objects, called *mechana*s (a coined word based on "machine" – the Fyorian word is *ahíinand*). It certainly *looks* like "magic" – but this is part of the art. As was already stated, the *ahíinor* are a secretive bunch, and they (not the Taennishmen) encourage anything that can make their art look arcane and mystifying. If nothing else, it keeps away from prying eyes (*ahíinu* can be extremely dangerous in the wrong hands) while impressing those who see it performed.

The *ahíinor* base their "art" on the Fyorian theory of the physical universe, divided into four basic elements, the same four known from ancient Greek, medieval European, and similar to some of those in Hindu and Chinese literature (fire, earth, water, and air – these are dealt with elsewhere in this volume). The Four, as they are known, exist on a purely theoretical level, however; *ahíinu* does not deal with them directly except for naming them as a part of the formulae said to the *mechana*s (and the *ahíinor* will admit that they don't really exist). Rather, they are used as symbols for various parts of the physical world that the Fyorians manipulate. And here is where things get interesting.

A casual glance at the symbolism of the Four reveals surprises about the nature of *ahíinu*. Kullándu, fire, mightiest of the Four (and by far the most fearsome) is associated with *dénkyas* (electricity), *súas ke shandáalis* ("power of the small" – atomic and nuclear power) and *tándu rotándu nel shandáalis* (matter/antimatter reactions). Certainly the Fyorians are not as non-technical as they would appear! Tandáalis, earth, is obviously associated with *fólu* (gravity) – it is worth noting again that the Fyorian concept of "earth" does not include fertility. Lornáalis, air, is associated with lights and illusions (the latter are holograms); and Kewándii, water, arguably the most interesting, connects all things which "flow", including time and space; it is also associated with life, and hence, DNA (the "spiral of life").

So much for symbolism. The fact that the Fyorians even have names for some of these phenomena (let alone appear to be able to manipulate them) is the most fascinating part of a culture that otherwise uses horses for transportation and has no indoor plumbing. How all of this came about is explained elsewhere in these volumes; here I will attempt to explain the physics behind what appears on the surface to be magic.

Manipulation of "the Four" is achieved obviously through technological means, but the *ahíinor* go to great lengths to obscure this fact. Or one should say that they *went* to great lengths – the time is long past when anyone in Tond has access to any machinery to sit down and invent a mechanical device. Most of the *mechana*s were made centuries ago, apparently of indestructible material (or, indestructible in *most* cases, though they were always made with a built-in "crush" mode. All have a sensor, capable of detecting a particular type of motion – in this case, a blow from a booted foot – which activates the self-destruct sequence. Any *mechana* can be crushed simply by stomping on it; but they are impervious to most other types of force.

During the Devastation they were scattered, and now are simply discovered lying around somewhere – either in the abandoned cities in the middle of the desert of Rhohándal, or else in plain sight but having been mistaken for something else. However, the "*mechana* factories" still exist, or did up until the time Tayon Dar-Taeminos made the Circle of Shining – and these "factories" are capable of producing whatever type of device that a person wishes, if he knows how to operate them. Thus the "factories" themselves are a type of *mechana*, according to the Fyorian definition.

The technology that went into making the "factories" was clearly beyond anything known in this world. The center of the "factory" consists of a "lore-floor" and a ceiling, between which pulse controlled blasts of quantum energy. In the front of this area sit one or more "tables" full of computerized levers, buttons, and readouts. Several detachable rods of metal (?) hang on one side. A person wishing to make a *mechana* instructs the computer and machinery what to make; this is accomplished with a great deal of lights and noise (which may be a genuine part of the process or may be simply to impress and intimidate the would-be manufacturer). The pattern is held as a hologram between the "lore-floor" and ceiling; then, as the *mechana* is completed, the metal from one of the rods (Tayon called them "swords") is taken and reformed into the outer shape of the *mechana*, now with the pattern embedded within it. The pattern of course consists of micro circuitry and miniature machines (nanotech?) used to produce whatever electrical, atomic, or quantum effects are desired. None of this is actually known to the person making the *mechana*; he or she merely knows that the "factory" will make the device that is wanted – thus, the computers within the "factory" actually design the circuitry and machinery themselves. They may even design the polymer from which the *mechana* is made; all of the *mechana*s appear to be made of metal (from the metal rods), with a small percentage of glass or wood, but actually consist of an extremely tough plastic. The entire process is powered by a continuous atomic reaction held within a magnetic bottle (see below), sometimes augmented with additional power from the *mechana* itself as it is being made. In this at least the *ahíinor* were wise in hiding their "factories" and making their *mechana*s appear arcane – as Tayon proved, it was all too easy to make something with unforeseen consequences.

The *mechana* "factory" also links the new *mechana* to an appropriate formula in Old Fyorian (these are set phrases), spoken through the four-pointed star. Four-pointed star devices are ubiquitous in Tond, and are the only *mechana* occasionally seen by non-*ahíinor*. They appear commonplace, merely metallic star-shaped ornaments that fit neatly in the palm of the hand; yet they actually increase the atmosphere of mystery about *ahíinu* by means of symbolism. The four points obviously stand for the four elements, which every Fyorian (*ahíinor* or otherwise) has heard about; and the shape as a whole is said to resemble a (short-bladed) sword or dagger, a reference to the Creator God Teilyándal' (who was, in his earthly form of Shar, slain and killed with a sword by the Karjan named Roaghrumtsuk).

But the four-pointed stars are more than symbols. They are incredibly sensitive machines capable of listening and analyzing ambient speech (they also detect motion). Obviously they listen for the set formulae of the *ahíinor*, but also they listen for set "oaths" such as the Mystery Challenge. They then react, either by remotely activating a nearby *mechana*, or by flexing one of more of their arms to alert their carrier of something worth noting. They can also carry written messages. All of this is accomplished again by means of high-tech circuits buried deep within the star: a sound processor, a radio wave broadcasting device (for the remote and to send messages), several pulleys to flex the arms, a small motor to run the pulleys, a radio receiver to detect messages being sent, a small-memory computer to record the written messages and a green LED readout to display the messages. It is all powered by solar power; the surface of the star is actually a translucent plastic which contains solar cells just beneath. All in all a wondrous bit of engineering, yet it pales when compared to the *mechanas* that it controls.

THE FIERY EYE – Several of the *mechana* work by bending "the flow" of space and time; these are relativistic and quantum effects. One of these is the "fiery eye", a fairly recent discovery as far as *mechanas* go, though like all the others it was built centuries before.

The mechanism for the Eye is hidden within a knife-shaped object, which is sharp and can be used as a knife, though it is rather short. The machine, when activated by a four-pointed star, turns on a directed beam of artificial gravity. This is achieved by means of an infinitely small "black hole" (*kúuras ke tyam*) hidden within the knife; the energy from this object is also used to produce a miniature anti-gravity well which keeps is suspended and out of harm (and prevents its infinite mass from being detected outside of its chamber). When the *mechana* is "opened", however, magnetic manipulations produce a small hole within the antigravity well, through which the gravity beam is directed. The resultant energy produces turbulence within the air; this appears as a flame. The gravity beam itself opens a tesseract, one end of which appears in the flame (the "picture" produced by the Eye); the other is a tiny "dot" which can be remotely directed (the "Eye" itself). The *ahíinor* first using the Eye after its rediscovery were apparently unaware that it was a wormhole; they thought it was merely a picture – and thus set themselves up for a nasty surprise when Gaeshug-Tairánda invented a device to widen the small end enough for a grosk to jump through. (Concerning the self-destruct mode: It is unknown how the black hole in this device was destroyed if one wished to crush it. Probably, since black holes do eventually disappear in the form of Hawking energy, the process could be artificially speeded up in the case of an infinitely small black hole, and it would simply dissipate into nothing as the *mechana* self-destructed.)

THE FLYFIRE – Perhaps even more fascinating than the Eye (and just as dangerous), the flyfires were a related form of *ahíinu*. They too created a form of tesseract by means of a directed gravity beam; in this case, however, both ends of the wormhole were in the same place (again resembling a flame), resulting in a small chamber that was essentially outside of the universe. This chamber was just large enough for a person to fit in, and it could be directed (by the same type of remote sensing that directs the small end of the Eye) to move from one location to another, usually through the air. It does not go through a wormhole itself; it moves at a predetermined speed. The person inside is carried along, in a manner that is rather uncomfortable until one gets used to it. There is no sensation of solidity to the edge of the chamber; and the chamber itself constantly flickers in and out of existence according to quantum effects. The result of this constant "opening and closing" is to let in air (it can also let in rain and well-directed sword blows); and to make the person inside appear to be suspended in the middle of the atmosphere, which can produce discomfort to a novice! It is also possible for a mordh to cause a flyfire to lose control by clinging to the outside of the chamber (it is not known how this is accomplished). All in all it is not a particularly comfortable or safe way to travel, though certainly the fastest in Tond.

The direction of the flyfire is controlled by the four-pointed star; though, like the direction of the small end of the Eye, the mechanism that does so is beyond any technology known in this world. It is curious that the direction of the flyfire also controls its visibility to some extent – flyfires can barely be seen as they pass overhead, but appear as "stars" or points of light when they are approaching or receding from the viewer. All of this may have something to do with the directed gravity beam (which, if strong enough, could influence light) but the *ahíinor* are close-lipped on the matter; they have probably forgotten as well exactly how it works.

THE PASSAGE – The passage *mechana*, only three

or four of which were ever made, simply opens wormholes, probably by the same mechanism that opens the fiery eye and the flyfire, though in this case there is no turbulence in the air and thus no appearance of flames. Again, the location of both ends is controlled by the four-pointed star, which can understand directions for locations.

ILLUSION STONES – Some of the *mechana* do not affect the flow of space and time at all. The most common of these are the illusion stones. These are irregularly shaped, slightly pinkish gray, and for all practical purposes appear to be palm-sized rocks. Their "power" is to cast illusions; actually holograms, which are pre-programmed by an *ahíinor* and can cover quite a large area. The pre-programming is done by verbal commands through the four-pointed star; the illusion stone then selects appropriate scenes from a matrix of possibilities stored (probably) on a chip. The scenes can be animated, but apparently this animation can last for no more than about ten minutes – close inspection of longer scenes reveals that they actually repeat (but if the illusion is an army of thousands, one usually does not stay around long enough to see if the image repeats!)

THE TRANSLATION STONES – Looking like the illusion-stones, the translation stones were the one mechana that the *ahíinor* were apparently still trying to perfect. These dealt with the mind, though with a certain amount of obfuscation created by complicated theorizing about the Four. The mechanism by which they worked is not well-known (because it dealt with the brain it could result in madness if not used properly) but it apparently "implanted" the knowledge of a given language into someone's mind, probably through the manipulation of the genetic basis of memory. How this was accomplished is not known. "Fires and lights" appear when the translation stones are used, but this could be part of the *ahíinor*'s show. For now, it is probably safe to guess that the manipulation was done with a microscopic device that makes the required alteration of the genetics within the brain, and then is dissolved into the body. Other applications of this genetic/nanotechnological type of *ahíinu* are discussed below (the *ahíinor* made no distinction between genetics and nanotech).

LEVITATIONS – These are apparently achieved with magnetism interacting with the earth's magnetic field; the Master of Light mentioned (at the Grand Council) a spinning substance that generates a field and interacts with a larger field. The exact process is unknown, but is used in the glowballs and the four-pointed stars.

GENETIC MANIPULATIONS – With the exception of the translation stone, the *mechana*s that influence the "spiral of life" (the Fyorian name for DNA) are the most horrific of the *mechana*s, and were used almost exclusively as a domain of evil (and thus shunned by the Taennishmen). The genetic manipulation is accomplished in two ways: either by designing a creature beforehand and using a nanotech *mechana* to construct its genes from some other creature, or, more horribly, designing some type of virus-like gene which could penetrate the DNA of a living creature and mutate it, changing that creature into something else. Gaeshug-Tairánda used both techniques, the former to make the lizard-men (derived from a bogy in Karjan folktales) and the *gruntagkshk*, the latter to make "grosk crystals" which could change men into grosks. (The first time people were transformed into grosks was apparently done with straight nanotechnology; the genetic system was invented later.)

This brings us to the discussion of Gaeshug-Tairánda itself. When Roagh decided to become this monstrosity, he did so with a design that had apparently been planted in his mind by mordhs, and thus it represents not only perverse human imagination but possibly the worst phenomenon that could be imagined by malevolent aliens as well. Gaeshug-Tairánda appeared shapeless, a mass of flesh inhabited by the twisting bodies of mordhs. Thus it was a fusion of organisms and machines (the mordhs were themselves basically cyborgs), a kind of super-organism invented specifically for evil. Its shapelessness was a purposeful plan; from this undifferentiated form it could instantly "evolve" any organ or orifice it wished. This was probably accomplished by fusing genetics with nanotechnology in some unknown form. This shapelessness also prevented the apparently parasitic mordhs from killing it; those who saw it reported that they lived within it "like giant maggots" but did it no harm even though they ate its tissues (resulting in the "festering" reported by everyone who saw it) – it simply and instantly rebuilt what flesh it needed, and perhaps could not even feel the pain that they must have created. At any rate, this shapelessness also resulted in the futility of trying to kill it; it rebuilt any organs that were destroyed. Its final fate, befitting such an intentional horror, is told elsewhere in the "Tond" books.

Other *mechana*s are mentioned from time to time, though these already discussed are those which have the most significance elsewhere in this story.

STEVEN E. SCRIBNER

Part Two

So, What Does it *Really* Mean? (Essay by the Author)

The question arises with fantasy (or with any) literature: does it mean anything other than its face value? Did the author intend there to be any symbols, metaphors, or allegory? Is there some symbolism there that the author didn't intend? Or is it all just for fun?

With Tond, there are two levels. On the surface, yes, it is just for fun, and I won't fault you if you read it that way. There are, of course, some jokes in it as well (Tayon's verbiage comes to mind).

Obviously I can't speak about any symbols that I didn't put in the book on purpose; but I did put in some intentionally. The following is a discussion of *those*; for anyone who wants to think that Tond is just fun and leave it at that, please read no further.

I'll begin with the most obvious: the *mechanas* and the *ahiinor*. It will probably be no surprise that the mechanas are stand-ins for technology – whether or not they are "magical" in the context of the book (and I go to some length to dissuade the reader from this view), they act as technological devices. The Eye assists communications (and spying). The Flyfire facilitates quick transportation. The various objects that manipulate the "Spiral of Life" stand for genetic engineering. The Circle of Shining could be an ultimate weapon (though it is never used as such) – a nuke or something even more destructive. The Blade of Azugh is unmistakably (a satirical comment on) commercial television – and it is just as entertaining, addicting, and finally, mind-numbing. More to the point, mechanas are symbols or amoral power, both beneficial and baleful: they make life easier and more interesting, but they destroyed civilization in the past and could do so again.

One mechana, of course, merits further attention. The Sword of Law was not Fyorian made (it is much older), and is the only example of what appears to be "magic" in Tond. Of course it is not really such. It brings judgement based on Law, while Shar brings mercy. The parallel with Old Testament Law vs. New Testament grace has been pointed out (by a Jewish friend of mine), though I didn't really have that in mind. I simply meant that both law and mercy act against evil. And, Rolan's final vision/voyage is seemingly dictated by (the power of) the Sword – but here I mean that laws (the scientific laws, made by God) govern the cosmos as well as earth (Tond).

What of the ahiinor, who wield the mechanas? Here we have a strange priestly caste, guarding the secrets of the Ancients' technology for themselves, refusing to let others use it – and (at least under the leadership of the Master of Light) willfully ignorant of the threat that is growing all around them. Some readers have suggested that I got the idea from the U.S. President and Congress waffling on global warming – but I made up the ahiinor twenty years before that issue had become known. To me, the ahiinor are *us*, humans in general: we strut around like we each own the place, guard our own money and possessions for ourselves and ignore the needs of others. We cling to narrow, narcissistic views which we proclaim to be the best, and we thank God that we aren't like others. In short, we behave like New Testament Pharisees or modern-day fundamentalists. It is the poets, musicians, artists, and those who take Jesus' words in the Bible seriously, who subvert the system that the rest of us have created. I like to think I am in this "subversive" group (everybody would like to), but I'm not all that certain that I am. At least I try to express its possibilites.

The mention of Jesus brings up another topic: religion in Tond. There are two religions in the narrative that I have developed to some extent. The "native" Tondish religion, that of the Taennishmen, Fyorians, and others – has obvious roots, though it is cross-cut with some other ideas. Taken at face value, Teilyandal', Shar, and the Lumaaris form a trinity – symbolic (and *only* symbolic) of the Father, Son, and Holy Spirit. (I have shied away from actually writing God – the Trinity – into a fictional narrative, and opted for symbols instead. They must not be read as what I think God would *actually* do in the situations presented – I'd like to think that I know what might happen, but I'm not qualified to answer that question.)

The interest comes from His relationship to the rest of the imagined Tondish world, and here I make some definite statements. Belief in Teilyandal' does not preclude belief in science (or vice-versa). It is the Fyorians that both believe in Teilyandal' and invented the mechanas. The Fyorians also invented the idea of "The Four" – the classical four elements of fire, earth, air, and water (expanded with various philosophical concepts). What is *that* doing in a religion that is symbolic of Christianity? Short answer: nature. God created nature. "The Four" stand for nature, as "scientifically" discovered by the Fyorians – and there is no conflict between science and religion. As I stated in the History of Tond, the Big Bang and evolution are all there – and anyone reading the Genesis account can't help but notice that the creation of animals occurs in the same order as what scientists discovered millennia later.   My own personal view is that the fact that evolution occurred proves that the Bible is not just a mere book – the ancient Hebrews who wrote the Bible down (after having it as oral literature for centuries) couldn't have *known* all that on their own.

There are, of course, several variants of this "native" religion (not including the supposed Sherványa polytheism – this is a misunderstanding on Tayon's part; it doesn't exist). None of these stand for any particular "denominations" of Christianity; none of them are really based on groups that actually exist. That said, one can of course find similarities. The Emb version is perhaps the most like American Protestantism, with its emphasis on direct, personal experience of God – but it also has strands of meditative philosophy which would be at odds with this subculture as practiced in the U.S.A. (It doesn't, however, show any similarities to pantheistic or "New Age" versions of the religion.) The Fyorian version is quite liturgical and systematized, though the Master of Light's fundamentalism generally ruins it. The mysterious Gleph version is perhaps the most important to the story (they forged the Sword of Law!), but I have deliberately left it unknown.

Before leaving the "native" Tondish religion, I must discuss the Taennish Folk – and I admit I don't really know what they are. I had originally conceived them as "unfallens" – that is, the fall of man happened one or more generations *after* the first humans appeared in

198

Tond, and some did not fall. I eventually abandoned this idea (though it is still suggested in the Song of Origins), and now I imagine the Taennish as something of another type of human, one that may dwell in a "magical" (though they deny this) realm, and appear as prophets and healers in the world outside of their homeland. While in their home, they seem to be able to communicate directly with Teilyandal', but this ability eventually disappears as they stay in "Outer Tond". (This is not saying that God is not all-powerful – it is merely saying that the Taennishmen, whatever they are, become like "normal" humans in Outer Tond.) Such separation causes them to become depressed, and they must return to their world to be revitalized. As far as symbolism goes, they don't really stand for anything except a possibility that is actually open to others: Rolan and his company enter into direct speech with Teilyandal' (through Shar) upon entering Taennishland as well, and this ability does not entirely vanish when they leave.

Taennishland is also in the Song of Origins, and here I draw a symbolic parallel with the Fall of Man story in Genesis. The "Spirit of the Void" tempts with the offer of "endless lands to conquer" – the primary temptation in the Tond stories is greed, and it is greed that motivates much of the evil in the stories. Greed becomes a lust for power – Tayon's downfall over and over – and the motivation behind Roagh's transformation into the monster. Greed also becomes pride: once one has taken everything for oneself, there is a pride in having attained everything – and such pride becomes arrogance. Others, after all, have *not* attained everything; their fate is to be squashed. So form evil empires.

What of the other Tondish religion, that of the Karjans? Obviously it's meant to contrast with the religion of the Fyorians, but it isn't a stand-in for any particular real religion. I suppose (at least on the Karjan Continent) it suggests Hinduism in the fact that it is ancient and has no particular founder, is polytheistic, and has spun off from itself through the millennia into various new and different forms. The particular variant that entered Tond is bloodthirsty, blatantly racist, and has none of the meditation or colorful exuberance that one associates with Hinduism. Rather, it is a distillation of religion gone bad: it is the Hinduism of Shiva and the Kali Yuga; the Buddhism of chöd and spirit possessions; the Islam of ISIS and Wahhabi jihadists; the Christianity of the inquisition and imperialism; the Aztec religion of Quetzalcoatl and human sacrifice. All of that, with a thoroughly unsavory bit of fascism.

Of the Karjan demon-gods (they must be seen as such, with the horrors inherent in the religion), I have really only bothered to develop two of them: Gaejtark-Bad'hani and Lijnan-Kwarhmaki. The former is somewhat drawn from C. S. Lewis' monster Tash in the Narnia series, though I've added genocide to its list of atrocities. Lijnan-Kwarhmaki was drawn from an *actual* case of Aztec or Mayan black magic, reported by a Pentacostal evangelist around 2005 (he had witnessed it some years before) – I have included it as a hint that there may be something even *more* sinister lurking behind abominations committed by mere humans.

That said, there is of course a "good" side to the Karjan religion too – as expressed in the *Katark* forces of creation. Not all religions are true, and some aspects of some may have been demonically inspired – yet, as the Taennishmen would say, "some truth gets through."

(Thus, I had Tayon admit that Karjan "lore" may express noble truths, despite what the more fundamentalist Master of Light has to say on the matter.) That doesn't mean, of course, that all are equally "good" – one must be careful. One must also be careful with *aspects* of religion. The Karjan religion itself is dualistic, allowing both good and evil (seen as creation and destruction) – and dualist religions often go bad because inherent in the idea of equal and opposing forces is another, less benevolent idea: that good and evil (i.e. God and the devil) are equal. I don't like to think where that philosophy would lead.

On to other topics. Some of my friends have noted the lack of "recognizable" ethnicities in Tond – that is, the "races" represented are all imaginary. This is intentional. When making up cultures, I feel it necessary to invent the ethnicities as well, so that no one will feel either that I am writing stereotypes or racism (which I do not wish to do) or misrepresenting such-and-such culture (which I don't wish to do either). Thus we have the Native Tondish (Fyorians, Shervanya, Kayantii, Drenn, and several groups in the south), the Karjans, and the Emb; none are representations of any civilization that is historically attested. (Ignore the mysterious prehistory of the Emb – if they *did* come from "here", they have been in Tond at least a thousand years and are thoroughly assimilated. Their original culture, whatever it was like – and I have deliberately left it ambiguous – is only a shadow of a memory.) What is important is that, with the exception of the invading old-style Karjans, everyone gets along. The borderlands between Rohandal and the Imperium also have a large percentage of people who are part Fyorian and part Karjan (Arnul, Ai-Leena, and Andri are all examples – it was an accident that their names all begin with "A"). One would have to assume that the analogous situation occurs near the borders of the Emb lands (Wuchk M'Brenya is such a person), though the books are not set there.

Lastly, there's the matter of the Tondish cultures. Here, I've simply let my imagination go. I don't intend any symbolism in the Sherványa Nocturnal Music, Emb spears, Kayanti black teacups or Karjan towers. They're simply expressions of creativity. As for the Fyorian love of adobe, mangoes, and edible cactus – this is because they live in a desert. Horn Hill probably came from listening to Mahler's Second Symphony. The Drennic Lands resemble both Puget Sound and Japan; I have lived in both places.

In conclusion, then, there certainly are symbols in Tond that I mean in a particular way, and there are a lot of details that mean nothing other than the fun of making stuff up. The reader should interpret the first group as I intended (if he or she wishes to read the stories as anything more than just stories) but the second group is wide open. If they must mean something, it's up to you, reader. Have fun. Welcome to Tond.

The Name Thing

These are some online discussions that I had with other writers and with some other friends (all are used by permission here). When it came to making up names, there were some unexpected complications.

ORIGINS OF SOME OF THE NAMES (posted 7/2/17)

Tondish place-names have been with me for a long time. Longer than I care to think about, or maybe not. Just for the curious, here are their actual origins in my mind (if you're not curious, I don't blame you; go on to some other, less self-indulgent post).

Fyorians: I can't really recall where the word came from; I'd been making up words along the lines of "Fee-yor" and "Fee-ore" at least since I was in 2nd grade. I decided that it sounded nicely non-English, so I used it when I started making up the world of Tond. (Most people still want to say it "furian", like a fury, anyway, but they're wrong.)

Karjans: This one went through a much more convoluted development. Maybe I'll just say that it went through several early versions; I was in 8th grade at the time and it kept sounding (inadvertantly) like distorted versions of names of other kids in my class. I finally made up "Karjans", who lived in "The Imperium" – those words didn't sound like anyone's name, so I went with them. Didn't stop a college buddy of mine from parodying them as "Garbijkans" in a fantasy role-playing game. Sound it out.

Sherványa: In the very earliest versions, the Sherványa were Tolkienic Elves (the spellbinding "Nocturnal Music" is a vestige of that legacy). Both "Sherványa" and "Lánnishar" were derived from "Lothlórien" by obscure processes that I no longer remember.

Kaii: I simply wanted something that rhymed with "Hawaii" so I could ironically put it in a cold northern region. The Kayantii people were originally Oroks, but I decided that it sounded too much like "orcs" so I dropped it. (I had actually invented "thorks" in another story – same problem.)

Tond: In sixth grade I found a reproduction of the painting "Vision of Tondalis") by a follower of Hieronymus Bosch. It was a scary painting – just right for the setting of a rather dark fantasy story. "Tondalis", I eventually found out, was a character in a legend, though at the time I thought it was a place. The place in my story got shortened to "Tond" in a comic strip in college, but Tándáalis still exists as the Fyorian personification of elemental earth or stone – and the *áalis* ending became the Fyorian collective plural (it changes to *áaris* in some cases).

Concerning the characters: four of the five major ones were already there in the earliest version, written when I was 9th grade. Arnul's and Tayon's names have not changed (actually I have no idea where those names came from; they were just "there" when I needed to name a character). Rolan was originally Rodan, a fictional but overused sci-fi/fantasy name. Ai-Leena's name has changed more: she was originally Rozaleen, after the unseen character at the beginning of "Romeo and Juliet" (remember, I was in 9th grade at the time, and we'd just finished reading that play in English class). I eventually decided that this reference was silly, so I changed the name. There were several versions, most of which I forget now, though I think all of them contained the "leen". The last main character, Shillayne, came along later as a composite of two earlier protagonists: Kelanna, the wife of a somewhat older Rolan, and a Sherványa woman named Tazzie who caused Tayon considerable consternation. One of my high school friends seemed to have a crush on Tazzie (as he read my stories, he kept saying, "More Tazzie! More Tazzie!"); but Tazzie was involved in a dropped subplot about swanlike aliens, so I eventually changed her. I made up the name "Shillayne" sometime in the late 1980s, ony to discover some years later that I had in fact *not* made it up – spelled differently, it was the middle name of a college friend of mine. It had been bouncing around in my subconscious for years. (More recently it's turned up several more times.) I got permission from the original owner of the name, and kept it.

THE OTHER TOND (posted 11/10/18)

The name things strikes again, BIG TIME. Somewhere, buried within the hidden annals of creativity, there is another Tond. The following conversation occurred on "The Writers Group" FB page and in private messages (edited, and used here by permission).

Ramsey Campbell: Ah! Did you find the name Tond anywhere?

Steven E. Scribner: Short answer: I made it up. Long answer: I once saw a painting called "Vision of

Tondalus" (with several alternate spellings). I thought "Tondalus" was a place (it was actually the name of a knight) and I thought I could set a rather dark fantasy story there. Later I shortened "Tondalys" to "Tond", which I decided means "earth" in a conlang called Fyorian. The final novel series has nothing whatsoever to do with the original "Vision of Tondalus", however.

Ramsey Campbell: This is why I ask (a summary someone else made of a book of mine):

"Far Away & Never: This is Dark heroic fantasy--stuff that Clark Ashton Smith and Lovecraft, Howard Phillips fans will devour....

Almost a "Tond Cycle" Anthology Far Away & Never only has 7 tales (not 8 like the backcover claims). The first 4 all star the warrior Ryre, which were all published first in Andrew Offutt's Sword Against Darkness series. Numbers 5-6 are also in Ryre's world Tond (without him) and were weird and dark, akin to Clark Ashton Smith's style. Number-7 is similar in tone and style, but is not part of Tond. The introduction by Campbell mentions another Tond tale called "A Madness From the Vaults" which debuted the "Tond" world...but this reference is not in this collection.

Steven E. Scribner: Hmmm, so there are two Tonds. I googled the word before I published the first book, and all I found was random words in French and Hindi. I'll see if I can find out anything about those other ones; if the two worlds are similar then one or the other could be fan fiction ...? (My earliest "Tond" was some comics by a friend of mine and I, published in the SPU student newspaper in 1981 or

1982; "Tondalys" predates that by roughly a decade but wasn't published.)

Ramsey Campbell: Forgive me if I was unclear. FAR AWAY AND NEVER is by me, and you will see from the listing that my first tale set there originally appeared on 1974, the rest later in that decade.

Steven E. Scribner: I don't see it on Goodreads. Where could I find a copy? I'd like to see if our worlds are similar. We could cooperate on a third series...? :-)

Ramsey Campbell: Really? I found it at once. I fear I don't collaborate - I couldn't even make it work with my old friend Poppy Z. Brite. Here is the Goodreads listing. (GIVES WEBSITE) And here's a more detailed review, sketching how I developed Tond: (GIVES WEBSITE)

Ramsey Campbell: I assume this is the painting you mean? (GIVES GRAPHIC)

Steven E. Scribner: Yes, that's the one. As my "Tond" stories evolved, they came to have very little to do with that painting, except for the Boschian critters called "gruntags" that crawl around from time to time.

Steven E. Scribner: The question arises if something should be done about there being two "Tond"s. (I suppose euphony rules in the world of fantasy!) Since your publication predates mine, mine could technically be called copyright infringement – but I had no idea... I could, I suppose, change my word "Tond" to "Tahnd", "Tahn", "Rond" or something like that, but that would involve changing a whole zoo of words in the Fyorian conlang: tánd (land, earth, or stone), tán (an individual rock or stone), táne (a "stone" or seed in a fruit, from a Japanese word), tándáalis (elemental stone – yes, I used the original "Tondalys" word there) – and I'd have to unpublish the book, edit it (including changing the title), and republish. I recommend that we leave it as it is; readers would be intrigued by how two fantastical worlds called "Tond" came to be; if they read one, they might want to read the other. There are two (real) places called Georgia, after all, and two (fictional) characters called Stargirl. A word of warning, though: my "Tond" contains Christian allegory – I hope that's okay with you if the two worlds are "linked" (I'm not going to change that part). What do you think? Also, do you object if I post this conversation and let others in the "Writers Group" comment on it?

Ramsey Campbell: By all means post! I don't think you should change anything. If there's an acknowledgements page in your novels, might it be worth saying there that the similarity is coincidental?

Steven E. Scribner: I'll add the acknowledgements at the back of Book Four — the (still unpublished) last book. Thanx for the suggestion!

Ramsey Campbell: That sounds good.

TRIVIA (posted 2/4/19)

In one of the appendices to Book IV, the Fyorian word for "lion" is listed as *ásalan*. The familiarity of that word has been pointed out. Obviously I didn't make it up, and the Narnia reference is likewise obvious. However, C. S. Lewis didn't make it up either. It's an old Central Asian word that has variants from eastern Europe to China:

Azerbaijani: aslan
Hungarian: oroszlán
Kazakh: aristan (арыстан)
Kyrgyz: arstan (арстан)
Manchu: arsalan (also erselen "lioness"!)
Mongolian: arslan (арслан)
Turkish: aslan

All of these languages except Hungarian belong to the (possibly theoretical) "Altaic" language family, which (also possibly theoretically) includes Japanese and Korean – though the latter two use completely different words for the big cat in question. (Chinese, belonging to another family, has another completely different word.) Japanese has ライオン, which if you know how to sound it out, is roughly the same as the English (and the writing in katakana letters indicates that the word is of foreign origin).

What does all of this have to do with Tond? Not much, really, except that I found it interesting and based Fyorian grammar/syntax on the "Altaic" model. There is also a little bit about comparative linguistics in Book IV.

Other than that, there are tigers.

Star Prologue

This is an unused first chapter to Book One. I decided to let the story of Rolan and Arnul unfold at its own pace without the introduction, though those who've read the books may find this interesting.

The four-pointed star was exactly the size of my palm; my fingers closed around it and felt its smooth surface.

"It was made in one piece," I commented, "I don't feel any rough edges where sections could have been put together. But I don't see what this has to do with..."

"You'd be surprised." George cut me off in mid sentence. "Made in one piece, you say. Made of what?"

"Well, plastic, obviously."

"What kind?"

I was getting a little impatient with this digression (I've heard some say that this impatience is a fault of mine) but I decided to play along for now. I inspected the surface of the star. Smooth hard plastic, cold to the touch, not exactly black; the outer eighth-inch or so was transparent, though it quickly darkened just beneath this skin. An idea struck me.

"You say this is some kind of technological device," I said. "The material looks like it's made to absorb light. A solar cell, of a sort."

George was now regarding me with a most

peculiar, and indeed unreadable, expression. There was a gleam of... something... in his brown eyes, and his lips were twisted into a slight smile. "Push your thumb into the center, between the arms of the star."

I did as he said. The plastic gave slightly, which surprised me because up until then it had felt hard as metal. The star flashed and sputtered a luminous green for a moment, then went black again.

"It's a light?" I asked. An odd shape for one, admittedly.

"Shout at it," said George.

This request was the most peculiar yet, but I still decided to play along. I put the star to my mouth, and yelled "WHY SHOULD I SHOUT!?" It lit up bright green, the same color, then went dark again. I lowered it, and my eyes showed my questions.

"It hears vibrations." George answered. "In fact it understands speech." He paused. "Well, maybe 'understand' is too strong a word. It's not like it has a brain or something. But there is a microprocessor in there that analyses sound. If we were speaking Fyorian, it would respond to certain phrases."

George's expression was still unreadable, but getting more intense. "Furian?" I asked, hearing the first part of the strange word like 'fury'.

George laughed. "No, Fyorian. Fyor, like a fjord. Fyorian, that's what I call it. *They* call it *Fyorándii*."

I'm no expert at languages, but I assumed that a language should be fairly well known if spoken in a major country that could make something as technologically advanced as this star ornament seemed to be. I was getting curious in spite of myself. "*They* would be the locals, of course. But where do they live?"

George's answer was unintelligible, because it

wasn't in English. He pronounced a few words in a polysyllabic language, rich in vowels; quite beautiful to the ear, actually, and he seemed fluent. He paused again, then said, "Actually I know a poem in it." And he recited:

Bríligh dárrum, zhen s'láidhu tóvis
Arn wéiv nii gáirenn gímlum.
Mímzum kaharn borogóvis,
Zhen mómu ráethis arn authgréivum.

Now my expression must have begun to match his, because he let out a hearty laugh. The poem's words were familiar, even if the language was unknown. "Alice in Wonderland, in that language?" I stammered. "Jabberwocky…?"

"Actually *Through the Looking Glass*. I translated it myself. '…And shun the frumious bandersnatch!' *Kein frkhándas, íilan frúumas ke váendrsnaesh yo!* You see, those nonsense words work in any language. But I'm getting off the point." He paused. "I believe your original question, even before I showed you the star, was if I had any theories about why technology, as we call it, evolved where and when it did. This star might be able to shed light on a possible answer. …But before I continue, I must ask you if you can keep a secret."

Now this was getting all too strange. "A secret? Whatever for?"

"Because I don't want a word of this getting out. Not to any of your friends who don't know me; not to any family, not to anyone. If this information was to get into the wrong hands, there's no telling what could happen. It could get ugly. Really ugly, really fast."

By now I was getting suspicious. I said nothing at

first, regarding that peculiar look that had cemented itself on George's face. I recognized it now as some kind of intense desire, mixed with more than a little fear. Desire for what? Fear of what? But for now the mind behind the expression was as opaque as a concrete block. For the first time (though not the last) I began to wonder if perhaps George had somehow become mentally unbalanced, though everything he had said so far was perfectly lucid if enigmatic. I realized, though, that he would not continue with his story (it was obvious that he had one), or answer my question (even though my original question had been somewhat casual), until I told him I'd keep his promise. I'd decide later if someone needed to be notified.

Since he asked if I could keep a secret, he had locked his eyes onto mine, and he had not moved a muscle.

"Okay." I said at last. "I can keep your secret."

He relaxed somewhat, though that expression remained, and his eyes remained fixed on me. He reached out, motioned for me to hand him the star. I did so. He sighed, then sat down in his leather bean-bag chair, gestured for me to sit on the sofa. I did so, noticing that his eyes would not leave me for a second. He was regarding my every expression.

"Okay." He said at last. He turned the star around in his hands a few times. "This star, uh, curio, is a technological marvel. Its whole surface acts as a solar cell to power it. Its whole surface also picks up vibrations; a kind of solid-state microphone; and it contains a processor that not only analyses speech sounds and responds to certain ones, but also links to a myriad other devices by remote control, using radio waves. My boom box can just pick up some of its frequencies. So it contains a radio broadcaster as well, all wired into its central processor. And you noticed the green light; an LED display, a dot matrix actually, though the dots are smaller than any pixels I've ever seen. It lights up when it hears certain sounds, and it does other things with that light – if you hold it up to certain machines, it picks up some type of code and tells you *what that machine does*. Letters appear on its upper side, in Fyorian, of course. You can also send messages with those letters. Wireless Internet of a sort. Also there are pulleys and cords inside; again, if it hears certain sounds, or if it realizes that it is being accessed by remote, it will flex and twist slightly, nudge you in fact, to get your attention. Like I said, it is linked up to hundreds, if not thousands, of other devices by radio waves; some of *those* devices are beyond any tech I've ever heard of; many of them operate on quantum effects and space distortions, among other things. Have I piqued your interest yet...?" He paused, waiting for the full impact of his description to sink in. Then he leaned forward, held out the star in his palm for me to see.

"You asked why I thought technology developed when and where it did. My answer is that it *didn't* necessarily. The Fyorians, the *fyoránya* as they call themselves, know otherwise. Their ruling class, the *ahíinor*, know that this... star... is over five hundred years old."

"Now wait just a minute!" I said. "If you expect me to believe that..."

"I'm not expecting you to *believe* it. Believing or not won't change it. I'm only asking you not to tell anyone else." And he added something in that strange language; actually he said it twice, and the star lit up for a second.

My thoughts raced. Obviously this was a joke, and this star thing was no more than a curio he had picked up at some game store. This had gone too far. I stood, ready to leave.

Or I tried to stand. I moved about an inch and my head struck something hard. Instinctively I reached up to see what the barrier was (I hadn't seen anything there before) but found that I whatever it was was blocking my hand also. In fact I could hardly move. My eyes raced around, but I could see nothing of the prison which now held me. I glanced at George, and now his expression had changed slightly, much more intense, though still quite unreadable.

"The Wall." He said. "Quantum space distortion; a directed gravity beam, made into a three-dimensional force field. Quite effective. The Fyorians use it from time to time, when necessary." He muttered something else in that language. "It's gone now." He said.

I cautiously raised my hand, found that the barrier was indeed gone. I stared at George, for the first time genuinely frightened.

"One of the devices that the star is cued in to makes the Wall." Said George. "I told it to surround you; remember that it understands speech."

I pronounced my next words carefully, slowly. "...And you're saying that this... technology... is five hundred years old."

"I am indeed."

I was beginning to understand. Something like that in the wrong hands, if it could affect more people, could be a hideous weapon... But the age of it was beyond reason.

"But why has no one heard of it? And how was all

of this...?"

George cut me off. "If you had made this five hundred years ago, would you have told anyone?"

The question was almost surreal. "Of course not. They'd have burned me as a witch. But that doesn't answer where I would have – where they, the fy-fyorians would have, gotten the machinery to make it in the first place."

"That's part of the problem. The old Fyorian civilization, which made these, kept them so secret that no one knew how they worked, though some people continued to use them. Your comment about the witch is actually quite fitting; by the time I found these things, all the Fyorians considered them to be magic, and it took me quite a while to figure out what was really going on. I had to read several hundred of their books, after my initial discovery at the Council that all of this was tech, trying to pick out the truth from their strange theories that looked like alchemy and were probably examples of intentional obfuscation. But eventually I got it figured out."

My next question was obvious. "How long did it take...?"

"I was in the Fyorian lands nearly seven years, after the War."

"Vietnam? The Gulf War?"

"The War of Talismans. See, there, that's the kind of thing I'm talking about. They call their machines 'talismans'. But there's nothing magical or occult about them. Oh, don't worry that you haven't heard of the War; it's not the type of thing that's well known. At least on this side of the tesseract."

"The what...? Did you say tesseract?"

"Of course. A bridge through the fourth dimension.

You didn't think that Outer Tond was somewhere near Portland, Maine, did you?"

"Outer Tond?"

"The Fyorian country."

"You've been there."

"Of course."

And this was exactly where he had wanted the conversation to go. It was obvious that he was on to something; that language itself would have been some kind of evidence; though one can make up words that sound like a language. But there was no denying the Wall. I regarded George again; his dark skin and eyes, his unkempt hair, his unreadable expression.

"So how did you get there?" I asked.

For the first time since that weird look had appeared on his face, he relaxed noticeably. "You don't think I'm crazy," he said.

There was too much evidence for that. It was all too weird, true, but now I was getting curious. "Tell me about it."

And so over the next few weeks I'd meet with George in his apartment after work, and he filled in the details. It must have been awful for him, to know about Outer Tond and not be able to tell anyone; so when I had asked about technology he had finally broken down. Now his mind was at rest as he told me how he had gotten there, what he had found, what he had done, and what had gone on before he got there, (he knew some of that from what the Fyorians had told him). I eventually was able to piece it all together, all the while studying the four-pointed star and a couple of the other Outer Tondish machines he'd brought back with him.

What follows is my pieced-together version of the first part of his tale, a detailed account of what went on before he even got there. It turns out that the Fyorians had kept a fair amount of it written down in book form, which George had taken the time to memorize nearly word for word. So it's also interesting from the cultural perspective; like he said, they know nothing of the technology which they are using.

Nocturne

This is a short story set in the world of Tond, taking place roughly fifteen years after the series. This story assumes no familiairy on the part of the reader with the world of Tond, and it could be the first chapter of a second series. Some of the words are re-spelled for easier reading as a separate story.

In the world of Tond, the Fyorian *aheenor* safeguard "lore" and wisdom, and seek to spread peace. But, an ancient hatred threatens to resurrect their enemy: a terrifying technological power that had destroyed civilization in the past. The power has taken a new form, and is disguised as something beautiful...

The sun had barely set when I arrived in the Shervanya town of Len. I met up with the elder *aheenor* Tulann, wanting to see if either of us could determine the source of the strong emanations I'd picked up two nights before.

I found him to be a tall man, not bent over with age, but his face was dark and weathered. In the eight days that I was with him there in Len, I grew to know him – if not well, then at least his outward quirks. His eyes sometimes seemed to point in slightly different directions, as if one were watching outward and the other looking inward at some old memory. His beard was thin and scraggly, though he wore it long, like all the elder *aheenor*. He tilted his head slightly when he spoke, as if listening to everything else besides his voice.

When I told him why I had come, he repeated my own ruminations, "The problem in locating most of the ancient's *mechana* is that they are well-hidden in plain sight. A very common object can be a machine of great power. For an obvious example, of course you know about the *mechana* for the illusions, and the glowballs."

Yes, I knew about glowballs. I had noted that he kept two of them in his hut, sitting one in either corner on darkwood tables, looking to anyone else like equipment for playing the popular game of ten-ball. Right now their gentle illumination kept the shadows away from our night meeting (and, as always, the light seemed to be coming from all directions).

Tulann leaned back in his puffy padded chair for a moment, and twiddled his fingers in his scruffy beard. He seemed to be thinking intently. From somewhere outside, a quiet music of bells and gongs began. He leaned forward again, regarding me with shadows under his grey eyes.

"There are no other *aheenor* in Len," he said at last, confirming my suspicions, "But a *mechana* was used here two nights ago. When my four-pointed star nudged me and indicated that a *mechana* was in use, I thought it was odd, but I didn't find anything. Then you came today, and said you'd felt it too..."

I had felt it too. The twisting of the four-pointed star in my side pocket had interrupted my conversation with a young Shervanya woman who was telling me that her grandmother knew some extra details about one of the legends that the *aheenor* have been trying to track down. When I'd excused myself from the talk and gotten a moment alone to check the messages on the amulet – about twenty minutes later – it was still flexing its four arms and flashing. "Powerful *mechana* in use. Purpose: unknown. Location: Len, Upper Shervanya Lands. All *aheenor* within three day's journey find Tulann Ras-Teliskar in Len."

"What did *your* amulet say?" I asked Tulann.

"Nothing really out of the ordinary, if there had been another *aheenor* in this town. Something like, 'Powerful *mechana* in use. Purpose: unknown. This town, exact location uncertain. Investigate.' I wandered a bit in the streets, but couldn't find anything. I asked a couple of people if they had seen anything unusual, but no one had. I stopped by the town center and listened for a couple of minutes – they were playing the Nocturnal Music, as it is tonight. But nothing seemed to be happening there either. I gave up and came home, thinking that its use – whatever it was – didn't seem to have done any harm, and maybe I could track it down later. Nobody seemed to have seen or heard anything yesterday either – all anyone could tell me was that they played the Nocturnal Music in a different mode. The only odd thing is that Sren – that's my friend, who's been telling me some of the Shervanya and Drenn lore that he knows – wouldn't talk to me much. He seemed to have suddenly found fear of me – though he's continued to tell me the details of the legend of Mayeyamusei. It's as if something's really scared him. ...Or, of course, he could be hiding something."

Tulann fell silent and sat back again. The quiet of the night was punctuated by the hushed tolling of the bells and gongs, now joined by flutes, and by the sound of crickets.

I asked, "This Nocturnal Music, and a different mode – Do you think there's some kind of clue in it?"

"Possibly, though I can't imagine what. I can't hear the modes either. I think I have socks stuffed in my ears when it comes to music. I couldn't even hear the notes right in the Fyorian music back home, and it's much less complicated."

We discussed it a little more, but could come to no conclusions, and I admitted I'd reached an impasse trying to investigate the mysterious *mechana*, at least for now. So I decided, probably just to change the subject for a while, to go hear some of the Nocturnal Music up close. I, at least, knew a little about music and was interested in finding out more. Tulann agreed to follow me.

Walking through the street of the city towards the sound of the music, I let my mind wander. I mused, first, how the strangeness of Shervanya cities had worn off. At first, I had been amazed (and somewhat taken aback) by the use of decorations on the outsides of buildings; even the walls of houses sprouted carved wooden foliage patterns or sported bright colored painted landscapes or abstract colors. I almost resented the waste of time that these ornaments represented. Back where I had come from, the Fyorian lands, nobody bothered to beautify the outside of a building because people spent most of their time *inside*. But gradually I had come to understand – the Shervanya lands were cooler than my homeland, and people could spend time out of doors – even at noon during summer (unbearable in the desert where I had lived); children played outdoors and adults who were not working sat on porches gossiping about whatever came to mind.

The Shervanya people were related to the Fyorians, I knew – they looked similar, with blonde or sandy hair and tan faces, and their language was similar – but at first I had regarded them as something like unwanted stepbrothers. They dressed in funny clothes – white drapery that looked like bandages up close and, from a distance, seemed to wrap around the body in a somewhat comical, tubular shape. I had thought they smelled strange, too – from the scented oils they applied to their skin and hair.

That was all five years ago. In the intervening time, they had grown to be my brothers. They no longer seemed strange to me, and I could speak their idiom. Their music, in particular, I was beginning to find fascinating – though as of yet I had not found anyone to teach me the theory behind it.

Tulann interrupted my thoughts. "Here is the music grounds," he said.

The street had come abruptly to a large grassy space, sloped slightly downward towards a pavilion at the far end. There were a number of torches here and there on the lawn, burning high up on poles so that their (rather dim) illumination spread out to cover the entire open space. Several wooden booths, tables, and chairs sat haphazardly around, here and there, made of the same light wood as the pavilion. All were vacant. The people were scattered about on the grass, mostly sitting and listening to the music, though some appeared to be sleeping and a few small groups were talking quietly among themselves. An old woman, seated by herself, sat on a mat a few steps away from us, watching us (rather suspiciously, it seemed) though half-lidded eyes.

My gaze followed the edge of the lawn down to the pavilion. It was large enough to hold at least thirty people, sitting comfortably apart, with their musical instruments. The sound of the music was coming from there, and certainly there were a large number of Shervanya there, though the light from the torches didn't penetrate far enough for me to make out many details. I recognized the sounds of the various instruments, though: harp-like *kitals*, *sulu* flutes, metallic *ketatangs*, bells, and gongs.

Tulann motioned towards a small table with two chairs beside it, and we seated ourselves. I listened to the music – half drawn-in by the spell of the strange and beautiful sounds, while Tulann looked about intently, seeming to focus on every detail and at the same time looking at something within.

"That's odd," he commented abruptly, "None of the Gleph seem to be here, again." I followed his gaze to a rickety booth by the edge of the square.

"Gleph?" I asked. "Here, in the Shervanya Lands?"

"Would you expect them to remain in the Imperium?"

I winced. His statement had shattered my tranquil mood. I ran through some of the details of the savage history in my mind. The Gleph had been the slaves of the Karjans – the rulers of the Imperium – who had brought the Gleph with them when they'd invaded southern Tond some centuries ago. All it took was one Gleph uprising, in which two or three Karjans were killed, to set off a campaign of butchery. The Gleph joined the "official" Karjan list of races to be annihilated. Surviving Gleph scattered to the far corners of Tond. Subsequent centuries had mellowed the Karjans somewhat, though an occasional *hrakezh* (as they called their aristocracy) still called for violence against others, and rumors still spread about Karjans hunting Gleph here or there. Most of these rumors, I told myself, were probably nothing more than ghost stories told at night, because I knew that the "official" policy of the Imperium had softened due to infiltration by *aheenor*.

Presently, a man approached, carrying a musical instrument. He was not a Shervanya; his skin was an odd grayish color (notable even in the dim light of the torches) and his hair, though mostly silvery, still had remains of a ruddy red. His stubbly beard was entirely white, and wrinkles marched across his face to gather at his eyes. There was something in those eyes, something hidden in their dark brown, that I immediately did not like – a fierceness, perhaps, or a veil of unfriendly secrets. He wore the typical off-white Shervanya clothes, bulky and tubular; sleeves wrapped around his arms, bandage-like.

"Arnul," Tulann addressed me, "I'd like you to meet my friend Sren. He's been playing in the nocturnal music the last couple of days. Sren, this is Arnul, *aheenor* from the Fyorian Lands."

"*Denhari*," I gave the Fyorian formal greeting, followed by the Shervanya, "*Tanaruyasei*. Pleased to meet you." I stood and bowed in both the Fyorian and Shervanya manner.

Sren replied with a greeting in a language that I did not recognize; one phrase with far more clicking sounds than any similar word in any language I knew. Then he informed me, "I-I saw you sitting here with Tulann, so I thought maybe you'd come to hear the music. I thought m-maybe I'd give you a little tutorial, since I figured you might not know what to listen f-for." He words were in Fyorian, though with an accent that I could not immediately place (he seemed to have trouble finding and holding a voice-pitch) and he spoke hurriedly as if he had limited time to get in as many words as possible, despite that slight (nervous?) stutter.

He set his instrument on the table in front of us. It was a collection of metal rods arranged in a wooden frame: four rows of eleven rods each, smaller to larger from right to left; but behind each bar and slightly raised, there were other smaller bars, two to each main rod, one on each side.

Sren explained. "It's a metal *kitál*." (I knew of the stringed *kitál* from the Fyorian lands.) "The first row, in the front, those are the notes for the *sheyándol* mode, the first mode to play. The raised rods behind them are the attendant tones, we call them; play them, you'll see what I mean. Play the m-main ones first." He handed me a padded mallet shaped like a hammer.

I tried it. I struck one of the rods on the first row. The sound was high and pure, a singing bell-tone. I struck a few of the others, from left to right, and they made a scale (with some notes missing, I thought, though it was very harmonious). I tried one of the 'attendant' tones; it was a slightly flat version of one of the others.

"Try it w-with this one." said the Sren, pointing to one of the main rows.

I played the two of them quickly together. The result was a blending and a shimmer; a beautiful sound more like audible light than anything.

"The main notes are the notes of the mode; the 'attendant' tones are eighth-tones. They are, as pitches go, very close together, too close to clash; therefore they make that shimmer. We call the shimmer the sound of the stars singing; even if there aren't any stars in the night, we like to keep their light shining." He demonstrated himself, with another, smaller, mallet; repeating a looping melody. The sounds leapt into the air and continued their sparkle. Gradually the sound began to change; Sren was introducing, very gradually at first, a note from the second row, and its 'attendant' tones. At first it seemed to clash, but he gradually dropped a note from the first row as well, and then moved entirely over to the second row. The entire sound of the music had shifted; it was somewhat darker yet paradoxically more harmonious, and the shimmers were more penetrating. "*Avalinkáalei*. The Wandering of the Moon; the second mode," he explained as he kept playing, his stutter gone. "That's how we change modes; the first note from the new mode is brought in as the 'enemy tone', but soon the other tones accept it, and it becomes a friend. If you listen closely, only one note has actually changed..."

I interrupted. "How many modes are there?"

"F-five," Sren stammered, too quickly. Then, immediately authoritative again, "Always the same five: *Sheyándol*, 'Darkening', as the sun goes down; then *Avalinkáalei*, 'The Wandering of the Moon'; *Ailíinya,* 'Silence' or 'Beautiful Clouds', the most mysterious mode during the darkest part of the night – that's what they're playing now – then *Avalantáalya,* 'The Traveling of the Stars'; and *Lomándol*, 'Brightening' – the final triumphal mode as the sun reappears."

I confessed that his list meant little to me, but commented that the Shervanya words for the modes (like many Shervanya words) were melodious to the ear. Then I mumbled, intentionally as if an afterthought, "I've heard something about another mode..."

Sren shot me a quick glance under his bushy eyebrows, and the muscles around his jaw tightened. Then, again, he seemed to recover just as quickly. "No, there are no other modes." Abruptly he grabbed the mallet from my hands and tucked the instrument under his arm. "I should rejoin the others." He left us.

"See what I mean?" said Tulann. "He's scared – though he's hiding it well. I was observing him carefully – I think he wants to alleviate some kind of suspicion, on himself. Obviously he knows that we're here to investigate something strange, and showed us about the music to try to get our minds to go somewhere else. He should know about that other mode."

But what could have scared him? And what suspicion could we have? – I wondered. I also noticed (at the same time) that the old woman on the mat was still staring at us. Then she averted her gaze, and quickly got up and walked away, out of the torchlight.

"Who was that?" I questioned Tulann, who'd seen her too.

"Her name's Elanna. She's one of the eldest in this town. That's all I know."

It was later that night (though the nocturnal music was still playing) that the elderly woman we had seen gently struck Tulann's door-gong. She told me that she could tell us something interesting. Tulann motioned for her to come in, and got her a mug of relaxing *némurath* tea.

She began her story. "...It was horrible, horrible... It was during the nocturnal music, the other night... The Gleph were there, as usual; they'd two carts of fruits and vegetables to sell..." She paused.

"How many Gleph live here?" I interrupted.

"Oh, they don't really live here – there are two families; let me see... nine, ten, no, eleven people in all. They have farms a few miles up the road, and they come here to sell their goods periodically. They've been there for, oh, probably fifty years. Some years back, the people of this town built the shed and the booths for them to use when they were here. I'm told they sometimes go to the next town, too. Anyway, all of them were here. They'd sold everything they had brought with them. Old Rendakh; he's the grandfather of one of the families and the eldest of all of them; he thought they should stay and enjoy the nocturnal music for an hour or so before heading back."

"The music had already started?"

"Yes, somewhat early, I think – that's probably why the Gleph families stayed. Usually they pack up everything and leave before sundown. But the moon and stars were so bright, they could travel in the dark – or even stay for the night – Nenu, the innkeeper, keeps a couple of rooms empty for them in case they want to stay. Anyway, they were all there; my grandson went over and played a game of ten-ball with Lakhmar, that's Rendakh's youngest grandson. The rest of us were just enjoying the music on a summer night. That's when it started..."

During her explanations, she had spoken matter-of-factly; but now her face tightened as if the full horror of what she was about to say had hit her. "...It started. Sren went up to the other musicians with his metal *kital*, and sat down with them. Some of those near him gave him a couple of suspicious glances, but he joined in and pretty soon they seemed to forget about him. They

229

just kept playing."

"Why would they look at him suspiciously? Isn't the nocturnal music for anyone who wants to play or listen?"

"Yes – but maybe some didn't think he'd know how to play. The modes are quite subtle, as are the melodies – and it is usually said that only Shervanya know them well enough to join in. ...Anyway, he played with them, and after a couple of minutes it didn't seem odd that Sren was playing too. Everyone listening started to get sleepy, which is the effect of the nocturnal music. I was just about to go home, when I heard the first jarring note. My ears pricked up – I've played in the nocturnal music for years, and know the modes by heart. There was an odd note in there – not the usual 'enemy tone', as they call the new note to shift into the next mode – but really a strange note... almost like a note that wasn't even in a scale. I looked down at the musicians, and some were glaring at Sren – obviously he'd brought in the strange note – I thought he might have made a mistake at first but he kept playing it. Pretty soon some of the others, the younger players who weren't as familiar with what tones went with what, started playing along. It was almost like they'd started another mode, different from the others. It was very discordant, and to tell you the truth, I didn't like it at all.

"I was about to leave in disgust. I've heard that younger players have no respect for tradition, and this proved it. I turned around, ready to give them a piece of my mind the next day. That's when I saw the Gleph – or where they had been..."

She paused, glanced around her nervously, and trembled slightly before continuing. "The Gleph weren't there. There was *nothing* there. I don't mean that the Gleph had left and someone had taken down their booth. I mean there was nothing there. A kind of blackness, or a mist, obscured my sight in that direction; there didn't even seem to be any grass or ground there. It was like the moonlight couldn't penetrate. I was confused at first, but not really alarmed until I suddenly made out the outline of one of the Gleph – I think it was Old Rendakh – standing within the mist. I saw him only for a second, then more darkness hid him. But what I saw… What I saw… It was horrible…"

She shuddered and put her head down in her hands. Tulann and I watched, not knowing what to say.

At last she raised her head and continued. "Old Rendakh was standing there, just standing – he didn't seem to be *doing* anything, just standing – but his face… His face… He had a look of absolute terror. I've never seen anything like that. His eyes met mine, and his mouth opened – in a scream, but there was no sound. No sound at all, even though the music was quiet. Then I saw he seemed to be bleeding. More of that darkness, or mist, hid him. I started to cry out, but found that I could not move at all. There was something surrounding me, holding me absolutely still, like a vice covering all my joints. I stared at that blackness, and saw him again, and he was *melting*. Literally – like a candle too near a flame. He still seemed to be screaming, and his… his… his face and chest caved in…"

"The darkness covered him again, and I didn't see him again for several minutes. I still couldn't move. Then the darkness faded. The booth became visible again, and I could see the two carts too. But there was no sign of any of the Gleph. They simply weren't there. I heard a voice, quietly, but menacingly, telling me that I was not to speak of what I had seen, to anyone, or the same would happen to me.

"Then I found that I could move again, and I noticed at the same time that the music had returned to its usual mode. I don't know why I noticed that... It seems that no one else had noticed it or seen what had happened, either."

Her speech trailed off, and she sat there for a second, rocking back and forth and staring at the floor. Then she fixed her steely gaze on Tulann. "It was murder," she rasped. "Cold-blooded murder. Sren did it. Oh, don't look at me like I'm crazy. What I saw means that the Gleph families didn't just walk away, and I know enough about the *aheenor* to know that you people have some powers, and I know those powers are capable of killing. I've heard that you try to prevent that, but sometimes others use your powers too..."

Tulann shot a quick glance at me, then back at the old woman. I said nothing, still trying to understand the implications of what she had said.

Tulann spoke first. "Let's say that you are right, and it *was* a murder – of one or all of the family of Gleph – and right in plain sight, though obscured in some strange manner. It would appear to be the use of an *aheenor* power." He glanced at me, then continued. "But how do you know that Sren did it? He is not an *aheenor*. Why don't you suspect one of us?"

She answered, "You've been here for years, Tulann, and there is no malice in you. That I am sure of. And Arnul, you showed up *after* the murder. You're investigating it, that I'm also sure of. Sren was the one who introduced the strange note into the music. That has something to do with it – that I'm also sure of; though I don't know what, or how, of course."

She finished her tea. "I'm afraid that I don't know any more," she said, "The menacing voice was Sren's, that I'm sure of too – and I'm sure anyone else that happened to see the killing heard him too, though I don't think anyone else had been facing in the right direction at the time. Most probably assumed that the Gleph families had gone home for the night. And I'm also sure that Sren will follow up on his threats. I'm old, but not old enough to leave Tond unless I'm called away – so if Sren asks either of you about me, I wasn't here." She shuffled out of Tulann's hut into the gloom.

Tulann leaned forward in his fluffy chair, the way he had when we first discussed the unknown *mechana*. "What do you think?" he asked.

"It sounds unbelievable – and ghastly – but why would she lie about it?"

"Exactly what I was wondering."

"...and... why would Sren be involved? He is not an *aheenor*; he is not even a Fyorian. Why would he have a *mechana*? And why would he, or anyone, want to kill those Gleph families with it?"

"None of it makes sense. I would think that Elanna there were making it up, possibly because she was angry with Sren about something, and wanted to slander him. But I don't think that's the case, because... Do you remember Sren's reaction when you asked about the 'other mode' in the music?"

"Certainly. He was hiding something, and he was frightened."

"The question is, why the murder, and why Sren...?"

There was something in the back of mind, a half-remembered thought that was trying to surface.

233

Something about non-*aheenor* from a certain part of Tond using *mechanas*...

"Help me think," I said. "Where exactly does Sren come from?"

"I thought you knew your geography. You saw him – grayish skin, reddish hair; odd colors except for people from the islands..."

"One of the Island Peoples, then, from the far west."

"Of course. He's a Drenn."

That was the fact I was looking for. "A Drenn. The Drennlands have a particularly complicated history... There are Karjans living there, aren't there?"

"Yes – though they call themselves by a couple of other names, and they have no allegiance to the Imperium. They don't hate the Gleph, like those in the Imperium do, or did."

"Are there *aheenor* there?"

"Not that I know of, except for an occasional wanderer, collecting legends like we all do, and looking for any signs of *mechanas*... and..." His voice trailed off, and suddenly his eyes grew wide. "Swords and daggers! That's it! The Tower of the Star!"

Yes, that was what I had been trying to recall. The Tower of the Star – known by its names in the various Karjan languages: Kfatsats Kweh'len, Kweezatz ag-Kweghan, Kvaz Kveranni – all complicated names meaning something like "Tower of the midnight starlight" – and its simpler Fyorian name, Lenkazan, the 'Star Tower'. The Karjans of the Islands had built it, centuries ago, in imitation of the larger towers in the Imperium, though unlike them it had never served as a military base. The Drenn had overrun it, run out the Karjans, and used it as a ceremonial center of power for their shaman/loremaster, the Chelloi – and then, after a long series of wars with both the Karjans and the Drellyans, another of the Island Peoples, had moved their entire civilization southwestward and left the Tower in ruins. Recently, rumors had spread that it was inhabited again, by someone rather mysterious and sinister – a renegade *aheenor*, who had left the *aheenor* Order because they would not side with the Karjans on some issue about the borders between the Fyorian Lands and the Imperium.

"Do you know who the renegade *aheenor* is, who is said to live in the Tower?" I asked, then added, "My own brother once tangled with a renegade who is said to have lived in that Tower at one point."

"I don't know who the renegade is. To tell the truth, I've always doubted the rumor anyway, as I do all rumors. But if it is true, then I wouldn't be surprised if it were someone who was a specialist in the *mechana* of sound... He might have something that is capable of strengthening sound vibrations in one place only, strong enough to vibrate a thing – or a person – apart... If he exists, he must have somehow kept it, or found it, after being turned out of the Order. The rumor *does* state that he was angry because we, the rest of the *aheenor*, I mean, would not side with the Karjans..."

"...And as someone who wanted to side with the Karjans, he would possibly hate Gleph people." I completed Tulann's thought.

Tulann stood. "Well, nothing to do but find out. Tomorrow, in the daylight when no one is playing the nocturnal music, I'm going to have a look at the instruments."

"Shouldn't we find out if the Gleph families really have disappeared first?"

"Of course. The problem is, I don't know exactly where they live or where to find them. I'll have to do some looking around. In the meantime, Sren may provide us with the answers whether he wants to or not. I have a feeling he'll show up if we start investigating the instruments. I may need to use one of my *mechanas*. You, take the usual precautions if you are going to come along."

Since the instruments for the Nocturnal Music were supposed to be for anyone to play, they were kept in the pavilion, open to all, when not in use. There they sat, unattended, as Tulann and I approached the next day. In the front, nearest the grassy slope where the audience would sit, there was a row of stringed *kital*s. Their strings were pulled tight, horizontally, across convex wooden planks; the metal strings of the higher-voiced ones glistened in the sunlight; the longer strings of the basses were made of silk. I plucked on of the latter; a deep resonance echoed. Behind them, were the rows of the metal *kital*s, like the one Sren had shown me; behind them, the deep gongs and bells – some as large as a small hut. There were several rows of other instruments, strings for plucking and metal for striking gently. I recognized some, and could even state their names – *ketatang, tong-tlong, goombuk, tiki-taka* – all suitably onomatopoeic. Finally, over to the far side of the stage, a shiny metal rack full of wooden *sulu* flutes. I mused that most of them were perfectly safe here even when everyone could get to them; all except the flutes and the smaller *kital*s were too heavy to move around easily.

Tulann busied himself by poking around the *kital*s, strumming a string here or there, tapping on a metal rod or on the wooden body of the instrument, or feeling underneath of them. Searching for a hidden *mechana*, I knew. I tried to do the same; I admitted that I didn't know really what I was looking for, but I knew that any odd object attached to an instrument in an out-of-sight place would be at least suspicious, if Sren hadn't removed it – and certainly I could feel it through the dulling effect of the protection field that Tulann and I had activated.

My thoughts were interrupted by a nudge from my four-pointed star amulet in my pocket. I was clutched by a sudden sense of danger. I glanced back at Tulann; he was inspecting what appeared to be the same *kital* that Sren had showed us the day before – and then his eyes raised and met mine. He had felt it too. In the shade, the vague ghostly shimmer of his protection field was visible.

Someone was approaching from the other side of the lawn. He did not take a second look, but proceeded deliberately towards us as if he had expected to see us here. In a couple of seconds he was close enough for me to make out his face; oddly grayish, though he'd wrapped his head with a cloth in the Shervanya manner and his red hair was hidden. It was Sren.

He said nothing, but walked up to the instruments (without a hint of hurry) and sat down on the bench by his *kital*. "Ah, *aheenor*, my friends. Would you like to play?" His manner was different from the previous night; overly friendly, and the fearful stutter was gone.

"I don't know how to play the Shervanya music," I commented. I was trying to stall for time, because something was clearly happening. The sun seemed to be dimming; the brightness of the day merging with the pavilion's shade. My four-pointed star nudged me again. "*Mechana* in use," I knew that it would say if I had dared to look at it.

"No matter," Sren said without apparent emotion, and produced two small mallets from a hidden pocket. He started to play a looping melody on the metal bars of the *kital*. Shimmering, metallic tones sounded. After a few seconds he spoke again. "Why is it that I find you here looking around in broad daylight?" He glanced around him with a strange smile – as if agreeing that the daylight was now quite dark. A wall of shadow was growing around the three us. "The light of day can hide things as well as reveal them," he continued, "Anyone looking at us now won't see that we are here. They might see a little wisp of mist, if they look closely."

"You have a *mechana* that alters Kullándu," muttered Tulann.

Sren chuckled, but continued to play his repeating tune. "So you Fyorians theorize, though I know that your names for the elements are nothing by symbols. Kullándu does indeed stand for light, among other things – but actually I'm altering Kewándi, 'the flow' – time and space, and light as a consequence, are acting differently around us." To the accompaniment of his kital, he began to chant from the Fyorian lore.

The first of the Four that was made is Kullándu.
Kullándu is fire and energy, power and change;
Now a soft flicker of heat in the chill air,
Now the roar of crimson destruction,
Now the burning passion to father anew and forge
*   beauty.*
But Kullándu cannot make or unmake by itself,
for Teilyándal' is the Maker.

The third of the Four that was made is Kewándii.
Kewándii is rain and river and sea;
Now the life-giving diamond-drops on the sand,
Now the flow of the river of water and blood and time,
Now the thunder of life and might at the edge of the
    sea.
But Kewándii cannot live by itself,
for Teilyándal' is the life-giver.

"Oh, do not be so surprised that I know your terms; I think you've already guessed it right. I have studied with the only *aheenor* in my country. Of course, the powers of the ancients do not need the intervention of *Teilyándal'*."

I flinched. Even if he hadn't claimed that he didn't need the intervention, himself, his speech was a confession of guilt of some kind type – *Teilyándal'* was the Fyorian word for the all-seeing Eye that personally watched and protected all it had created – the entire universe.

Tulann said, "So it *was* you, then…"

"Indeed," answered Sren, "And I think I owe you an explanation before you join your Gleph cousins."

I shot my eyes to Tulann. He knowingly glanced back. We had both heard it, and I knew that both of our four-pointed stars were recording the conversation.

The darkness was complete around us. I could see only Tulann, Sren, and several instruments – about to a foot in either direction; we seemed to be illuminated by sunlight but in all directions there was merely blackness. Sren seemed to take no notice; he merely kept repeating his melody on the *kital*. "The Karjans know nothing of *Teilyándal'*," he went on, "but only of the two competing forces of creation and destruction.

Both were equal, it was said – but of course if both were really equal, then everything that was created would be immediately destroyed. So says the teachings of Hrenchuk."

The name was familiar – the first of the Karjan prophets. In fact I had heard much of this before, in my early days as an *aheenor* in training.

"And it was Ch'pfarchduk who told the way out of the conundrum," Sren explained, though I knew this too. "One of the powers of destruction had defected to the creative side – thus tipping the balance. Finally, it was Tarshkn who told us his name – Gaejtark-Bad'hani..."

Tulann cut him off. "I have heard of these names. They are not of the makers of the *mechana*s; they are not Fyorian words, that have so many consonants strung together. They are words from the bringers of destruction."

"Indeed!" laughed Sren, and now he began to introduce a strange, dissonant note into his melody. I saw that he was striking one rod from the last row on the *kital*; he was mixing modes in a way that would never happen in the Nocturnal Music. "Indeed, Gaejtark-Bad'hani makes by destroying – for truly he was originally a destructive force. He makes the empire for the Karjans by destroying all of those who had come before. As I am doing with this music now, making a new mode by destroying those that came before. *Kayef grechdamwsh arjala!*[1]"

"I have heard this before, and I grow weary of it," said Tulann, speaking now solemnly as a grand *aheenor*

---

[1] *Kayef grechdamwsh arjala*: – motto of the Karjan Imperium during its most warlike period. It is usually translated as "We come to conquer!", though its meaning is much stronger.

in council. "The Karjans believed it out of arrogance, and the Fyorians had to stop them by destroying civilization itself and hiding the powers of their *mechanas*. ...And you are not a Karjan anyway, to be allied with their falsehoods." (I flinched again. That was the speech of a knowledgeable but unwise old-style *aheenor* – astute in the ways of the Fyorians but as haughty as the forces he was fighting. It would merely make the confrontation all the meaner.)

But Sren merely continued to play. The new mode was now more obvious; the strange note was clearly asserting itself harshly over the others. "I am not a Karjan," he explained, "but I learned their ways while living near the Tower of the Star. ...And this new mode is based on *their* music theory. It is the new, replacing the old." Then he added, quietly, *"Break protection field."*

For a second I didn't know why he had said that – it was not related to what he had said before – then I felt a sharp stab of pain in my left arm, the instant that he had struck the strange note. I hazarded a quick look. There was a gaping wound just below my elbow, small, but deep. Blood was beginning to ooze from around its ragged edges. My protection field was gone and the power of Sren's *mechana* was penetrating, activated by the combination of notes.

Tulann seized Sren's instrument with both hands and overturned it. The metal slabs clattered apart on the ground. Sren responded just as quickly; standing, he produced a spike of metal from under his Shervanya tunic, and he brandished it at the two of us. "That was what I had been waiting for," he said, with a change in his voice: it now suddenly sounded cheerful, almost perky. "Hidden people, please show yourselves."

What happened next was so unexpected, so unbelievable, that I could merely stand there gaping. Several people stepped into the darkness surrounding us. All of them were dressed more or less in the Sherványa manner, though the material was darker, drab brown and grey. Their hair, likewise, was not Shervanya blonde or brown, but black; their faces were broad and round, with high foreheads. I would have mistaken them for Karjans from the Imperium if not for the scruffy beards that the men wore. All of the women wore their hair long and tied back in a pony-tail. There were four children.

They were Gleph. I knew immediately that they were the Gleph families that Elanna said were dead! There were eleven people in total, just as she had said. As if to confirm my identification, Elanna herself toddled into the light, wearing a bemused smile.

Sren gently set his sword down among the scattered slabs of the instrument. He was laughing, "I hope I did not frighten you too much. You see, I had to make absolute sure whose side you were on..."

Tulann stood there scowling, his arms folded across his chest. "Explain yourself, Sren."

Sren mumbled something inaudible, and my arm itched where the wound had been inflicted. I glanced; the bloody gap was gone. "An illusion," Sren explained, "though quite effective when the sensations are worked into it along with the sights. You see, there is something evil starting, and I had to make sure that you were not part of it." He gathered the pieces of the instrument, and showed us the underside of one of the slabs: a pinkish stone had been glued to it. An illusion-stone; one of the Ancients' most sought-after mechanas. "You were right in guessing that there is an aheenor in the Tower of the Star, and that he has learned the worst of the old Karjan ways. You were incorrect, though, that he only wishes to kill Gleph; he has even more slaughter in mind. And, you are correct in thinking that he has found a mechana that amplifies sound in a particular, small, place – and it may be used to dissolve things; as a horrible weapon. I took it from him, and fled here."

Tulann asked, "Then why did you try to make us think that you were using it?"

"Grendar – the aheenor in the Tower of the Star – is looking for me, and he has spies. I have already been attacked twice in two cities on the way here. So, when I found that you, Tulann, were here – I decided to make a test. I did in fact use the weapon, though not *on* anyone – I merely had it affect the air above my head. That was enough for the four-pointed star amulets to respond; indeed, it brought you as well, Arnul. The rest of it was an illusion, and Elanna didn't actually see anything."

The elder woman nodded. "I was part of the plot."

Sren continued. "I laid a trap. You see, it came down to when you broke my instrument. If you had taken the pieces to look for the weapon, I would have known that you were spies for the Grendar and were trying to take it back. You wouldn't have found it, by the way. But since you merely tried to destroy it, I knew that you could be trusted. You are not on his side."

"We could have been looking for it, in order to destroy it," I commented.

Sren laughed (and this time, Tulann with him!). "Oh, but I am aware that you might not know how to destroy this particular mechana. It is a very powerful one," said Sren.

In the end, I stayed in Len for five more days. Tulann and Sren were obviously friends again, and the two of them made rather vague plans concerning fighting Grendar. I was not sure if I would join them. On the fourth day, Old Rendakh and his family invited us to their home, apologizing for the fright they had caused us, and gave us a feast of Gleph roasted, spiced lamb and vegetables. Then we all ventured back to listen to the Nocturnal Music.

Ussers out of the Blue

This is the first chapter of my next writing project, a novel that is not fantasy (but eventually develops a tenuous connection to the Tond series). Intended for a YA audience, it is nonetheless more experimental than "Tond". It is fiction, but also semi-autobiographical. The different typefaces are an intrinsic part of the writing.

So I guess, before we continue, I have to tell you how I got involved in all this gibjabj.

What? Gibjabj? That's my special word for garbage. Or it could just mean "stuff", which is really anything. In this case, I'll say it's just "stuff".

I have special words for a lot of things. What? Why ask why? I call garbage or any kind of unidentified stuff gibjabj. Also I say "company" as numpa-c'nuggamy, "stupid" as stoodle-poopid, and "probably" as prob-kabob-kabayobob-kabayo-bubbita-blubby because anything ending in "blubby" is automatically funny. All of that – I call it "longspeak".

My name is Tony Bradner. You know that already. Tony's not my real name. I'll tell you later why I chose it. I live in Seattle, Washington. You know that already too, but you don't know I call it See-acka-taw-t'lucky, in the state of Wa-shawwing-taw-tucky. I'm just about to graduate from high school, which is a fact tied up with the gibjabj I was *referring to in the first paragraph.*

So, um, I guess I'll start at the beginning. Really, it's the best place to start. There might be some irrelevant details in it. But then again, maybe it'll shed some light on how all of this got started.

So, exactly how far back is the beginning? I'll skip the big bang and the Cambrian Explosion and the extinction of the dinosaurs and the art of Hieronymus Bosch and the music of Mahler and all that. It's just extra gibjabj for now. I'll come back to it later.

Maybe I'll start with the first thing I remember. Importance to this story: profound. Grand cosmic significance: probably nil.

Blue looming, dimensions unknown. Maybe there were two or three white streaks in it, but otherwise it was just blue. It cast no light. It held no darkness. It exuded no joy. It contained no sadness. It held no promise or prohibition. There was no warmth, no cold, no distance, no proximity, no stillness and no motion in it; nothing came before it and nothing came after it. It was just blue – just a single entity of blue, and it is my earliest memory.

What? Not so interesting? I thought I described it rather well. Well, let's try my next memory, then. I must have been two or three.

Fear. Dread attacking as a blood-freezing moaning sound. It arose spontaneously from the space beyond my crib, beyond the pale walls of my room. It groaned under the door and into the safe space and lingered crying in the half-light of the shaded room.

I awoke, shreds of nightmare still clinging to my ears. Had I imagined the noise?

Moan again, infinitely remote, very near. It burst into dark icicles of panic.

My mouth exploded, "Mom!"

It was only trucks on the freeway, my mother said. She had come into my room and listened, at first not able to hear the faint sigh, then smiling at me with reassurance. The freeway was only a few blocks away and down a hill, she said. There were trucks on the freeway, she said, and they made that hum as they drove by. The sound was nothing to fear, she said as she left from my room.

I was silent in my crib. Sleep began to overtake me again.

The moan returned. It's only trucks on the freeway, I told myself, but I was not so sure. It was a sound after all, and sound could be my enemy or my friend. Sound could break into my sleep, break into my serenity. Or, sound could soothe me, ease me into slumber, still my anxiety. I sat there in the dim for several minutes, listening. The moan was quiet, but near.

Then I decided that it was my friend, and I went to sleep.

Yeah, I had to decide about it. Most sounds affect me in that way: they are either my enemy or my friend. There are no neutral sounds to me. Sometimes I can decide which they are, but usually not.

Sound, prob-kabob-kabayobob-kabayo-bubbita-blubby, is one of the reasons that I got involved in the gibjabj that I keep referring to.

The other reason is the imagination.

Again, I was two or three years old.

The dream of the coughing usser. That was my next memory, still from the time before reason.

What was an usser? It was something alive, but not really an animal; not a pet, but nothing wild either. It was rectangular, the size and shape, perhaps, of a slightly flattened shoebox; more like a geometrical solid than an animal, and it clung to walls. It was opaque and beige. The top half of its front surface was a perfectly hemispherical dome, the same featureless color and texture as the rest of it. I did not know what the dome was for.

Why was it called an usser? I was before the age of linguistic games as I was before the age of reason: an usser was not something that went around "ussing" things. Nor was the name political in any way (those were the times that the two superpowers of the world were haranguing each other as "Godless Communists" and "Decedent Capitalists" – I knew none of that); I did not name ussers after the USSR. The name was as mysterious as the creature itself. It was just called an usser, in the same way that other beings were called dogs or rabbits or goldfish.

One afternoon during my nap there was an usser clinging to the wall above my crib. It coughed. I watched it through half-lidded eyes. It coughed again, many times. I could not see where its mouth was (nor was I curious), but by now ten or twenty people had heard it and were crowding in from all sides to watch it and listen to it cough. There was a woman with curly brown hair and a red flowered dress. There was a man with a large tan hat.

I sat up. I looked around. The people and the usser had gone out of the room as I awoke. I regarded the place on the wall where the usser had been. The wall was blank, with a hint of the interplay of sunlight and shadows of a tree, streaming in from the open window.

Nothing was out of order. I went back to sleep.

Well, enough of when I was under the age of two, even though those incidents do relate to what I'm about to tell you. Really.

I'll fast forward to the age of five, and go to Kindergarten.

It was a bright autumn day outside, and the leaves on the big maple tree outside the classroom were deep red. A little breeze was blowing.

Inside of the kindergarten, it was too hot, as always. We sat there around our tables, waiting for the next activity (though at that time I didn't understand the concept of staying still). The teacher said it was time for an art project. She handed out geometrical shapes cut from colored paper, and told us to paste them on a larger piece of white paper to make a picture.

I stared at the shapes. Red squares, yellow rectangles, green circles, blue triangles. I arranged them in various random ways. They didn't make anything that I could think of.

Maybe I'd paste a green circle on a yellow rectangle and make an usser; but immediately thought better of the idea. It was too easy, and besides, it was the wrong color – ussers were beige all over, not bright green and yellow.

Actually nothing I knew of was bright green and yellow.

I looked outside at the maple tree. A leaf fell just as I looked. A rich, vibrant brownish, purplish, red leaf. That was a color worth looking at, not like these bright generic paper forms.

I stared at them again. Hmmm, maybe the green circles were peas. Peas were the only green circles that I knew. So I pasted nine or ten green circles on the paper and a couple of the yellow rectangles around the edges just to make it interesting. I looked at my picture from several angles. Yes, it looked good. Peas coming out of a peapod.

I left my seat to go see what the other kids had made. I found that Rick had ignored the colors and put the triangles, squares and rectangles together to make a house. Renee had ignored the colors too, and made a person, using the green circle to make a head; the other shapes made the rest of the body. Those were clever, I thought – I hadn't thought of ignoring the colors.

Marcus had made an airplane. Cindy had made another person (the green circle was the head again). Jana had done exactly the same thing. That wasn't odd, I thought, they were sitting right next to each other.

Joe had made another airplane. Jill had made another house. Tom and Michelle had both made people again. Duane had made yet another house. In fact, everyone had made people, houses, or airplanes! What was going on? Only people, houses, and airplanes? Nothing interesting! No animals, no plants, no dinosaurs, no planets, no rockets, no musical instruments, no fireworks, no apple-coring machines. Why was everyone so boring?

And, after I'd told Renee that mine was supposed to be peas coming out of a peapod, she laughed at me: "Nobody knows what a peapod is." And that was true. They were all staring at me. None of them knew what a peapod was.

Wow. I decided I'd need to show them something

interesting, so the next day I brought a record of Beethoven to kindergarten. The teacher said she'd take it home and listen to it, but not play it for the other kids. Was that why they were so dull? The teacher was keeping all the good *gibjabj* for herself?

Well, yes, you heard that part correctly. I did bring a record of Beethoven to kindergarten. That may have been the start of the problems.

I had heard my parents play some classical music on the record player, so I asked for a kids' record player and some records of that "music that grown-ups listen to" for Christmas. My mom and dad obliged. They gave me a used multiple record set called "Treasury of Light Classical Music". It had an impressionist painting of some people dancing the waltz on the cover, though I knew nothing of impressionism or waltzes. (For that matter, I didn't know that "light classical music" wasn't really "classical music".)

I decided that I liked Tchaikovsky best (though I called him "chai-cow-skee").

Capriccio Italien

Trumpet signals, "Awake!"; brass answer.
'Cellos intone with a sad song.
Stirrings begin. Sounds grow, summiting a
    mountain, burst of radiance, trumpet signals
    again "Awake!"
The sad song again. Then silence.

Oh, something new. There's a happy tune. A little
    dance with the birds.
More instruments. The happy tune grows.

**Other instruments answer. There's a flute,
    skittering.
There's violins, singing.
There's a horn, calling.
There's timpani, commenting on the others, ba-
    boom.
And another happy tune, shining.**

**Something's wrong. The sad song again.
Repeated notes. Scurrying. A spider in music,
    slithering multi-leggedly across the strings.
Music lurches, staggers, stumbles.
Oh! There's the first happy tune again, louder! Now
    all is well!
Now a forward rush, gallop, triumphal galumphing!
Cymbals crash! Din of drums! Awake!!**

Of course I didn't just sit there alone and listen to it. Sometimes my mom or dad would listen to it with me (though they always seemed to have something to do, so couldn't listen as long). I listened to it over and over as I built fanciful cities with my Lego blocks and Tinker Toys.

And usually, Butlabush listened to it with me.

Butlabush was my friend. Nobody else could see him. He lived in a little house in a little city underneath my bed. His name was strange because people from that city had strange names. One of his friends (whom I met once or twice) was called Skoobdidup.

I remember a particular incident with Butlabush. It was a Saturday, not long after the day of the peapods, when we went out to look for kimlimtimles. There were a lot of fir-trees in the back yard, which shaded a dirt patch where grass couldn't grow. That was the best place to find kimlimtimles, said Butlabush, because they came down from the trees during the day to forage among the fir-needles on the ground.

"What do they look for?" I asked.

"Kimlimtimle food," said Butlabush.

Kimlimtimles were about the size of dachshunds, though with longer legs. They had a whole bunch of legs, in fact – probably ten, though I never saw one close enough to count them. They had oval bodies and round heads, with kind-looking, almost human faces; their mouths almost seemed to smile. Their ears were high on the top of the head, and stuck up like a cat's but were longer and tended to curve (indeed, flop) forwards. Their tails were an exact match for their ears – shaped like a cat's ears at the base, but longer and curving or flopping downwards at the end.

Butlabush and I went out early that Saturday morning to look for some kimlimtimles. The air was damp and chilly, though the sun was already up. My parents were asleep in their room, the way that grown-ups always did when there were more interesting things to do.

Butlabush cautioned me to be quiet and not wake them up. I agreed. I didn't want to have to explain what we were doing. There was no way that they'd know what a kimlimtimle was, or what we were going to do with one when we found it.

"What *are* we going to with it when we find it?" asked Butlabush.

"Feed it. They like that. Then we'll play tag or checkers with it, and listen to Tchaikovsky. Then we'll let it go."

He agreed that this was a good plan, though he said he didn't know if they liked to play checkers.

"Of course they do," I assured him, "...and besides, I thought you were the one that knew all about them."

"Only where to find them."

"Oh."

We put on our clothes and jackets, and quietly padded out of the bedroom and into the hall to the living room, and through the back door. "Don't let the door make any noise," Butlabush reminded me. I closed it as quietly as I could, and we went out into the pine-scented woodland of the back yard. I grabbed my blue plastic sand bucket from the garage on the way out.

We waited a couple of minutes in the shade, but didn't see or hear anything. Butlabush began humming quietly, then suddenly burst into song.

Libbadee, labbadee, labbap skaboo,
Labbap skabunga loooooooba.

"Shhh!" I shouted. "Mom and Dad will hear you! What is that nonsense, anyway!?"

Butlabush's face reddened. "Sorry." He was quiet for a minute, and then, "It's a song to attract kimlimtimles. It's in their language."

"What's it mean?"

"How should I know? I'm not a kimlimtimle."

I agreed that this made sense.

"Look! There's one!" Butlabush exclaimed. Something darted under the pine needles at my feet. I quickly slammed the overturned bucket down on it. There was a crunching, snapping noise, and an animal bolted out of the newly-made hole in the bucket and disappeared behind a tree.

"I'd forgotten they could eat plastic," Butlabush

commented.

We waited a couple of minutes. The animal didn't seem to want to move from behind the tree, and neither Butlabush nor I wanted to approach it lest it spook and run away completely. I passed the time thinking all I knew about kimlimtimles, which wasn't much.

"How do you *spell* 'kimlimtimle'?" I queried.

"I don't know, but I think it starts with a capital *kim*," Butlabush replied.

"There's no letter called 'kim'! It's a girl's name. She's in my class at school!"

"There is so a letter called 'kim'! Haven't you read Dr. Seuss!?"

"Oh – On Beyond Zebra..."

"Of course."

"But there's no letter called 'kim' in there either. And besides, those aren't real letters. If you make up a real new letter in the alphabet, you have to make up a new sound for it to stand for."

"I never thought of that." He then told me that he could spell 'thimle' and 'foom' correctly.

(A thimle, by the way, was like a kimlimtimle but it only had four legs. "It has fewer letters because it has fewer legs," Butlabush reminded me. Foom was something else entirely. Foom was what the clouds did when they got tired of raining or snowing. Foom was large, soft, multicolored blobs that looked rather like cantaloupe-sized pieces of painted popcorn. It fell only on Tuesdays when nobody was looking, and the second you saw it, it would melt into ordinary water. The clouds were very secretive that way.)

A rustling from behind the tree interrupted our thoughts. The animal emerged slowly, snuffling at the ground. I circled around the tree slowly, trying to position the animal between my house and myself, and stepping lightly to not make any noise. The creature raised its head and glared at me – I'm sure it glared, not just looked at me – and then abruptly bolted towards my house. Butlabush ran after it, and I, impulsively, grabbed a stone from the ground and flung it at the running creature, thinking, perhaps, to scare it into running a different direction.

The stone missed the animal completely and bounced up into air. There was a horrible shattering, smashing, splintering sound as shards of glass crashed to the ground and the rock sailed into my parents' room. I gasped. The animal turned and disappeared under the neighbor's fence.

The next day in kindergarten, I told Marcus what had happened.

"You threw a rock at your parents' bedroom window!?"

"Yeah, I was trying to hit the kimlimtimle."

"What's a kimlimtimle?"

I told him.

"Wow. Is it anything like a skubbyloofer?"

"A what?"

"A skubbyloofer. It's a green walrus about as big as a cat."

I smiled. So other kids could make up things too.

"Does it like to play checkers?" I asked.

"I don't know. I've never played with one."

"Oh. Does it like Tchaikovsky?"

"What's that?"

I stared at him. How could he not know? "Music," I answered.

He stared back at me. "It's cool to make up animals and things, not music."

"I didn't make it up."

"Well, you're weird then." He got up from his seat and walked away.

That was odd, I thought, but then again, Marcus was one of those kids who'd made an airplane with the colored shapes because he didn't know what a peapod was. So, I went home and played with Butlabush (while I was grounded for throwing a rock through the window) and imagined what it would really be like to have a pet usser.

About the Author

Steven Eric Scribner is a high school teacher, freelance author, blogger, and avant-garde pianist/composer. He graduated from Seattle Pacific University. He has lived in the suburbs of Seattle, in the San Francisco Bay Area, and in Japan. The roots of his "Tond" series go back more than forty years to imaginary tales he used to invent while walking to and from school. The landscapes in northern Tond (seen in Book Two) were inspired by the forests and mountains around Seattle and in Japan, those in Rohándal by eastern Washington State; other aspects of the Tondish world are purely a product of his imagination.

As mentioned in the "The Name Thing" chapter, similarities between the name "Tond" and names of imaginary lands in works by other authors is coincidental.

CPSIA information can be obtained
at www.ICGtesting.com
Printed in the USA
LVHW010256240322
714225LV00003B/504

9 781675 972847